MARIËTTE WHITCOMB

BINDING
LIES

ISBN Paperback: 978-1-990988-63-9
ISBN eBook: 978-1-990988-64-6

I dedicate this novel to every person who has not been in control of their own lives. To those who cannot make their own decisions and are forced to believe the lies others feed them.
And to every person who lives in fear of those closest to them.
May truth, and justice, set you free.

One

Porcelain shattered, crashing to the floor – an ironic symbol of my life. The mug should've smashed into his face, but his reflexes were better than a cat's. Not even loathing is a strong enough word to describe what I felt. Every single day I had to remind myself why I couldn't kill him. Remind myself that the day would come when their blood would drip from my hands. It's a good thing babies can't hear their mother's thoughts; if they could, mine would've had to go for in utero therapy.

"What the hell, Ley?" he demanded, staring at the white pieces scattered behind his bare feet.

I grabbed the meat cleaver and let it hang lax from my hand. A sneer consumed my face as I lifted the blade towards his chest. "Lesson for the day – most men are killed in the kitchen during domestic disputes, and seeing as we are forced to live together, I call this domestic. Stop pushing me or you won't like how this ends."

"I only touched your stomach, stop overreacting. I want to touch my child, Lizzie does it all the time."

"My child. *Gabriel*." I spat out his actual name.

"Dammit, Finley. My child is growing inside of the woman I love, and you won't let me be part of anything, do anything for you. Nothing."

"Remind me again how it came about that this child is yours?"

He turned his broad back on me, slamming his fists on the granite counter. "The story won't change. I did what I had to do to keep you safe and ensure you don't have a serial killer's child."

Story? Interesting word choice. Each time he lied to me, said anything about the man I love and need more than my next breath, I kept a tally. One day he would pay for every last word and act. This was not that day.

I focused on the chicken fillets and sliced them into strips, imagining I was cutting his face. It's a good thing my baby was exposed only to my nutrients and oxygen. But this child grew under hostile conditions. Circumstances beyond my control. I needed to gain control, I had to get away from Gabriel and his lies. More than anything else, I longed for Aidan. After everything we went through to have our baby, our rainbow baby, it wasn't fair that he wasn't sharing in my pregnancy, seeing my tummy grow with his child. For the time being, it was best that Gabriel kept believing he had fathered my child.

Eli stormed into the kitchen. "Can you keep it down? Lizzie is trying to sleep."

I spun around, meat cleaver pointed at my sister's fiancé, a man I had once considered my friend. "Get him out of my face or I will silence him permanently." Two weeks of being their prisoner, I could no longer keep up the charade. "I want to go home. Now!"

Eli pushed his hands through his dark hair and sighed. Gabriel smirked, crossing his arms over his bare chest. "You're not going anywhere, sweetheart. Not until your serial killer husband is arrested, or better yet, killed."

I closed my eyes and breathed deeply as heat spread through my body. When I opened my eyes, Eli blocked my view of the man I had every intention of whacking to death with a skillet. "Unless you want your child to grow up fatherless, you better move," I said, gripping the handle of the cleaver so hard my hand cramped. I ignored the pain, the ache in my heart much worse. I had carried it for two weeks.

Two weeks of living a lie. Not knowing whether my husband still breathed. Fourteen days of listening to the men standing in the kitchen, the very ones who had framed Aidan for two murders, spew their nonsense.

Two weeks since I had activated the tracking device once we had arrived at this house in the middle of nowhere. I had sent a single signal to a private satellite owned by none other than my father-in-law. The reason Ryan Walker owned it I had learned on my last night with Aidan. Still, Aidan hadn't come for me. There could be only one reason – he hadn't eliminated the mastermind behind Gabriel and Eli being inserted into my life and that of my sister. Tom Anderson, my godfather, a man I had once loved, adored, and looked up to, stood in the middle of this anarchy my life had morphed into. The reasons for his betrayal were still unknown to me.

Thirteen nights of not falling asleep in Aidan's strong arms, without his scent hypnotising me into slumber. A familiar copper taste filled my mouth. The only way to keep myself from telling them that I knew what they had done.

Eli stepped closer and placed a hand on my shoulder. "Tomorrow morning, you and I are going out for breakfast. You're the only one who hasn't left the property yet."

Once a week, Eli and Lizzie drove to the city for groceries. Gabriel stayed with me.

"This will be over soon, Fin; Aidan can't run forever. This is the only way we can keep you and Lizzie safe. Aidan made it clear in the letter that he will not live without you, and that he wouldn't even spare Liz if she tried to keep you away from him."

Again, I closed my eyes, my nostrils flared, but I didn't say a word about Aidan never writing the letter they kept referring to. He had been out of our home even before I drove through the gate. One benefit of receiving a former safe house as a wedding gift from my in-laws.

Gabriel, or Ari, as he had called himself when he slithered into my life, Eli, Tom, and whoever funded their little operation didn't know the family I had married into. To be fair, neither did I until my last night with Aidan. After Aidan found a tracking device on my G-Class, he had bought me a GLE and left a burner phone hidden under the driver's seat.

The second I was alone after we had arrived at this prison, which others might describe as an ideal mountain retreat, I had tried to switch on the burner phone. The battery was dead. Out of utter frustration, I had opened it and remembered that Aidan had told me about the satellite and the tracking device hidden inside the phone's casing. Rage and grief had made me dumb. Or perhaps pregnancy brain was a real thing, a reality I couldn't face when the biggest war of my life surrounded me.

I transferred the cleaver to my other hand and stretched my aching fingers. "Going out for breakfast sounds like a good idea. Do you think Lizzie will be up to joining us?"

"Doubt it. She believes she has a double dose of morning sickness because you didn't have any."

Gabriel leaned his hip against the granite counter. "I'll stay and take care of her. Maybe absence will make your heart grow fonder, *Ley*."

The blade lifted on its own. Eli moved with me, keeping me from unleashing my rage on a man I once thought I was falling in love with. It's funny how you can perceive something to be love, and when you find the real thing, no past relationship measures up to the reality of what it truly is. I can never love anyone as much as I love Aidan Walker. Glancing at the faint bump under my black tank top, I bit the inside of my cheeks. They would never see my tears.

"One of these days I will stand back and watch her kill you. Will even clean up for her." Eli shook his head and moved to take the knife from my hand.

I plunged the blade into the cutting board and marched out of the kitchen, out of the house, heading towards the ravine. Forty meters below my feet, water sped over black rocks.

I lifted my eyes skyward, tears streaming down my face. "Aidan, where are you?"

Two

Rows of trees sped past us. To my right, the gorge held no answers. Ahead of me, a road I didn't know. I had asked Lizzie for information about where we were being held. The city where she and Eli had gone grocery shopping – Coopersville. Coopersville lay cross-country from our home, Marcel. They had driven an hour north to reach the grocery store. When Eli and I had left, I had grabbed the keys from his hand and turned left as we exited the dirt road. There were no sentries standing guard at the gate, no visible security cameras. Still, I knew they were there. Just as they had hidden them inside our home, and Aidan's office. I glanced at the watch Eli kept twisting around his wrist. Neither he nor Gabriel had worn it before the day we had left Marcel.

"Lizzie is looking better today," he said to the passenger side window.

"I took her some crackers and water before we left and forced her to eat. If it doesn't get better by Monday, we need to take her to a doctor. It's not good for her or the baby." My knuckles turned white on the steering wheel. Of all the things I wanted to say to him, my sister's health was not at the top of the list.

"Finley."

"Yes, Eli? Is that even your real name?" I shook my head. I had trusted the man next to me with my sister, had given my blessing and helped him choose a ring before he proposed. My Krav Maga instructor, Aidan's instructor, and our friend. As I had watched the footage of him placing the rifle inside the safe in Aidan's office, I realised he was on the list of people I would have to kill. Aidan had said that killing is overdramatic, and I reminded him how I respond to people who hurt my sister. Or people who betray us.

"My full name is Elijah Levi Netanyahu. For as long as I can remember, my friends and family have called me Eli."

"At least you never lied to me about your name." Aidan had told me their true identities that last night. He had whispered so many things to me that night, things I still couldn't wrap my head around.

Eli's betrayal burned in my core. Gabriel's hatred towards Aidan I could understand, but not his. Eli covered his face with his hands and exhaled hard. He stared at the wristwatch; from where I sat, the screen appeared black. "Do you know where we are going?"

"No." I increased the volume and music filled the inside of the SUV. Gabriel's SUV.

Eli reached for the control panel, but I swatted his hand away. "Don't. When I drive, we listen to my music."

"Ari's vehicle. His music."

I switched off the music, hating that Gabriel and I shared an appreciation for heavy metal and hard rock. The only thing I wanted to share with him – a heavy rock crushing down on his skull. "His name is Gabriel. Now that the truth is out, you can drop the act."

Eli laughed, the sound bitter. "When we met, he introduced himself as Ari, that's what I've called him since I was eighteen years old."

"I find it hard to believe he lied about his name when you both joined Aman." Aidan had shared the highlights of their military background with me. How he possessed classified information about the years they had spent as part of Sayeret Matkal, I didn't ask. Once he mentioned the satellite, I had my answer.

"You know things you shouldn't, Finley."

I slammed my palms against the steering wheel. "I don't know diddly-squat. All I know is that I'm carrying *his* child, something I never consented to. My sister fell pregnant while on the pill, and here we are, hiding from my husband. Aidan believed you were his friend. He trusted you."

Eli looked at me, his hazel eyes unreadable. "Finley, *you* got into this vehicle and left with us. For your protection and Lizzie's. Aidan is unstable, he killed two of his patients' husbands, the exact way the Marcel Sniper gunned down several people years ago. You need to face the facts that the man you love is not the real Aidan Walker. He's a psychopath, Fin. You of all people should know there is no magic pill to cure him. Aidan is a cold-blooded killer, killing people not to protect his country, you, or himself. He enjoys it."

Not as much as I will enjoy killing you. "What? So, because I have a doctorate in Psychology and I'm a qualified profiler, I should've seen the truth?" The truth I referred to wasn't about Aidan.

"Love blinds us." He shrugged. "I also didn't see him for what he is, and I've been surrounded by more psychopaths and narcissists than I care to count."

"I'll count for you. One – Gabriel."

"He's not a psychopath. His only issue, if I can call it that, is that he's committed to the woman he loves. You."

I laughed, struggling to keep the vehicle in the lane. A deer darted from between the trees, stopping in the middle of the road. My foot pressed the brake to the floorboard. The squeal of tyres filled the silence. The deer disappeared into the thin line of trees on the other side of the forest towards the cliff. For a split second, I noticed a vehicle in the rear-view mirror. The first and only I saw during the drive towards, at that point, I didn't know where.

"Are you okay?" Eli asked.

I placed my hand to my stomach and glanced down. "Yes, I think so."

"Do you want me to drive?"

I turned to Eli and rolled my eyes.

"No need to get childish. I thought, considering what happened to your parents, you might be shaken up?"

My nails dug into the leather covering of the steering wheel.

"I've driven since my parents' accident."

"Sorry. I forget you and Lizzie process things differently."

I turned to him, my jaw tight. "Yes, Lizzie and I process things in our own ways. I didn't identify their bodies. If I hadn't been held captive at the time, I would never have let her do it. Why didn't Tom do it? You're his buddy, his pal, why not him?"

"I wasn't aware that you were being held captive when your parents died. Only the time the Scarecrows abducted you," he said, looking at his watch again.

I ignored him, removed my foot from the brake, and continued driving south, taking the first road we came across. No signage or any indication of what road we were driving on. We were in for a bumpy, dusty, ride.

An hour and fifteen minutes after we left the house, we drove into a small town. The word quaint created for a place just like this. The wooden buildings looked as if they were straight out of a previous century, the five vehicles parked in the main road more modern, but not new. As we drove along the dirt road leading in and through the town, I realised this was it.

I parked the SUV and got out. A sign hung above the door of what appeared to be a restaurant – Welcome to Pepper Gorge. Eli and I walked towards the establishment and as I glanced down the street, I saw what I believed to be the vehicle I had spotted in my rear-view mirror, park at the edge of the town.

I asked for a table close to the air conditioner. The outside humidity didn't compare to summer in Marcel, but the heat remained unbearable. Eli took the chair to my right. Neither of us ever sat with our backs facing a door or open space in an unfamiliar place. I scanned the restaurant; none of the people were glued to their mobile phones. No one took selfies. The two waitresses greeted everyone by name. They directed curious glances towards our table.

Our waitress, Nicol, disappeared into the kitchen after

taking our order. I stared at the man next to me; he had been different since we left Marcel. Come to think of it, he had been acting strange since we returned from Vietnam.

Eli tilted his head and met my stare. "Is there something you want to ask me?"

The list of questions I had were as long as my arm. They had been milling inside my head since I had watched him frame Aidan for murder. I reached for the glass of water the waitress had brought us when she had informed us that today, they only served boiled eggs, sausage and toast, and returned it to the table without quenching my thirst. The desire for knowledge doesn't make me thirsty. My need for vengeance, however, is a different matter.

"Are you excited about being a father?" Where the question came from, I didn't know, the answer didn't matter to me. No way would I allow him to be a part of Lizzie's or their child's life once this was over. When Aidan came for me.

Eli tapped a finger against the wristwatch and smiled. "Of course, I thought Lizzie and I would get married first and then start a family, but sometimes life works out differently to what we had planned."

"You've been engaged for close to two years, why did you guys never keep to the dates you set?" I thanked the waitress for my juice – half orange, half strawberry – and waited for Eli to answer.

"Work has been busy for both of us. Lizzie signed with the new distribution company and I had several important projects which required my attention."

Ice clinked against glass as I stabbed at the ice cubes with the straw. "I'm calling bullshit. You asked her to marry you, you moved into her house, and don't forget you were the one who kept pushing the date back. As much as I respect the work you do, it's not something someone else couldn't have overseen while you took a week off for a honeymoon. Lizzie's assistant, or I, could've helped with the arrangements."

He shook his head, glancing towards the door. "You didn't

have time with your thesis and the hours you put into hunting Sophia."

The previous year had been one of the worst; not only hunting a serial killer and completing my thesis, but also losing our baby and undergoing the fertility treatment which had given me the life growing inside me – Aidan's child.

"You and I share a special bond, Eli. The least you can do is be honest with me about your plans with my sister." In my mind he had been the closest male friend I had ever had, more a brother than a friend.

He dropped his head forward. "As soon as we eliminate the threat, I will marry Liz, and we will raise our child together."

"Are you trying to convince me or yourself?"

Eli didn't look at me. "Dammit, Fin, why can't you just accept that I love your sister? The fact that we aren't married yet doesn't change how much I love her and want a future with her. In case you forgot – your husband is the reason we're hiding in the middle of nowhere."

Heat spread to every part of me as I pushed back my chair. "I will be right back." Eli got to his feet. "I'm going to pee, if you must know, not running away. Where will I go? My sister is with Gabriel. Do you think I will take off without her?"

Eli sat down, hard, mumbling under his breath.

A woman appeared in the mirror as I looked up from washing my hands. Even though we had never met, I recognised her bicoloured eyes. I turned to face her; she held her hand out towards me. It wasn't the first time a stranger had approached me in a bathroom and showed me something they wanted me to stick in one of my orifices. This time, I wouldn't leave the person bleeding on the floor.

I placed the device inside my ear. Not only did the device transmit sound, but it also picked it up. Invisible to the naked eye, and waterproof. It will never be available on any kind of market, including the black.

"I've missed you, Mrs Walker."

Tears streamed down my face at the sound of his voice. "Come get me. I can't do this anymore."

"Seeing you throw the mug at his face made me laugh almost as much as the day you shot into the fireplace. Did you miss on purpose?"

"What do you think? Wait. You saw it?"

"I've been watching you since we hacked into their surveillance cameras. Fifteen seconds after you activated the tracking device. FYI, none in your or Lizzie's bathrooms."

"Then you know I'm a breath away from killing them both and ending this. I'm leaving with her. Today." I stared at the woman who smiled back at me, her eyes filled with compassion.

"There's nothing I want more than to hold you and have you and our child back where we belong, but, Finley, this isn't over yet. We still don't know who, or why. I'm sorry for failing you."

"Send a team to extract Lizzie, I'm ordering them to take Gabriel out. Right now, Aidan. We can take Eli in; I will make him talk." My entire body trembled.

The woman placed her arms around me. I pursed my lips, fighting against the wave of emotions swirling inside me. The ever-present darkness clawed at me and I yearned to let it in. Allow it to consume me and unleash it on the people who forced me into standing in a bathroom, listening to my husband's voice. I had no idea where he was. "Where are you?" I stepped back and away from the sympathy this almost complete stranger offered.

"Europe. A step closer to the truth."

"Europe is big, my love. Be specific."

"Not France. Not Germany." I could hear his smile.

"I love you, Aidan Walker. If you don't end this soon, I will put a bullet between Gabriel's eyes, one in each of Eli's kneecaps, and shoulder sockets for good measure, and then I'm going to hunt *you* down." If a stranger wasn't standing in front of me, I would've told him exactly what I had been fantasising about doing to him as soon as I saw him.

Aidan laughed. The sound filled my soul, yet broke my heart. I would've given anything to see the way his face changes when he laughs. The fine lines become more pronounced around his eyes, and the colour always reminds me of the sky after a storm. Mischief dancing in those very eyes. His boyish grin. We had met as two broken people and become whole on our own; well, as whole as can be expected considering what we had both survived and done. Two halves do not make a whole, but two broken wholes are a perfect match. We merged into each other's broken parts and became stronger in our union, embracing each other's flaws and never passing judgement. I ached for him.

"Mrs Walker, I promise in less than 336 hours, you will stand in front of me. I will push my hands through your beautiful hair, drop my mouth to yours, and kiss you until your legs fail. Then I will hold you up, pulling your gorgeous body closer to mine, and keep kissing you until your jaw hurts. Feathering kisses along your jaw, neck, collarbones, and make my way lower until I'm on my knees. I will reclaim every part of you with my mouth, my tongue, and hands. What will follow is best shown in person."

I closed my gaping mouth, willing my heart to beat. Remembering the taste of his mouth, the strength in his hands, the feel of his warm body moving against, and with, mine. Exploring the perfect lines of his muscles with my tongue and the sheer joy of him filling me. The next 336 hours would be the longest of my life.

The woman shook her head with a hint of a smile on her face. She jerked her head towards the door behind her and pushed me into a cubicle. She locked the door and instructed me to sit. Pressing her back against the brick wall, she lifted her legs and placed her feet on the opposite wall, anchoring herself.

"What's going on, why can't I see you? Quinn, tell me what's going on," Aidan said.

I lifted my eyes to the acrobat still pressed up against the cubicle's walls. She met my stare and shook her head, pointing at her eye. I pressed my forefinger to my lips.

"Where did you get that?" I recognised Nicol, our waitress' voice.

"Henry gave it to me."

"Where did he get it? You know what will happen if you get caught with it."

"Will you calm down, no one will find out. At least now we can see what's going on. What time does your shift end? Do you want to go with me?"

"I'm here until closing. Can tell my mother we are going to the waterfall or something. Is Henry coming with us?"

"I haven't asked him yet, he wasn't at breakfast. Will head home now and ask him to join us. He said he has something to tell you."

"Did he ask your dad for permission?"

"My dad said yes. He will have to clear it with the others, but you, my friend, will be married soon."

A strange thudding sound came from the other side of the door.

"I'm going to marry Henry. Nicol Bailey. I've always liked the sound of it. I wish I could be his only wife. More than that, I wish he could be my first. I don't want to do it."

"It doesn't matter, he's in love with you. Why it bothers you is beyond me."

"Keep quiet." A shuffling sound on the other side of the door. "Hello, is someone in here?"

A knock on the cubicle's door. I opened my mouth, but the woman answered first. "No comprende inglés."

"I didn't realise there were Germans scheduled this week. And why are they bringing their wives with? To watch? Freaks."

"It's Spanish, you idiot. She said she doesn't understand English."

"My apologies, your highness, not all of us have the extra classes you have. Listen, I need to get back to my tables. Strangest thing, this couple came in and I swear if the woman doesn't stab the man before they leave, my name will not be Nicol Bailey. She practised on the ice in her glass."

Laughter followed them out of the bathroom. The woman eased down as Aidan spoke. "Why are you in Pepper Gorge?"

"I turned left instead of right when I drove out the gate. Aidan, our waitress can't be more than sixteen and she's already talking about marriage."

"Not all girls are into guns and warfare at that age."

I rolled my eyes and sighed.

"I saw and heard that. Since when do you roll your eyes at me?"

"Since you're watching me through surveillance cameras and whatever this woman has in her eye. Whatever it is, I want one. Then you can see what I do."

The woman in question handed me a small tin. "Way ahead of you, Wife. Quinn has more gifts for you. I trust you will appreciate them until I can give you the one I'm dying to give you."

"I take it she can hear everything you're saying?" I shook my head at Quinn's smile. The photos I had seen of her in Aidan's parents' house in Wild Bay didn't do her justice.

"Yes. You need to go back to your table. I'll talk to you as often as I can, so keep the device in your ear, especially in the shower. I love you, Finley Williams-Walker. Tell my baby I love him or her."

"We love you. You have less than 365 hours, Dr Walker. Remember, if you're on time, you're late."

Quinn turned to me, placing her hands on my shoulders. "You need to get your head in the game. Aidan won't say it because he loves you, but your aggression will undo all the sacrifices he's making to put an end to this. If you don't get your act together, you may as well have gone with him. He can't hunt when he's worried about you, or what you might do."

She shook her head and squeezed my shoulders. "Whoever is behind this is watching your every move. I can assure you they're wondering why you left with Gabriel when you look at him with nothing but hatred. Two more weeks, that's all Aidan is asking of you."

My heart clenched. "Two more weeks?"

Quinn shrugged. "336 hours." She pulled me closer and hugged me tight, whispering in my other ear. "You have an ally with you in that house, and I'm not talking about Lizzie."

She disappeared as quickly as she had appeared, through the manhole in the ceiling. *336 hours. Two weeks.* Aidan knew I sucked at mathematics. I smiled, realising why he had said hours and not days. "If you're still listening, I love you, Aidan. You get me, you know me better than anyone ever has. You're the glue that keeps me together. I'll do better, play my part. I ache for you, to be home with you. Hurry. Please." Nothing.

I wiped my eyes and stared at myself in the mirror. *Of all the masks I've ever worn, this will be the most important.* "Game time, Walker."

"I love it when you're just Walker, not Williams-Walker," Aidan said in my ear, his voice filled with promise.

"I've been Walker since the first time I laid eyes on you."

"Finley, I..."

"I know."

Aidan sighed. "No, you don't. Gabriel's speciality is death."

"If he's an assassin, who hired him? And why hasn't he killed me, or you, or whoever his mark is?"

"Your guess is as good as mine."

Three

Somewhere in Europe. (Not France. Not Germany.)

"Why did you lie to her?"

"If I tell her, she will hunt him down on her own. I won't allow her to put her life, or our child's, in danger. Finley will hear the truth when I can serve him hog-tied on a platinum platter to her." Aidan leaned back in his chair and stared at the ceiling. *Two more weeks.*

"Here's what I don't understand – why are you both set on hunting on your own when you're the perfect team? Hell, you both served in the military, not to mention the years you worked for me, yet you've both decided to put your old lives behind you? Together you will be unstoppable."

Aidan nodded, closing his eyes. He hadn't slept more than a few hours at a time since the night he had last held his wife in his arms. Frowning, he leaned forward and tilted his head to the side. "What do you mean, with our old lives?"

"Remind me, what was The Hangman's final body count? Although, knowing your wife, she probably took offense that the authorities never considered a woman could be responsible."

Aidan forced a shrug but didn't play ignorant. "Forty-eight, if I'm not mistaken."

"Forty-nine, counting the death of the wanna-be necrophiliac who raped her sister. Don't look at me like that. It's my responsibility to know everything that's going on in the world, or at the very least, pay people to stay on top of everything."

"You knew?"

"Of course, why do you think your mother and I welcomed her into our family with open arms? She's the perfect fit for this family and she doesn't even realise it."

"Dad, she can't go back there, it almost destroyed her. I will do whatever it takes to avoid her being in a position where she holds someone else's life in her hands again."

"We can show her a different way."

"No. Finley's reasons for putting it behind her are the same as mine. I will lay them all at her feet and it will be up to her to decide whether she kills them or not. I hope we will need the rooms I have asked Chester to prepare."

Four

Upon my return to the table, I noticed Nicol had brought our breakfast. Taking my seat, I reached for the decaf cappuccino. The mug was cool against my fingers.

"Where the hell have you been?" Eli asked.

"In the restroom, bathroom, toilet, ladies, whatever you want to call it."

"For ten minutes?"

I sighed and leaned back in my chair. "One of the many things a pregnant woman has to endure is constipation. There, I said it. I'm constipated."

Eli's cheeks turned red. "I'm sorry. Is there anything you can take to help you, you know?"

"Prunes, fibre-rich cereals and food. I drink enough water. Just another part of being pregnant." I forced a shrug and dug into my scrambled eggs. Not as delicious as the Eggs Benedict Aidan made me.

Eli leaned closer. "Something's going on in this town."

"Tell me why you say so, and I will tell you what I overheard while in the bathroom. Oh, when the waitress comes around again, I speak Spanish, it's a good thing you ordered for us."

He placed his knife and fork on the plate and moved closer. "From now on we are husband and wife, having a lovely breakfast on our way through town."

I nodded, forcing affection into my stare.

"A woman rushed in screaming that they found another body. The guy sitting by the front door stood and said something to her. I couldn't hear what he said, but the woman looked at me and stormed out. After she left, he told me she's delusional, always making up stories. Nicol stood outside the door to the kitchen, her face as white as bleached teeth. Okay, your turn."

I told Eli what I had overheard between Nicol and her mystery friend. "Did the woman say a name or only that a body has been discovered?"

"Just a body. What do you think Nicol meant when she spoke of the tourists bringing their wives with them?"

"No idea. How old do you think Nicol is?"

"Fifteen. Sixteen. Why?"

"She's talking about marriage and wishing she could be this Henry's *only* wife. Did you see the girl who came out with her?"

"Yes."

"How old would you say she is?"

"Nicol's age. Don't girls that age dream about getting married?"

I didn't know. Teenager-me focused on perfecting my aim with any gun I could lay my hands on and building cars with my father. Lizzie had her schoolwork. Even though at sixteen we had both started dating, neither of us ever mentioned marriage. I made a mental note to ask Lizzie when we returned to the house.

"When Nicol comes to our table, ask her for the newspaper."

Eli did. *The Pepper Times* was printed once a month and the newest edition had been delivered that morning. No mention of the body found the day before or any other deaths in the four-paged A5-size pamphlet. Calling it a newspaper would be a gross exaggeration.

After finishing our breakfast and ordering another round of drinks, caffeine-free for me, Nicol made her way to the restroom. I followed her.

"Nicol, what you tell me of body found?" I butchered a Spanish accent.

She spun around, her face pale. "You speak English."

I nodded. "Si. Uhm, yes. You see dead person?"

Nicol headed for the door, but I grabbed her arm. Tears filled her eyes. I cupped her face and smiled at her. She dropped her head forward, taking a step back.

"How many bodies have been found?"

She jerked her head up, frowning.

"Sorry I had to deceive you, I'm on an undercover assignment in Coopersville." Not a complete lie. "I work with the police." I had in the past. "If there's something going on here, I can help you."

"Why are you here? No one ever comes to this hellhole unless they..." She shut her eyes, shaking her head.

"To help."

"If you work with the police, then you're one of them."

I reached for her. She stepped back, pressing her back against the wall. On instinct, I stepped back to give her some personal space. "I'm not a police officer, but I do work with the police as a profiler. Do you know what a profiler is?"

Nicol shook her head. "Nothing is going on here. Someone died, it's part of the cycle of life." She shrugged and wiped her eyes.

"How did this person die? And how many others died before him or her, and how?"

"I can't..."

"If something is going on here, you need to tell me. As a profiler, my work is to help the police apprehend criminals. To stop the terrible things they're doing. It's much more complicated than that, but that's the just of it. What do the Germans do when they come here?"

Again, she stepped back and realised her back was already pressed against the wall. "To see the waterfall."

I rolled my eyes at her, a new habit which irritated me more than anyone else. "Tell me the truth and I can help all of you. Faster. Please."

"Get back in your car and forget about this place. Nothing good comes from asking questions."

This time, when she moved towards the door, I didn't stop her.

***

On our way back to the house, I told Eli what Nicol had said, and what she hadn't. Fear had rippled off her in waves. More than once he glanced at me and opened his mouth, only to look away and stare at the wristwatch.

Eli walked ahead of me, and I sank down on the top step of the porch, scanning the surroundings. The reason they chose this place had been apparent the moment we had arrived. Isolated. Far from the main road, with only one road leading to the house close to the top of the mountain. The surrounding trees offered camouflage, even if a helicopter passed overhead, they wouldn't be able to spot us. Similar to the town we had stumbled upon.

I made my way to the room I occupied and locked the door. In the bathroom, I removed the tin Quinn had given me from where it was strapped to my thigh and opened it. Inside the tin was a switchblade and contact lenses. Putting a contact lens in for the first time isn't the easiest thing to do, but I did it, and felt proud of myself for succeeding on the first try.

"I have visuals," Quinn said in my ear.

In a low voice I said, "Can you please not listen when I'm on the toilet? Or watch when I'm showering?"

Quinn laughed, the sound made me smile. "Don't worry, Finley, it will only be me with you at all times. I'm sure Aidan is used to your bathroom habits."

Aidan and I had both been adamant that certain aspects of our personal hygiene had to remain a mystery, and we never walked into the bathroom when the other person occupied the throne. It didn't matter that he's a doctor, a gynaecologist, an obstetrician, I'm his wife, and he had to believe I did nothing more than urinate. *Urinate.* I've never liked the word, and pee is crass. Tinkle? Perhaps.

"So, you're the ally in the house?" I whispered.

"Yes and no. It's not my place to tell you, and you're an intelligent woman, Dr Walker, you can figure it out yourself."

Never before had anyone called me Doctor Walker. I never had time to process the reality of obtaining my doctorates.

"Once this is over, I look forward to getting to know you."

"And I you, Finley. Game time. Gabriel is heading towards your bedroom door."

Before Gabriel could knock, I opened the door and stared up at him, tempering down my rage, and realised he couldn't be the ally Quinn had referred to earlier. *Eli?* "Gabriel, what can I do for you today? Stab you? Shoot you? Smother you in your sleep?"

He rested his hands at his sides. "Funny. Smothering me would be easier if I slept next to you. If you tire me out, as you once loved to do, I won't be able to put up a fight."

"Aidan never got tired." A smile spread across my face.

"They say serial killers have a lot of stamina."

And assassins? "Get to the point, Gabriel. I want to check up on Lizzie, and then Eli and I have some work to do."

"Ah, yes, your little wild goose chase. Are you so bored you need to look for people to save? Always the protector. One of the many reasons I love you."

"I recall we had a similar conversation before Sophia's arrest. This time I won't say anything about shoving it in your face." I held up my hands. "Something is going on in that place and Eli knows it as well. So, either help us or keep quiet and stay out of my way."

"Stress isn't good for our baby."

I laughed. I tried not to, but couldn't help it. "You think being in the middle of nowhere, confined to this house, with *you*, isn't stressful?" Remembering my promise to Aidan and Quinn, I continued. "Gabriel, it will take time to get used to the idea of my child being yours. You had no right to switch your sperm with Aidan's, no matter what you believe about my husband. I was desperate to have a child, and you tainted this for me. You're my ex, for crying out loud, and to be honest, I don't even like you anymore. You lied to me about your name. If you can lie about something like that, how can I trust anything else you said, say and will ever say to me?"

He stared at his shoes. "I came to invite you to dinner, as

a peace offering. Whether you want to come to terms with it or not, my child is growing inside you, and I will be a part of his life."

His life? An idea came to me. "It might be a girl. I'm sixteen weeks pregnant. We could go for a sonar, ensure the baby is still growing as he or she should, and that the stress of the past two weeks hasn't affected the baby, or me. A doctor might be able to tell us the sex of the baby. Due to my age, the torture my body has been subjected to, and the baby I lost, this pregnancy is at a higher risk. Going for regular check-ups will be a good thing. Wouldn't you like to see your child?" The feeling that spread through me was akin to what I believe evil witches and stepmothers in fairy tales feel.

Gabriel's smile reached his eyes. I hadn't seen him happy in a very long time. "Yes. I want to see our child, hear his or her heartbeat, and of course your and the baby's health is the most important thing to me."

"Lizzie is around eight or nine weeks pregnant, so now will be a good time for her to go for her first check-up. Gabriel, seeing as I don't have internet access, can you please find us an obstetrician in Coopersville? One who specialises in high-risk pregnancies."

He lifted his hand to my face, dragging his thumb along my cheekbone. I wondered how many people had died at his hands. "Will get on it right now. Finley, thank you."

My smile was forced, but he didn't notice.

"Will you have dinner with me? Meet me at six on the back porch."

After agreeing to his invitation, I went back into the bathroom. "I'm working on it," Quinn said.

"Thank you. Under no circumstances must Gabriel learn the sex of this baby."

Lizzie lay on her side, facing the window. I settled next to her and brushed my fingers over her hair as I had when we were children.

"I asked Gabriel to find us an obstetrician in Coopersville. We can go for check-ups and you should be able to hear your baby's heartbeat."

"Thank you." She kept her eyes on the window.

I leaned closer, pressing my lips to her temple, and whispered, "Two more weeks and this will be over." Her golden hair like silk between my fingers. "Do you remember when we were young, and we communicated without saying a word?"

Liz nodded.

"I wonder if our babies will be able to do it? When last did we even try?"

"We haven't needed to since we got mobile phones and started texting each other." Lizzie turned to me, a sorrowful smile on her delicate face.

"Remember when Mom saw the messages we had sent and took our phones away for two weeks? It seemed much longer."

Lizzie nodded, a hint of a smile tugging at the corners of her mouth.

"How are you?" I laid my fingers against her forehead.

"Better. Gabriel made me some ginger tea while you were out and opened the windows. The air is fresh up here."

"If you feel up to it, we can go for a walk. Getting out of this house will do you good."

Lizzie agreed, and together we walked through the forest to where the property ended at the edge of the ravine. Gabriel had been reluctant to let us go out on our own, but Eli told him it would do us both good.

I took her hands in mine and pulled her closer. "Aidan made contact today."

"I knew it. Your eyes are brighter and the dark cloud hanging over you isn't as dark. Why are we here? Has he figured out what's going on?"

"He said no, but I think he has, he just doesn't want me to worry. Liz, Aidan confirmed there are surveillance cameras throughout the house and parts of the surrounding property. The ones out here face the ravine. If you need to be alone, go into your bathroom or come here, it's the only places they can't see or hear us."

"I still don't understand why." Lizzie rested her forehead against mine.

"I've been racking my brain trying to figure it out. If anyone can get to the bottom of this, it's Aidan and his father's organisation. I'm in constant contact with one of their operatives and Aidan checks in on me whenever he can. We aren't alone anymore."

"I'm sleeping next to one of them, carrying his child. I love him, Fin. How can he do this to me?"

Answers I didn't have. Not until I have the opportunity to make him tell me. Everyone has their breaking point. Since we had left Marcel two weeks before, I hadn't stopped trying to dissect the circumstances. Gabriel's return to Marcel. Eli's reluctance to get married. Tom's obsession with proving Aidan is the Marcel Sniper. Gabriel and Eli framing Aidan for two murders. Why?

If they were after the money Lizzie and I had inherited from our parents, there are far wealthier heiresses in the world for them to have targeted. Eli's one of the best hackers in the world. With just a few keystrokes he could steal unfathomable amounts of money. Gabriel's an attractive man, he could con any woman he wanted. Anyone but me. Not anymore, at least.

Had Lizzie fallen pregnant while on the pill by chance or human hand? Too many questions. No answers.

"The operative told me we have an ally in the house, and I think she referred to Eli. Maybe he's playing both sides. Either he's the best actor in the world, or he loves you. We will know soon enough. For the time being, we keep sticking together. Can you keep faking morning sickness?"

Lizzie laughed. "I get to read novel after novel and not cook or clean and Eli's at my beck and call. This is the best vacation ever." She shook her head. "Vietnam was the best. This is our lives and not a vacation. I'm sorry."

"For what? You're having fun and getting the rest you

need during your first trimester. Enjoy it. Two more weeks and we will be back in Marcel, back at work and preparing for our babies' arrivals. Savour the luxury, even under the circumstances."

"How does this thing with Aidan and the operative contacting you work?"

I told her about the device inside my ear and the contact lens which had a microscopic camera imbedded in it.

"Aidan, if you hear this, thank you. Fin is her old self. Hurry up and get whoever is behind this. It's time we all go home."

I waited, but Aidan didn't answer. *Where are you?*

As Lizzie and I made our way back towards the house, I thought about what she had said, 'Fin is her old self'. If only she knew of the darkness festering inside me. What I'm capable of when I embrace it.

I joined Eli in the dining room, and he shared what he had learned about the town we had stumbled upon. Nothing.

"What do you mean Pepper Gorge doesn't exist? Did we both hallucinate it?" I pulled his laptop closer and searched for the town using Google Earth. Once I located it, I turned the laptop towards him and leaned back in the chair, crossing my arms over my chest. "And they call you the brilliant hacker."

Eli laughed without malice. "That I found. The town itself isn't on any map, it doesn't have an area code, nothing. The road leading there isn't an official road either. What made you decide to turn down a random dirt road?"

I shrugged because I couldn't tell him I suspected we were being followed and I wanted to know if the pursuers played for their team or ours. My hunch paid off big time. "I've been confined to this house for two weeks; I needed to get out, see something, anything."

From the kitchen, Gabriel cleared his throat. "So, the town doesn't exist, and the person who mentioned the body is said to be delusional. Teenage girls talking about marriage. Shocking."

Eli and I shared a knowing look as realisation dawned on us. I said it first. "There's a place you haven't looked."

He lowered his voice. "Are you sure you want to open that gate to hell?"

Did I want to tumble down the hole which the abyss, the dark web, is? No. *Yes.* It had been my hunting ground once. The place where nightmares breed. Nightmares I still have.

"Send out one of those Trojan horse thingies or worms or whatever you do to find stuff no other person can ever find without it taking months, if not years." If Eli had been on Team Hangwoman, I could've saved myself a lot of late nights hunting the vilest of human predators.

"Are you sure? Think about what happened last time." He placed his mouth against my cheek, and I willed my body to remain in place. "When Aidan hears of this, he will kill me."

"No, I won't," Aidan said in my ear. It was like having a deadly guardian angel on my shoulder. Well, two, both on the same shoulder, considering Quinn also made her presence known. "If this puts you in any danger, then I will kill him."

This, I decided, must be how people with schizophrenia live, and authors whose characters talk to them. I turned to Eli and mouthed, "Tell me."

He nodded, took my hand, and pulled me to my feet as he came to his full length.

Five

Somewhere over Europe. Location: Classified.

He touched her face on the screen with his forefinger. He smiled, wondering how long before the voices in her head would irritate her.

"The plan wasn't to tell her, not until this is over." Ryan Walker poured himself a whiskey and one for his eldest son. He settled next to Aidan and refastened his seatbelt.

"Quinn blew it by telling her she has an ally in the house. After I told her Gabriel's speciality, it would've been a matter of minutes before she put two and two together." Aidan savoured the taste of the Jameson. "She needs to know she's not alone, Dad. Finley was heading towards killing them both and I don't want her to have more blood on her hands, more deaths weighing on her soul. Eli proved himself by making contact, and *his* fingerprints weren't on the blister pack of the contraceptives we found in Lizzie's bathroom."

"Involving him is risky considering we're talking about your wife and child's lives here. Not to mention what *he* will do to Eli if we're unsuccessful."

Aidan closed his eyes, reminding himself that his father had his best interests at heart. *Failure isn't an option.* "I've known Eli for two years, we are friends. Family. You know how he came to be involved in this and when he made contact. He loves Lizzie and will do anything to protect her, just as I will do anything to protect Finley. At least Eli's armed, should Gabriel get a kill order."

"Why do you think the Williams sisters weren't eliminated? This is an elaborate ploy considering how easy it would be to take them out. Neither Finley nor Lizzie know the truth,

28

otherwise the men working with Gabriel would've found what they're looking for when they ransacked your homes."

"Tom Anderson struck a deal with the devil, but he underestimated the lengths Duncan went to in order to protect his daughters."

Aidan contacted Quinn and instructed her to aid in any way possible with Finley and Eli's investigation into Pepper Gorge. If it came down to it, she could even share the contents of the file his father's organisation had compiled on the unofficial town.

Finley needed this distraction to keep her centred and her mind focused on solving whatever was going on at the farm rather than willing away the next 358 hours.

Six

The sun hovered above the horizon; the shadows cast by the trees reached towards the back porch where fairy lights hung from the rafters. Across from me sat a stranger. The man I had met, began to fall in love with, even longed for after he had left, had never really existed.

Everything I knew about Gabriel I had learned from watching footage of his sessions with Doctor James, his therapist. The ironic thing – I had a serial killer to thank for discovering the truth. Hearing how obsessed Gabriel had become with me, and his desire to have children, a family, a normal life. Could an assassin be capable of living a normal life?

Aidan and I had realised long ago we could never live a life the general populous consider normal. Neither of us deluded ourselves into believing we could; to an extent, we embraced who and what we are, always fighting the ever-present darkness which hung over us, suffocating us at the best of times. Its name? Vengeance.

Aidan had spent his life trying to fit in when he had been born to be different. Circumstances had moulded me into who I am.

"Thank you for agreeing to have dinner with me." Gabriel reached for my hand, but I picked up the glass of water and lifted it to my mouth. "Admit it, you're tired of my cooking." I forced a smile.

"Never. What I will admit is how much it bothers me that you still wear your wedding ring." Gabriel glanced at the rock of a blue diamond on my left hand.

Time to test the mask. "I'm not ready to take it off. I miss Aidan and a part of me will love him forever." I covered my face with my hands, forcing tears.

"Ley, I hate it when you cry. He never deserved your love. He's a murderer," said the man who took lives for money. "How long did it take you to get over me? To put the love and passion we shared behind you? Don't you think it's strange that he came into your life right after I left?"

"I met Aidan *months* after you left. Not to hurt you, but you can't compare what you and I had to the life Aidan and I share."

Gabriel moved his chair to my side of the table and took my hands in his. "I will spend the rest of my life making you happy, taking care of you and our child. Children, if you want more. I love you, Ley."

I stared up at the man next to me, aching to plunge the steak knife lying on my plate into his neck.

Aidan's voice filled my head – his actual voice. "You're the apex predator. Look at the orca tattoo on your wrist. Remember who you are. The Scarecrows didn't break you, neither will he."

I pulled my hands free and stared down at the tribal ink covering a scar Aidan had stitched when he saved my life. Again, he spoke. "That's my wife."

"Why?" I asked Gabriel.

"Why what?"

"Why does Gabriel love me? Ari never existed. The man I could've fallen in love with was an illusion. Everything we shared was a lie, even your name. None of the conversations we had about my time as a prisoner of war, the things they did to me, things I shared with a person I trusted, it meant nothing to you. I thought Ari was a soldier like me. A man who fought against the evil in this world. Like me. The worst thing is, I gave my body to him after I was...none of it was real. *Lies.* All of it." Tears streamed down my face and I pushed away from him, heading towards the dying light.

My tears weren't from being hurt by his actions, or his lies. I cried because the alternative would be to kill him. Rage swirled deep inside me, moving closer to the surface. This man framed my husband for murder, tried to impregnate me, and still had the gall to say he loves me. *Neutering him with a wooden spoon might work.*

"If you kill him, this entire operation blows up in our faces. Believe me, I hate this more than you do. But I promise the day of reckoning will come." The control in Aidan's voice grounded me.

Footsteps came to a stop behind me, and I felt him towering over me. "The bravery you showed when others would've crawled into a corner and withered away. Not you, not my Ley. No, you fought back and righted some of the wrongs in this world. You survived captivity twice. You're loyal and love your family more than anything. The commitment you showed hunting Sophia and finishing your thesis while you suffered a loss and underwent fertility treatment was nothing short of inspiring."

I spun around, and my palms connected with his chest. He stammered backwards. "A loss? Losing my baby almost killed me. If not for Aidan, I wouldn't have survived. How dare you bring up the death of my baby? I held that embryo in my hands and you dare call it *a loss!*"

Gabriel dragged his hands down his face. "I'm sorry, Ley. I didn't mean to upset you."

"Tell me, seeing as you claim to love me, what's my middle name? What's my favourite meal for breakfast? Name three of my favourite bands? What's my favourite colour? My biggest pet peeve? My first love, what is his name and where did we meet? I had a dog growing up, what breed was it, and bonus points if you can tell me the gender and name of said dog?"

As I asked each question, Aidan answered. He had known the answers since the night we first met. When he had opted to get to know me rather than get naked with me. At the time, my hormones didn't agree. His boyish grin is the biggest turn on ever. Not to mention the effect kissing him has on me. After two years of kissing him, butterflies still scurried inside me.

"Your middle name is Duncan; you were named after your

father. After school you completed your master's in Psychology and Criminology at the University of Marcel, and then you enlisted in the army where you held the rank of sergeant until you were taken prisoner during an ambush. During your captivity, your parents died in an accident. You carry two guns on you at all times, a SIG holstered by your hip and a Glock at your right ankle. My apologies for taking them from you, but a pregnant woman shouldn't carry a loaded weapon. You identified the Angel Taker as a former classmate at UM and a police officer."

It sounded like he was reading from a list, one he had committed to memory. I realised they must have a file on me, and perhaps one on Lizzie, too. *Why?*

"Who killed the Angel Taker, Tony Andretti, and saved my life?"

Gabriel flinched, and for a second I relished in the small victory. A hired killer couldn't be proud of missing a target as big as Tony Andretti. "The police never identified a suspect. The calibre of bullet was the same as used by the Marcel Sniper when he murdered innocent people."

I guess an assassin would call paedophiles and the sister and her roommate who sold a fourteen-year-old girl to be raped *innocent*.

"My middle name, I've never told you."

"Lizzie mentioned it, or Eli."

"You know general things about me. Yet the things that make me who I am, you don't. Say you love me again and you will consume your food through a straw for the rest of your life." I left him standing alone and headed back to the house.

Gabriel caught up and grabbed my arm. "Not knowing silly little things about you doesn't change the fact that I'm in love with a woman who is fierce, loyal, and deadly. I've never met anyone who survived the things you have and fought your way from being a killer to a profiler. You keep protecting the innocent people in this world. And you're the most beautiful woman I have ever been with, ever laid eyes on."

I bit my tongue. Without a doubt Lizzie is the more beautiful Irish twin. Not that I would've admitted it when we were teenagers. Trivial sibling rivalry aside, she's by far my intellectual superior. To my advantage, my husband's IQ is far higher than hers; perhaps rubbing up against him enough could transfer some of it to me. It's worth a shot. *Two weeks.*

Interestingly, Gabriel kept referring to my dark side, yet he has no idea who I am in the light. The things that make me laugh, the movies that make me cry. My guilty pleasures – not considering Aidan being my biggest. "Killer?"

"Well, it's not like they decided to commit suicide on their own. The autopsy reports listed all the various injuries they had suffered pre-mortem, including malnourishment and dehydration."

"Who gave you access to autopsy reports?" *Dig yourself in deeper.*

"During the six months I stayed with Tom, before Sophia abducted me, I came across the case files in his office one day when he was out."

In all the years I had known Tom Anderson, my godfather and my father's best friend, he had always kept his home office locked because of his work, first as a detective and later as a state prosecutor.

"Then why wasn't I arrested, if you believe I'm the Hangman?" Ugh, that sexist word.

"Because the people who know love you and will protect you no matter what. The people who died by your hand, or however you want to phrase it, deserved it."

"Has every person who died by your hand deserved it?"

Gabriel turned his back on me and stared out into the darkness. "Tonight was supposed to be a new beginning for us. I'm tired of fighting with you. We need to find a way to make this work. I refuse to let my child grow up in a house where both parents aren't living together."

The only way that would happen was if this child was his and Gabriel lived locked in the basement.

"Finley, I made appointments for both you and Lizzie with a Doctor Duvall in Coopersville for Tuesday. She can squeeze you in on short notice."

"Thank you for doing that for us. If you want, you can be present when the doctor check's the baby, but as for my check-up, you will wait outside."

"Like hell I will leave you alone with a stranger."

"Well, I have news for you, buddy, you will not be present when the doctor checks my cervix."

"I know every part of you, with my eyes, hands, mouth, and I've been inside you, Ley." Memories flashed in his eyes.

"You impregnated me without my consent. If I had a say in the matter, I would never have had a child with a liar. I will never forgive you for the men Sophia killed because you couldn't be bothered to tell the truth. Your games lead to innocent people dying. No. End of discussion."

"Take that ring off your finger and I will remind you of what we shared, what we can share again."

"Correction, what Ari and I shared for a brief time. But you destroyed his memory when you told me your real name. So, no deal. Thanks for dinner, *Gabriel*. Eli and I have work to do."

Seven

Somewhere in Europe. Location: Classified.

Aidan smiled. Finley toyed with Gabriel, just as he expected. He marvelled at her, his wife, his best friend, the mother of his child. Slamming the laptop's screen shut, he leaned back in his chair and stared out the window. On the other side of the glass, the city teamed with pedestrians and traffic. This wasn't his first time here, and if everything went according to plan, it wouldn't be his last. He had to get to Coopersville. The day they learned the baby's sex, Aidan wanted to be next to his wife.

"Why were you saying random things?" Ryan asked as he walked into the sitting area.

"Gabriel made the mistake of telling Finley he loves her. She asked him why and listed various things she knows he couldn't know about her. I guess she realised they have files on her and Lizzie."

"Were your answers correct?" Ryan asked, the corners of his mouth quirking up.

Aidan shook his head and returned his father's smile.

"Does she know *everything* about you?"

"Of course."

"And, what was her response?" Ryan settled on the couch across from Aidan.

Aidan smiled, remembering the look on Finley's face. "She asked me whether I had enough playtime. If my brothers still wanted to play with me, if I could win in almost every game."

Ryan laughed, the sound filling the room. "They never wanted to play hide-and-seek with you. I remember they only asked you to play TV and computer games when they couldn't

36

advance to the next level." He leaned forward, resting his elbows on his knees. "That's not the typical response you get when people learn your IQ is over 210."

Shaking his head, Aidan closed his eyes, the memory of what Finley did after she found out, so sweet, so typical of her.

"What are you thinking about?"

Aidan mimicked his father's body posture. "She asked me to play with her, but with her own spin on it."

"What was her spin?"

"Strip-hide-and-seek." Glad he leaned forward, so his father wouldn't see his body's response to the memory of that night; a lifetime ago, yet her laughter still sounded in his ears. As did the sounds she had made later.

"You were never made to fit in. Aidan, you're as close to unique as one person can be, considering everything you have done so far. Your mother and I are proud of what you have accomplished. The wrongs you righted. The countless lives you saved as a doctor and an operative. We will forever be most grateful that you found Finley and married her; you're making a wonderful life together. She understands you, respects you as a man, for your uniqueness, your abilities, and your quirks. We need to end this, for all of you."

Ryan stood and walked to the window. "When the time comes, you will not be a part of the mission. I will not let you put your life in danger." He held up his hand, his back still to the room. "You took a calculated risk letting her go with him, and if not for Eli, you wouldn't have. Strategically it was the right thing to do, but as a man, this tears you up inside. The control in your voice when you speak to her isn't real. Your eyes belie your inner torment. Therefore, as your father, and the head of this organisation, you will not be present when this goes down. It's too dangerous."

He turned to face Aidan. "You fought hard to have a normal life, marrying Kate when you knew in your heart she wasn't the right person for you, but still you stayed with her because that's who you are. You're honourable to a fault. Let me do what I should've done for you when you were a child and protect you against your own brilliance, your capabilities. Finley is going to need you safe and unharmed when she learns the truth. She will need you to ground her. To help her make the decision she will be able to live with for the rest of her life."

Aidan clenched his fists. "If she doesn't kill them, I will. For her, Lizzie, and their parents." He joined his father at the window. "How dangerous is the situation at Pepper Gorge? If a single hair on her body isn't the way it was when I left her, I will take out every one of them."

Ryan patted Aidan's shoulder and squeezed. "Ah, you forget the reason you let her go with them. Your mother's assessment of him has been faultless thus far. Gabriel's obsession with her consumes him to the point where there is nothing he will not do to keep her and the baby safe. It goes far beyond what he shared with Dr James. Dr James didn't have access to the records your mother worked through. Perhaps the good farm-folk will solve one of your problems for you."

Growing up with a psychiatrist for a mother hadn't always been easy, but Heather Walker had yet to be wrong in her assessment of a criminal. For as much as Finley Williams-Walker still had to learn about the depths of human depravity, that's where Heather had swum for years.

Eight

I could've made it easier for everyone in the house by allowing Gabriel into my bed. Allow him to touch me, kiss me, do the things he had been vocal about doing the previous night. Not even to save my life would I cheat on Aidan.

Coffee never tasted the same when not made by my husband and brought to me while I still lay in bed. My barista, wearing nothing but a towel riding low on his hips, showcasing his delectable abdominal V. I returned the mug to the table and stared at the Saligna Gum trees. It wasn't much of a view. Only row upon row of trees standing sentry, keeping us in and the world out. I thought of Pepper Gorge and wondered what Eli had found during his research the previous night. Eli had refused to allow me to sit with him while he scoured the dark corners of the abyss for answers.

Years before, the dark web had been my hunting ground where I located paedophiles, rapists, and killers. The abyss, the hunt, their righteous deaths had consumed me until I no longer knew myself at a time when I had already been a fragment of my former self. Four months as a POW changes you; the deaths of my parents while I was in captivity had cinched my implosion.

I still hadn't found time to talk to Eli, to gauge whether he was the ally Quinn had mentioned. Gabriel strode past, his bare back a moving target as he jogged off into the woods. A part of me hoped he would trip and crack his skull on a rock. This was my childish part, that danced with vengeance when I had to control it.

Why did they frame my husband for murder? Why did they have this place set up, awaiting our arrival? The furnishings were beyond the comfort one would expect from a house on a mountain top, which should rather be classified as a brick cabin. Even the bedding and curtains were to my and Lizzie's individual tastes. Flowers in her room, an orchid in mine. I didn't have the heart to let it die, so I took care of it as best I could without a tinge of green in any of my fingers.

Eli and Lizzie joined me, bringing three plates with them. I thanked them and dug into the omelette. This baby needed food. We spoke very little while we ate; Lizzie mentioned she felt better, Eli had information to discuss with me. As we headed to the kitchen to load our dishes in the dishwasher, Lizzie proposed we go to Pepper Gorge for lunch. Eli refused.

"Are we having this discussion again?" She crossed her arms over her chest and leaned the back of her head against the refrigerator.

"It isn't safe, Liz. I only just started finding information on the place, and I don't yet know if the source is reliable." Eli placed his hands on her shoulders. "On Tuesday, we're all going to Coopersville, and we can go for lunch after our appointment. Celebrate our baby, our future."

"I'm tired of being locked up in this house. Come on, honey, Aidan would never hurt Fin or me. Let's go home. Gabriel is not moving back in with us."

The back door slammed shut. "I wasn't planning to. As soon as it's safe to return to Marcel, I will find a home for Finley and myself. Close to you, of course, so you can see each other often and the babies can have more than enough playtime. Family is everything."

With my back to him I asked, "Tell me about your family, were you close? Are you still in contact with them?"

"They're dead." Gabriel marched down the passage and disappeared into the living room where he slept. The house only had two bedrooms. For all I cared, he could've slept in the garage.

I glanced at Eli. He shrugged and shook his head. "Liz, if you don't mind, Finley and I need to talk about what I learned last night." He pressed his lips to her forehead.

"When will you realise you don't need to protect me from everything? I took care of myself before you came into my life. And I..." She pursed her lips. A single tear rolled down her cheek. Lizzie disappeared into their bedroom, closing the door without a sound.

I grabbed Eli's hand and pulled him along as I stormed out of the house. Spinning around to face him, I instead came face to face with his wristwatch. He shook his head. As I pushed up onto my toes, I wrapped my arms around his neck and pressed my lips to his ear. "You need to tell her." Increasing my hold on him, he did the same. "Thank you."

Eli kept me against him and pressed his cheek to mine. "Thank me when this is over. I love Lizzie, our baby, and you. Aidan is the best man I've ever known, he's my friend. None of you deserve this. No, I don't know; Gabriel never told me why."

The kitchen door slammed shut and Eli and I both turned. Gabriel leaned his shoulder against the post. "Are you going to tell Lizzie, or am I?"

"Tell me what?" Lizzie appeared behind him.

"Elizabeth Williams, the reason you and Eli are not yet married, he's in love with your sister."

Aidan's laughter filled my ear, and I bit my bottom lip so as not to do the same.

"Oh, I'm aware of that," Lizzie said and walked over to where Eli and I stood. She wrapped her arms around both of us. "Fin and I will be sister wives."

Laughter erupted from my core. I bent forward and steadied myself with my hands on my knees. Once my breathing returned to normal, I stared at Gabriel where he stood, separate from the rest of us. "If you want, you can take my room, the beds are big enough for three people. None of this *one night with you, one night with me* nonsense."

I turned to Lizzie and Eli. "If we're going to make this work, we sleep together every night and we make love together. Only rule – Lizzie and I don't touch each other. I've done a lot of things in my life, and I still have a number on my bucket list. Incest isn't one of them."

The kitchen door slammed shut. Eli pulled Lizzie into his arms and told her to head in. He wanted to take a shower with her. She looked at me, confusion in her eyes. I answered with a slow blink.

As Eli and I watched her disappear into the house, he said, "We joke. For others it's their way of life. Fin, we need to talk about Pepper Gorge."

I sat at the dining room table, cursing under my breath as I couldn't key in the correct password for Eli's laptop. Aidan had been silent since his abrupt laughter earlier until he started rambling off a series of vowels, consonants, numbers, and an exclamation mark and hashtag in between. Of course, it was Eli's password. I sighed aloud and shook my head.

"It's like vertigo when you do that. Please don't." His voice ignited a spark in my core. I ached for him. His scent, the familiarity of not hearing him move around the house.

I shook my head again and laughed.

"I miss your smile. Remove the sticker from the webcam. I need to see you."

Sticker in hand, I drew my bottom lip between my teeth and arched an eyebrow on a smile.

"Wow."

I shut my eyes and pursed my lips. Drawing a deep breath, I held it and fought against the tears. Never had I wanted to cry as often as I did during the preceding two weeks. *Hormones.* I was neither the mother of the oestrogen nor the progesterone dragons. Both I rode like a boss, or so I thought until they scorched me.

"Woman, if you cry, I might cry with you. I will call my mother over and she will cry with us. My dad will cry when he holds his grandchild. He didn't cry when I was born, but I suspect age is making him tender, like an excellent piece of steak."

"I heard that." My father-in-law's familiar voice comforted me like my father's would've had he still been alive. For a moment I allowed myself to wonder how Duncan Williams would've reacted the first time he held his grandson or granddaughter. I stared down at my belly, where my hands rubbed.

Aidan's breath caught. "I can see a bump."

Tears dripped onto my hands as I nodded. I didn't have the heart to tell him it was more bloat than baby. He's an obstetrician, he would figure it out. This moment he needed as much as I did.

"I like you, Dr Finley D. Williams-Walker, but I love you, my wife," he said.

Still staring at my hands moving over my extending belly, I said, "I love you more than all the best and happiest moments of my life combined. You're the culmination of everything I hoped for, prayed for, and will continue to fight for. This is a symbol of the goodness which radiates in the dark. You're my home. As long as I have you, I will always know who I am."

"Sticker back on, Eli's at your six and Gabriel's stepping onto the front porch."

I returned the sticker and closed my eyes. Every time Aidan called me his wife, it stirred something deep inside me. He only ever called Kate his wife when we spoke about her. Not once did he refer to her as such to her face or to anyone else while she had been alive. To the casual observer it would've seemed cold, but knowing Aidan, understanding how his mind works, it made perfect sense to me.

Kate had been his attempt at creating a life he considered to be normal. After completing high school at fourteen and his medical degree by nineteen, Aidan had been yearning for what others take for granted and enlisted in the army. His brothers never wanted to play with him and he, just like me, had never been one for team sports. Aidan longed for the camaraderie, the sense of belonging, being a part of something, not just watching other people live. He wanted to make a difference.

For him it was the best fit considering his exceptional marksmanship. His longest kill shot had been at a distance greater than three-and-a-half kilometres. At fifteen, he was already hitting targets at that distance.

Kate had been a nurse, a homemaker, a caring and attentive person who he thought would make him happy. Aidan had been miserable. She only saw his intellect and brought it up in every conversation, even their own. He admitted he shouldn't have married her, but he had hoped to fall in love with her despite contemplating divorce. She had brought it up first; they had both made a mistake. The day before they met with the attorney, she realised she was pregnant. Their last desperate attempts at connecting, physically and emotionally, had created another life. Aidan did the honourable thing and asked her to try for their child's sake. It wasn't such a hardship considering they had been friends before they had started a romantic relationship.

After Kate and their unborn son had died in a car crash, Aidan had been tormented with guilt. If only he hadn't tried to live a normal life. If only he hadn't agreed to marry her when she had proposed. If only she had found the love and happiness she had deserved. If only he could've held his son and not carry his casket to the grave he would forever share with his mother.

I realised once he told me about her and their life together why he had been adamant we abstain from having sex. He was giving me an out as sex complicates things, forces feelings which should grow on their own. Kate had been his first. He had loved her as a friend, not the way a man should love his wife.

After their deaths, Aidan spiralled. He yearned to connect with someone and had a few brief relationships. Not once did he tell any of them about his childhood, or his years in the military. None of the women ever asked. Our first weekend together he had told me everything, except about Kate and their son. I've kept his story to myself. Aidan is so much more than a genius, a soldier, a sniper, and a medical doctor. He's funny, non-judgemental, and sexy without realising what the sight of him does to me, and every woman who lays eyes on him.

Aidan reminds me of who I am when the darkness creeps up on me and I yearn to plunge into it headfirst. Long before I become aware of its presence, he fights it for me by making me laugh, keeping my mind busy whichever way he knows will work best. A cold case he read up on with the intention to distract me, his boyish grin, late nights in our swimming pool, bringing me coffee every morning wearing a towel, sometimes letting it come loose. Aidan didn't leave when the abyss screamed my name. Ari had.

"Who are you talking to?" Eli asked as he joined me.

"The baby."

He leaned over my shoulder and asked how I knew his password. I recited the password, forgetting one hashtag.

"Of course."

I turned to him and frowned.

"I created that code. It can unlock any computer in the world, no matter the level of security during start-up." He laughed and went into the kitchen, returning with a glass of water for both of us. Ice clinked against the glass as he placed it on the dining room table.

"I have a question, thought of it now. Don't know why I haven't asked it before. Whose house is this?"

Eli glanced over his shoulder. "I don't know."

"Gabriel's employer," Quinn said in my ear. "Did you notice how similar the furnishing is to your lake house? Aidan picked up on it the second we accessed the surveillance cameras."

"Why did he leave?"

"He's here somewhere."

"No, I mean why did he come into my life and as soon as we got serious and I opened myself up to him, he left? Was there no one else who could've gone on the undercover assignment?"

Eli glanced at his wristwatch and met my eyes. "He asked to go."

"Then I was right. All of his declarations of undying love are bullshit. Why?"

"Perhaps the immensity of your connection was too much for him. You know how hard it is to reintegrate back into civilian life, albeit his return wasn't to civilian life. Neither was yours." Eli readjusted the wristwatch. "Sometimes people need to step back and let things run their course. The food chain has a way of taking care of itself. Let's talk about Pepper Gorge."

Eli filled me in on what he had learned about Pepper Gorge. I made my way to the living room and dug in the television cabinet until I found a piece of paper and a pen. Taking my seat again, I turned to Eli. "I need to write this down for it to make sense. Henry "Pepper" Andrews purchased the farm in 1811. Over the years, his four brothers and two sisters joined him and there they lived until they died, leaving the farm to Pepper's son, Henry the Second. Since then, the family has lived there." I looked at Eli, he nodded.

"Do you mind if I use your laptop? A normal Google search will suffice."

"Okay, but I'm not going anywhere."

I wondered if this formed part of his act. After I had told him the password he created, he must have known I was in contact with someone on the outside world. Computers and technology are not my friends. Eli was. How? I didn't know. I had watched him place the incriminating rifle inside the safe in Aidan's office. Gabriel had opened the safe's door once Eli had disabled the electronic lock.

After an hour of online research, I didn't quite understand what I had read. Was it or was it not a problem? Then I read about an ill-fated Spanish king. If only Aidan had been there to do the math and calculate the probabilities for me. I shook my head, staring down at my notes. Nothing. *Where are you?*

This time I would have to figure the math out for myself.

Again, I looked at the family tree on the website and estimated the same amount of people had lived in Pepper Gorge since 1811. Two hundred and nine years.

"If we look at this family tree, I estimate seven generations since Pepper and his siblings started the farm. That's seven generations of genes crossing over and doing whatever it is that genes do." What's a generation or two to a non-mathematician? Ask me about the criminal mind and I can talk for days. Medical jargon is not my forte, apart from body decomposition, wounds, and death.

"Yes, but I read there aren't always deformities or medical problems." Eli listed the various things which can occur when cousins or siblings reproduce. Blindness, hearing loss, neonatal diabetes, limb malformations, schizophrenia, and disorders of sex development which can lead to infertility. Not to mention a higher infant and child mortality rate. Of the more visible, one might notice fluctuating facial asymmetry, cleft palates, clubfoot, dwarfism, to name a few.

"We need to go back there and this time *look* at the people."

"Finley, don't you think either of us would've picked up on something? Come on, give us some credit, we're not your average Joe Public."

I rolled my eyes. "Or Joe-Anne Public."

"Fair enough. You forget about the delusional woman. Couldn't schizophrenia account for this?"

"Yes, it can present as delusional thinking. Then again, she might have seen an actual body, and the man who spoke to you didn't want outsiders to call the police. What else did the writer say?"

Eli had found a site where people shared information regarding organisations they had been associated with. Not the business kind, but those who sit on the line between community and prison. He concluded that either the writer no longer lived at Pepper Gorge or hid their anger well.

"There are five families know as 'The Originals'. They make everyone else feel like outsiders, as if they need to prove themselves worthy of being there."

"Why would anyone be outsiders if they all stem from the same bloodline?" Eli shrugged, I continued. "Five families? Pepper plus four brothers plus two sisters equals seven." *Yay me, I can count.* Even though I hadn't realised 336 hours equate to two weeks.

"Perhaps two siblings and their families moved away, and their departure isn't worth noting."

It was my turn to shrug. "Did the writer identify him or herself in any way?"

"Whoever wrote it didn't sign it, but the person said his or her role had been that of a 'hunter'."

I stood and paced the length of the dining room. Eight steps, turn, eight steps, turn. "Okay, so we have nothing except maybe incest and the possibility of another body. Not knowing how many other bodies have been found *if* this woman isn't delusional. No way of knowing whether a person perhaps suffered a heart attack and dropped dead in the woods, and this woman came across said hypothetical body."

"Finley…" A creepy voice sang-whispered in my head. "Finley…"

"Man, that gives me the creeps." I rubbed my hands over the goose bumps on my arms, the hair on the back of my neck trying to avoid contact with my skin.

"What?" Eli spun around to face me.

"Incest." I'm okay with dead bodies, in the woods or not. Only the bodies of children will haunt me forever. When I close my eyes, I still see the bloated, decaying faces of three little blonde girls. If the Angel Taker could be killed again, I would be first in line.

"Nice save, Walker." Quinn laughed, no longer whispering. Still not my favourite person at that moment.

"I agree, but unless the marriage isn't against the law or the children have been molested or raped, there isn't anything we can do about it," Eli said.

"Most countries have laws prohibiting first cousins from

marrying, and this one sure does. There is such a thing as age of consent to consider."

"Okay, but what if they're first cousins once removed, or twice removed? I don't even know how this removed thing works."

"Neither do I. If there's a common ancestor, it's a no from me."

"Then you shouldn't do further research on inbreeding."

I asked why as I again took a seat at the table and rubbed my belly.

"We are all descendent from the same ancestors. Due to small populations, cousins often married."

"I don't want to think about it."

"Perhaps what you should consider is the things Eli isn't saying. Ask him what else he has uncovered," Quinn said.

"Eli, is there anything you're not telling me?" I held up my hand before he could answer and excused myself. I returned with a tub of strawberry flavoured yoghurt and a few more questions in my mind. "The writer – why did this person leave the farm? When did this person leave? How sure are you it isn't someone who stumbled onto the farm like we did and came up with a ridiculous story?"

"Unless this person is delusional or a fiction writer, coming up with such a detailed story isn't something someone will do just for kicks. They would've sold it to a newspaper or posted it somewhere online where it would garner attention."

"What are you not telling me?"

Eli pinched the bridge of his nose between his thumb and forefinger.

"Ask him what the hunter hunted." Quinn became like a second brain, one that thinks for my pregnancy brain.

"What did the hunter hunt?"

"The hunting is twofold." He refused to say more.

"People?"

Eli nodded.

Nine

Location: Classified. Final destination: Coopersville.

Aidan unbuckled his seatbelt and stood to stretch his legs and back. He rolled his shoulders and turned to the person watching him. He hated flying with his parents. Their need for security and anonymity he understood, but being stuck for hours, confined and unable to escape his mother's prodding, wasn't his idea of onboard entertainment. Business class was his idea of luxury travel, not that he didn't appreciate the Boeing 787 9 Dreamliner VIP for its aesthetics and capabilities.

Since the day he had introduced Finley to his parents, his mother had a tell-tale 'I-told-you-so' expression on her face. She had told him, he hadn't listened the first time and married a woman his mother knew wasn't right for him, or he for her.

"What's going on in your beautiful mind? I can see you're thinking of something you haven't before." He hated how well his mother could read him, another disadvantage of living with a world-renowned psychiatrist.

"I need to be a part of it, for her."

"Your father is right, it's too dangerous. Finley will need you." Heather Walker crossed her legs and sipped at the espresso. Aidan had stopped wondering why she didn't wait for it to cool when he was four.

"There is another option we haven't considered. The margin for error is smaller, but the risk and possibility of casualties are both lower. His unexpected schedule change works to our advantage. I can be home with my wife on our first anniversary."

"Will you return to the house after they invaded your privacy the way they did?"

"It's our home, Mother. Your wedding gift to us. How did you know we would need it?"

Heather changed her position to better face her eldest son. "Thomas Anderson has been on our radar for quite some time. After you told us he confronted you about you being the Marcel Sniper, we did what parents do."

Aidan sank down onto the seat and covered his face with his hands. He scratched his beard and wondered what Finley would say if she saw him now. She preferred the light stubble which left bruises on her inner thighs. She didn't complain when he couldn't get enough of her. Moan she did. Aidan's heart clenched. His wife, the lover he never fathomed could exist. His.

The desire to be with her, to be one with her, had consumed him from the night he had lifted his eyes to find her standing in Alias' door. Why he had thought joining a singles bar, with the sole purpose of people meeting for a one-night stand, had been a good idea still baffled him. Little did that. Finley's two sides captivated him, for it mirrored his own. He often wondered if other people had two duelling sides.

Aidan met his mother's eyes, a knowing smile on her face. The gesture so comforting, he wanted her to hug him and tell him everything would be okay, as she had done when he came home crying because the older kids didn't want a little boy to eat lunch with them. Learning he had loved, but socially he couldn't cope. Heather had spent countless hours coaching him, teaching him how to interact with others. Which things to say and which not. With Finley, all of it flew out of the window. She's the only person with whom he can simply be.

"Will you teach me how to be a father?"

Heather walked over to him, leaving her trademark high-heeled Louboutin's standing in front of her seat. She wrapped her arms around him and pressed her forehead to his temple. Their hair a similar sun-kissed brown, and his vivid blue eyes the same as his father's.

"Honey, you will be an amazing father. You already are.

Just look at the sacrifices you made to keep your child safe by letting Finley go with the enemy, knowing it was the only way to make them think they have won. You're selfless, Aidan. You feel more and deeper than most people. Look at how well-loved you are by your patients. Your father told me about the twins who were named after you. The only thing a child needs is unconditional love, your full attention, and honesty." She pressed her lips to his hair.

"You weren't always honest with us. Rowan believed Santa was real until I explained to him it was impossible for one person to deliver gifts to all the children in the world in one night. Come on, Mother, he was twelve." Aidan bit back his laugh.

Heather roughed his hair. "You didn't have to mention that if Santa was real, and if he was good, he would've informed the police where all the children who are victims of trafficking were being held."

"It's true." Aidan shrugged and leaned his head on his mother's shoulder. "Aren't you glad I didn't explain to him what trafficking entails?"

"Only because your father lured you out of the room by taking you to the shooting range."

The indoor shooting range at their home in Wild Bay had been his parents' gift to him on his fifteenth birthday.

"Aidan, what other options do you have to get your hands on the one who pulls the strings?"

Ten

I got used to Quinn's voice interrupting my inner thoughts as I contemplated what Eli had told me about Pepper Gorge. "Eli hasn't found everything."

It had also been my conclusion. Something was going on in that place, but I couldn't quite put my finger on it. The previous night I had lain awake, staring at the ceiling, yearning for the nights I had done the same in my and Aidan's bedroom. The nights the nightmares kept me awake. Without fail Aidan would turn, wrap his arm around me, and pull my back against his warm, bare chest. He always said the same thing, 'Sleep, Wife, I'm here to slay all your demons'.

Yet he hadn't been there the previous night, or any of the other since Lizzie and I had left Marcel with the two men I believed to be the biggest enemies to my and Aidan's happiness. They were nothing more than puppets in this game my life had turned into. Although it appeared as if Eli had cut a few of the strings which bound him to an invisible force.

"Is he the ally you mentioned?" I asked Quinn.

"Yes. But it's for him to tell you the entire story."

"I'm getting tired of people saying that to me. Where's Aidan?"

Quinn sighed. "Neither here nor there, but closer than you think."

"You're enjoying this, aren't you?" I pulled my hair back and tied it with the band I had snapped on my wrist after I had showered. A haircut had been in my future; I had missed it as I had scheduled it for the day I last saw Aidan. When Captain Taylor told me about Aidan's imminent arrest, the world beyond us had ceased to exist.

"Which part? Being the guiding voice in your head – yes.

A man I consider a brother being away from the woman he loves because of circumstances beyond his immediate control – never. I would trade places with Aidan in a heartbeat."

"You've never been in love, have you?" No person, no matter how much they loved another like a brother from another mother, would want to be in this position. To be away from the person who is the air you breathe, sustenance to your soul, the parts of you you didn't realise were missing until you found them. Not when you didn't know whether you would see that person alive again. For all I knew, and I had thought about it the night before, Gabriel was biding his time until he could kill me. I still didn't know what his end-goal was, or why he did all of this to me. All of this, much more than an unhealthy obsession.

"It's not on the cards for me, not in my line of work."

"Will you be there when this is over? I've been wanting to meet you since I saw your photos in the house at Wild Bay." Quinn the unofficial sister-cousin of Aidan, Nathan, and Liam. The first girl Rowan ever noticed.

"I can't promise to be there, but if work allows it, I will. For now, let's focus on solving the riddle of Pepper Gorge."

"No riddle. Incest."

"Are you sure that's all there is? Have you been inside Gabriel's garage? I'm sure he has some toys in there which might aid in your investigation. And while you're at the garage sale, Eli should dig a little deeper. He hasn't even spotted the tip of the iceberg."

"If you know so much about Pepper Gorge, why hasn't it been shut down? Or social services called out?"

"It came onto our radar a little over a month ago, when that post was first made by the unknown writer or hunter. We dug as deep as we could without going out there to investigate for ourselves. The information was passed on to the Coopersville police three weeks ago."

"Have they launched an investigation?"

"They concluded the writer was nothing more than a

'crack-pot', direct quote. Said everything we uncovered was created by the writer's imagination. Another direct quote – *There is nothing of concern going on at the farm known as Pepper Gorge.* The people they claimed to have interviewed said they were all there out of their own free will."

"You're not convinced?" I started to make my way back to the house from the ravine. I missed my lake house, the lake, the feeling of being home. The place where Aidan had saved my life, and I his.

"Free will doesn't mean they aren't breaking the law if cousins or siblings are getting married, or having children for that matter."

"That's what Heather said. Finley, the things we uncovered, the Coopersville police made them out to be the creation of the twisted mind of the writer. If those things are factual, incest is the least of Pepper Gorge's evils."

Gabriel lay on the couch with a leg up on the back support. A man his height and size couldn't be comfortable sleeping with his feet dangling off the end. *Did he think I would share my bed with him?* He sneered without opening his eyes. "Are you enjoying the view? Come here, bet we can snuggle real nice on this couch with the way your body moulds into mine. Do you want to watch a movie? Perhaps make our own?" He showed his teeth.

"As repulsive as that sounds, I came here to ask you for the garage's keys."

"Why?" He opened his eyes and placed his hands behind his head.

"Knowing you there are various items either in there or somewhere in a hidden room inside this house which I can use to investigate Pepper Gorge."

"You're like a dog with a bone." He laughed. I knew where his mind crawled into.

"Either you help me, or I break the door down."

"Good luck, sweetheart; it's steel-reinforced and the walls

and ceiling are solid concrete. A bomb wouldn't get you through the door."

"I believe Eli has a knack for locks, perhaps I should ask for his help." I rubbed my hands over my belly. This baby was growing. The only good thing in all the darkness, and that Lizzie was with me.

"I'm excited to see our child tomorrow. It's a boy, I can feel it. My son is growing inside of you, Ley." An idea played behind his dark eyes. "Ari and Finley, Ri and Ley. Riley is the perfect name for our son. Or daughter if I'm wrong. Doubt I am."

Riley. The little girl we had saved from the Angel Taker when he had dumped her in the lake and left her to drown. That night, the Angel Taker had lost his arm. If only Gabriel hadn't missed. Then again, the Marcel Sniper wouldn't have had a reason to save my life. How could someone as deadly as Gabriel miss? The opposite shore, only eighty metres away. Even at night, he shouldn't have missed.

"Don't you dare mention her name. I haven't spoken to her in two weeks, and I never had the chance to say goodbye or explain why I wouldn't be able to call her." Riley and I had spoken every week since that night. Some weekends I took her for ice cream or to the beach. After intensive therapy, her nightmares had stopped. Mine never will.

"Ah, another reason you can hate Aidan."

"Two things, Gabriel: give me your satellite phone and the keys to the garage. I will speak to Riley *today.*"

Quinn cleared her throat. "Aidan has been sending Riley's mother emails from your email address with photos of your vacation in Vietnam last year. He told her the cell phone reception isn't great over there, and that you will bring her a gift. Don't worry, he's got your back. And left it up to me to find a suitable Vietnamese gift for a little girl."

Motionless, I stood. Unable to smile, unable to thank Aidan for being who he is. I couldn't even thank Quinn for telling me and lifting the weight off my shoulders. Deep inside the pit of my stomach, rage coiled. A snake ready to strike its prey. "Garage key. Now."

"No." Gabriel closed his eyes, the grin still in place. "First you need to do something for me."

Bile rose in my throat. "If you bring that thing close to my mouth, I will bite it off."

He clenched his thighs. "No, that wasn't what I was thinking, but thank you, I will remember the magic your mouth is capable of later in the shower."

I gagged audibly. The mask slipped. Quinn told me as much through fits of laughter. "What do you want, *Gabriel*?"

"A lot of things, *Miss* Williams. For now, be nice to me. We once had a very special bond, which led to us being lovers. Let's get back to being friends. Why you're so angry is beyond me." He eased himself up, not taking his eyes off mine.

If I had to list all the reasons I loathed him in one session, I would need an energy drink. But being pregnant, it wasn't an option. Some of the reasons I would still end up hating him for I didn't even know yet. I hoped he would tell the truth after hours and hours of breaking him down. There is only so much torture the human body can take. Even I had my breaking point, and the scars to show for the days it had taken me to lose my will to live. I hoped it would take Gabriel as long, if not longer.

"Okay. Key. Please."

He sneered. "I love it when you beg."

I have only ever begged one man, and still Aidan had refused to have sex with me. After we did, I started begging him for different reasons. There's a reason forbidden fruit is delicious. If I had known before what being with him would be like, I might have used harsher begging methods, if such a thing even existed. A man that good with his hands and mouth, had to be amazing inside me. Amazing – such a laughable word considering the reality.

"I used up my nice quota for the day." I turned on my heels.

"What is it you hope to find in there?"

"I'll know when I see it."

The garage, to me, was what I suspect designer shoe stores are to other women. Women like Lizzie and not my mother-in-law. Despite her impeccable sense of style and her trademark high-heeled Louboutin's, she rarely wore shoes when not needing to be Dr Heather Walker, psychiatrist, and head of the organisation's interrogation division. Some call it interrogation, I call it what it is – torture. The people they capture aren't your run-of-the-mill bank robbers, traffickers, rapists, or murderers. No, the people they hunt could last through years of conventional interrogation. *I love my in-laws.* They right wrongs made in the grey. Ryan helped me realise things aren't always black and white. Mix the two and that's where they step in.

I spun around, drinking in the room. Better than a whiskey distillery. I'm not one for candy, although I was craving something sweet, at the time unsure whether it was chocolate or revenge. Both, perhaps.

"I haven't seen you this ecstatic since the night I opened my previous SUV's back-door and showed you my toys. The night we saved Riley." Gabriel stood by the door, he had locked it after we entered. "Pandora's trunk."

I stared at him, frowning.

"Don't you remember?"

I shook my head, even though I did.

"You called the compartment Pandora's trunk, but filled with only good things."

"It was years ago. You can't expect me to remember everything, considering what happened afterwards."

I made my way through the items, trying to hide my confusion. Some I had never seen or heard of, let alone knew how to use. During my time in the military, we didn't have any of it. The standard items I knew – handguns, rifles, grenades, and blocks of C4. Even the body armour was different. Lighter than what I had worn the last time, the day we were ambushed and taken hostage. Prisoner.

"I shouldn't have left you," he said to my back.

"I wasn't referring to what happened between us or that you left."

"Finley, can you pick up the box to your right? Check the serial number for me?" Quinn requested.

I complied, not knowing what I held in my hand. "What's this?"

Gabriel walked closer and removed it from my hand, returning it to the rest of the stack. "Nothing you will need."

"What is it?" I asked again.

"Something we were told had been destroyed." Anger rose in Quinn's voice. She told me what I had held in my hand.

"Anything else you have for me to look at which might be useful?" I asked Gabriel, hoping Quinn would get the hint.

The woman is a quick learner. "Keep moving, take your time. I'll tell you if I see anything."

A mosquito buzzed around my head and landed on my neck. On instinct I slapped myself.

"What the hell? Do you have any idea how much that thing is worth?" Gabriel stood to my left, shaking his head, his jaw lax, the remote control clutched in his hands.

"Insect-size spy drone," Quinn said, anger still dripping off her every word. "In the wrong hands, capable of doing much more than just surveillance."

"How did you get your hands on a micro drone?"

"Part of my job." Gabriel still stared at me in disbelief.

"What job would that be, Gabriel? You led me to believe you worked for the good guys when in actual fact you have these bullets in your possession, which tells me who and what you are." I lifted the box Quinn had asked me to check.

"One woman's villain is another woman's hero." He took the box from my hand and returned it to its unlawful place. "What do you even know about these bullets?"

I couldn't remember all the technical words Quinn had used. "They're the size of a shotgun slug. The exterior is made of a soft metal or alloy-like element which explodes on impact, releasing whatever the hollow centre is filled with." Quinn hadn't given examples, so I improvised. "Agent Orange, Sarin, Botulism, Mustard Gas, etc. A different take on a deadly bullet."

"You know things you shouldn't, *Miss* Williams."

I turned my back to him, my jaw clenched. If he called me *Miss* one more time, I would grab the closest object and hurl it at his face, this time taking into account his feline reflexes. "Perhaps I do, Mr *Berkowitz*. Tell me, how did a Polish-born Jew end up in Sayeret Matkal?"

"You're poking an atomic bomb. Careful, Mrs Walker." The sound of Aidan's voice caught me by surprise, yet not as surprised as Gabriel must have been. I refused to face him, and kept my grin hidden. I had asked Quinn whether there were any surveillance cameras in the room before following Gabriel out of the house. She had said no.

Strong hands grabbed me and spun me around; his fingers dug into the skin of my upper arms. Defiance burned in my core until I realised my feet were dangling above the ground. Adrenaline kicked in. My breathing stilled. Forwards and backwards my head thrashed. Not by my doing.

Two options. One – head-butt him. Possible outcome – he drops me, I fall, the baby can get hurt. Two – kick him in the testicles. Possible outcome – he drops me, I fall, the baby can get hurt. Both options will enrage him even more.

I stared into black eyes. The face, not Gabriel's or Ari's. This was the assassin shaking me like a wet rag. Fear filled me, numbed me. *The baby.* I hadn't felt so terrified, or powerless, in my life. Not even being tortured by the Scarecrows, or in that bunker. Gabriel held more than my life in his hands.

"If you...if you...I can lose the baby!"

Aidan cursed, something he never did.

Still, Gabriel didn't release his grip. Pain seared through my biceps, burning into my shoulders. "You'll end up like the cat if you keep asking questions." His expression turned serious, concerned even, as he lowered me to the ground. "Finley, you know things you shouldn't. Nothing good ever comes from the truth." He rubbed his hands over my arms and pressed his lips to my forehead. "I'll never rape you, Ley. I love you." Gabriel stepped back, not meeting my eyes.

My entire body shook as I wrapped my arms around my belly and scanned the shelves. *I will kill him before I live through that again. Or lose another child.*

"Finley, step down. That's an order. Think about the baby. I'm getting you both back alive." Aidan never took that tone with me. The authority and fear in his voice grounded me, reminded me I wasn't alone, despite being locked in a room with a murderer.

I lifted my eyes to the ceiling and inhaled musty air.

"I'm sending Quinn for you. This ends today," Aidan said.

Gabriel stood with his back to me, shaking his head.

"No. You won't," I said to Aidan. We had come too far, gone through too much; I wouldn't allow this to derail our mission. I could protect myself, and the baby. As long as Eli or Lizzie were around, we would be safer. *Never out of harm's way.* I needed a weapon. Something.

Memories surged through my brain of dust, men, and pain. My soul dying more every time they did what they had done to me. The memory of holding the embryo in my hand. Two unrelated events collided, rendering me breathless. No longer fearless.

"What?" Gabriel kept his back to me.

"I will always say *no*. You claim to love me, yet you can hurt me like this. I'm *pregnant*. Who are you? I never thought Ari was capable of this, and I empathised with Gabriel for being held captive and for being raped. I will die before I have to go through that again. How dare you do this to me? I told Ari everything. He knows what they did to me, how they grabbed me. Like you just did." Tears streamed down my face, I wiped at my eyes. I wouldn't allow him to see my fear.

Gabriel placed his hands on the door and leaned his head

against the metal surface. "Finley, I'm sorry. I'll never touch you like that again, I swear. Please don't say that surname. And as for Gabriel, I wish I had never told you the truth. I'm weak around you, Ley. You'll be my downfall." He grunted a laugh. "You already have been."

"Finley, Aidan has gone all primal, Heather's talking him down. I warned you, if Aidan does anything irresponsible, you will answer to me. There are things going on you can't begin to comprehend. Get your anger, pregnancy hormones, frustration, heart break, whatever it is, under control. Do you have any idea what it did to Aidan to see another man touch you like that? He's punching holes in the door. You've never seen Aidan this angry. There are sides of him he won't show you because he loves you. It's my responsibility to be your friend right now, your voice of reason in all of this. Dammit, Finley! I get this is hard for you. I understand."

Quinn's voice caught. She cleared her throat. "Keep in mind that Aidan's preparing to wage a silent war on the person responsible for you being where you are. Don't make him a casualty because he's worried about you and his child."

An invisible fist connected with my gut. Quinn was right, saying what I needed to hear. The veiled compassion in her voice made me realise she understood my fear.

I kept getting absorbed in my end of this war, forgetting Aidan stood on the frontline. All I could do with Gabriel within earshot was nod. My sore neck forced my head to make big, promising movements. To keep my head down, until this ended, and then to unleash my wrath on Gabriel for everything he had done, including what had just happened.

"I'm sorry." I meant it for Aidan and Quinn.

Gabriel turned to face me. "Sometimes it's best to never know. The truth is a heavy burden to carry."

Eleven

Water fell around me, covered me. Steam rose, creating a cocoon. The tiles were no longer cold beneath me. Quinn had been right. Aidan's always right; one of the many reasons I love him. He's my voice of reason, my constant in every storm.

During our fertility treatment he had been my rock, more so than at any other time. Inside me, our miracle baby grew. Seventeen weeks since the IVF cycle started. Seventeen weeks of living in constant fear of losing this child as I had lost our first. My anger and frustration were born from my fear of not being worthy of carrying a child to term, of not giving Aidan the one thing he had wanted for as long as he could remember. He told me once that he worried about not being a good father. The way he had spoken to me the night before, I knew he was prepared for the terrible twos and teenage years. And every other stage.

I often wondered if I have enough patience to take care of another human being, a child who still needed to learn everything we take for granted. No one is ever ready for the life-altering experience of being responsible for another person. Parenthood is not for the fainthearted. I wrapped my arms around my waist and asked the baby to forgive me for failing him or her by being too caught up in this war. When you fight for your life, for the lives of everyone you love, it's war. *Will the ever-present darkness inside me allow me to be a good mother?*

To the baby I vowed to be better, do better, and ensure we got back to his or her daddy unharmed. With eleven days left until the deadline Aidan had given, I knew how to keep my mind busy, focused, and allow him to do what he does best. Strategise. Execute.

I turned my face into the spray and thought about the countless women who have no one looking out for them. No one keeping them safe. When the person they love is the very person they need protection from. With no chance of escaping their nightmare. The women who are punched, and kicked, and stomped on until they miscarry. The women who raise children in the middle of active war zones. Where you never know which of your loved ones will see the sun tomorrow morning, or the moon tonight. I had seen the torment on their faces.

Tears mixed with the water spilling down my face. For the powerless. For the women and children a piece of paper will never protect. Protection orders do nothing when you're in the fight of your life, for your survival. I cried for women I would never meet, for the ones I do when they come to live at Tabula Rasa. Anger filled me for not being able to do more than keep them safe, offer a warm bed and food when they had eventually found the courage to run. In that shower I vowed to do more for them, be more proactive in pushing them to complete or continue their secondary and tertiary education, and to claim their own identities as survivors.

I cried for the men who suffer in silence. They will continue to do so as long as society keeps constructing a deceitful reality where men are always the aggressors and never the victims. For the countless children who witness hatred between the two people who should teach them about love and feeling protected.

I cried. The memories of what I had endured returned with a vengeance the night before. Instead of dreams, I saw the cold, rage-filled eyes I had seen before. Every day for four months.

Steam kept rising. I let go of a fear I had forgotten and realised it never left me. It would forever be a part of me, the person I became when I could do nothing but survive and move forward. No amount of therapists can ever cure you of the constant fear of being at the mercy of another human being. It burrows into your soul and latches on. Soulless dark eyes, the colour peach, a song, a single word. We all have a trigger.

During the time I spent in the shower, Quinn remained silent until she whispered, "It's time." Her voice was a mixture of compassion and excitement.

The compassion in her voice meant only one thing – she understood this fear.

Coopersville is a far cry from being what I call a city. To call it a big town would be generous. Dr Duvall's receptionist called me in first, and my stomach clenched. I was grateful that sonars are black and white and at seventeen weeks, Gabriel wouldn't see this child had no resemblance to him. As we walked down the passage, he placed his hand on my shoulder, I pushed it off. Even knowing that he was an assassin, I never expected he could get violent with me, or any other woman.

Dr Duvall sat behind her desk, her hair an auburn I had seen before, her face almost identical. I bit down on my bottom lip to keep from smiling. Behind me, Gabriel stopped in the doorway. *Sophia Blake.* The woman who had abducted Gabriel and held him captive for six months before whacking him on the back of the head with a shovel and leaving him for dead in a shallow grave.

Was it wrong of me to wish her aim and strength had been better? Or that she had used a deadlier weapon?

"Sir, are you alright?" Dr Duvall pushed to her feet.

I turned to Gabriel; his expression ashen. "Gabriel?" I asked louder than necessary, still fighting to hide my smile.

I wanted to throw my arms around Dr Duvall and tell her she's my new best friend. I wanted to make her a charm bracelet, braid her hair, have a sleepover, and consume litres of margaritas with her. Of course, the latter only once I was no longer pregnant or breastfeeding.

He nodded and stepped further into the consultation room; his hastened breathing visible because of his too-tight shirt. If we were friends, I would've bought him the correct size shirts for Christmas. Without shaking Dr Duvall's hand, he slumped down in the chair, his eyes fixed on her face.

I reached for her extended hand and gave it a squeeze. This close, I couldn't miss her bicoloured eyes. The only indication this wasn't the woman of Gabriel's nightmares. Not yet.

"How far along are you, Mrs Jones?" Dr Duvall asked as she settled into her chair.

Jones? Missus? I pulled at the sleeves of my shirt, trying to hide the bruises with the black material. Dr Duvall noticed the movement of my hands.

I cradled my bump with my palms. "Seventeen weeks to the day. Doctor, I'm not sure whether he shared my medical history with your receptionist when he booked the appointment. I suffered a miscarriage, and this baby I conceived through IVF. My body has been subjected to quite a lot over the years, and the fertility specialist had been adamant this pregnancy is high risk. In my mid-twenties, I had a Lletz done to remove aggressive pre-cancer cells from my cervix."

Dr Duvall made notes in the file and met my eyes. "I will measure your cervix, but I'm sure you would like to see the baby first? It's still early but I might be able to tell the sex, if you want to know?"

Gabriel nodded and pushed to his feet.

"Mr Jones, you can wait right here while your wife undresses."

"I'm not his wife." Again, I pulled on my sleeves, the bruises left by his pinkies visible despite my efforts.

Dr Duvall scanned the file. "Says here you are."

Gabriel found his voice. "We're engaged and hope to get married before the baby's born."

The only formal occasion we might attend at the same time will be his funeral.

Dr Duvall dropped her eyes to my hands rubbing over my belly. "That's quite a diamond, you must love her very much to have given her one of the rarest diamonds in the world, not to mention one that size."

"Only the best for my Ley."

I considered pushing it down his throat so he could choke to death on the diamond Aidan's parents had purchased for his future wife when he had been twenty-four. They also bought diamonds for his brothers' future wives. They never gave it to Aidan when he and Kate had gotten engaged. The first time they had met me, his father had told him it was waiting to be placed in a setting of our choice.

I undressed and covered myself with the gown hanging in the cubicle. As I got onto the bed, Dr Duvall and Gabriel walked into the examination room.

The gel the doctor squirted onto my stomach was much colder than I expected, the spatter hitting my face even more so. Dr Duvall apologised despite my laughter.

The baby's heartbeat filled the room as Dr Duvall moved the probe over my stomach.

Gabriel stared at the screen and grabbed my hand. I couldn't yank it free from his grip, too mesmerised by the sight of baby Walker on the screen. The baby kicked and one tiny arm moved towards his or her face.

"Is it a boy?" Gabriel asked.

"The baby's leg is in the way. Even if I move the probe over here, I won't be able to tell. Sorry. The baby will still move around a lot. We might be in luck at your next appointment in two weeks." She turned to me. "Are you ready for the internal exam?"

No one is ever ready to have a probe longer than the average male penis inserted inside them. The only time a woman truly appreciates a condom. That little stick is like a gigolo on Viagra with a major debt to pay off.

I nodded and pursed my lips, pushing the sleeve on my arm closest to Dr Duvall up, exposing the purple-blue spots left by Gabriel's fingers. Dr Duvall didn't miss the slight movement.

"Mr Jones, please wait in the reception area."

He turned to me, his expression unreadable. "I'm not leaving you alone with a stranger."

"There's only one door which leads into the consultation room. Get out. I'm not doing this with you in here." I stared up at him, grinding my teeth.

Anger flashed in his dark eyes. "I've seen that part of you better than you have. I'm not leaving."

Dr Duvall stiffened her spine and placed a hand on my arm. "Sir, my patient asked you to leave and you need to respect her privacy. As for the bruises on her arm, I will contact the police if I believe you're responsible or that my patient is in danger."

Gabriel stared down at my arms and swallowed hard. Without another word, he left, shutting the door behind him. I turned to Dr Duvall and thanked her. Mischief and rage duelled in her bicoloured eyes.

Lowering my voice, I asked, "Is he here?"

She shook her head and covered my hand with hers.

"I'm sorry, Finley. If I have to be in the same building as him, I will shred him to pieces with my bare hands. We haven't won the war yet, but we will. Let her do the internal examination, I need to be sure your cervix isn't funnelling. Fin, our baby is healthy and growing strong. That's the most important thing right now. Let's find out if we're having a boy or a girl."

If only I had kept my mouth shut the previous night, Aidan would've been there with me. Tears streamed down my temple, disappearing into my hair. "I'm so sorry, Aidan. You should be here with me to share in this moment."

"I'm always with you, but I don't trust myself not to kill him after the way he touched you last night, for making you remember. Never mind everything else he has done. For the time being we can't overplay our hand."

Dr Duvall slipped the condom over the probe and squirted more of the cold gel on the tip. Either she had experience or Aidan had given her good instructions. I hoped the latter. Aidan didn't have to tell me what to do; this part I knew all too well thanks to annual check-ups and the fertility treatment.

"The baby is healthy, and ahead of the growth curve.

Despite what happened last night, the baby and everything else looks fine. Thank you for not fighting back."

Quinn inserted the probe, a feeling one never gets accustomed to, or at least I never will.

Aidan continued, "Your cervix looks good, but we will monitor it throughout your second trimester. In two weeks, you will be back with Dr Brown and I will be back at work, so if we need to check in between your consultations, I can do it."

Being married to an obstetrician has its advantages. I understood why it would be unethical for Aidan to be my doctor and deliver the baby, but I trusted him more than anyone else with our child's life. Even more than I trusted myself.

"Dr Duvall?" He laughed at Quinn's use of his mother's maiden name. "Can you please zoom in? I believe today we will learn whether the baby is Ryan or Aly."

"What do you think of Ainsley for a girl?" I asked.

The three of us, and Gabriel, walked down the street from the offices of Dr Rhodes and Associates and made our way towards the restaurant where Eli and Lizzie had said we would enjoy lunch. Enjoy being a relative term.

Dr Rhodes and Associates consisted of Dr Rhodes, the general practitioner who also served as the area's obstetrician and gynaecologist, Dr Manning the dentist, Dr Xavier the psychologist, and Dr Choi the surgeon. Their offices doubled as a day clinic where minor surgeries were performed. Critical patients, and those in need of major surgeries, are sent to the nearest hospital in the closest major city, 200 kilometres away. Why Lizzie considered Coopersville a city remained beyond my understanding.

Ryan Walker had contacted Dr Rhodes himself and offered him a well-deserved vacation. Dr Rhodes hadn't asked any questions; I had a lot. Weeks later, I learned that Dr Rhodes and Ryan Walker had a history. Another family helped by my father-in-law's organisation. Dr Rhodes' sister had been arrested for drug trafficking when she flew out of an unnamed South American country. Her friend had asked her to check-in a suitcase for her while she went to the bathroom. The suitcase contained more than clothes and toiletries.

The government had refused to get involved due to strained relations with the unnamed country. One night, Dr Rhodes' sister had disappeared from the prison where she awaited execution. My in-laws had helped her with a new identity. She now runs a rehabilitation centre for drug addicts.

Dr Duvall, who stood in for Dr Rhodes, had held me while I cried after Aidan told me the gender of our baby. Tears of gratitude for a healthy baby and tears of frustration that Aidan couldn't be there with me because I had poked the atomic bomb. As I had walked out of the examination room, I realised the atomic bomb Aidan had referred to the night before wasn't Gabriel, but himself.

Shops passed me in a blur. My head spun with the joy of seeing my baby again and hearing Aidan's voice. One thing was for sure, the bicoloured eyed woman and I would become best friends. I hoped she realised it, too. Across the street, a shop's sign called to me and I changed course.

Gabriel called after me. "Where are you going?"

In the reflection of a shop's window, I saw him reach for my arm, but his skin didn't touch mine. I ignored him and headed in. Lizzie on my six.

An hour later, we walked out and headed for the restaurant. Gabriel and Eli had sat in the waiting area, paging through magazines and looking a great deal agitated. I didn't care, neither did Lizzie. She grabbed my hand and intertwined our fingers. Inside her, my baby's cousin grew just as strong. She cried when I told her the baby's gender and promised not to tell Gabriel.

I needed this time with my sister, doing something we once took for granted. Finding the right hairdresser is like finding the right man. There are a couple who are good enough, but a perfect fit is rare. If I wasn't so happy with Antoine back in Marcel, I would've considered commuting to Coopersville, by train or car. I hate flying. Danielle had done exactly what Lizzie and I asked. Lizzie's golden hair brushed the top of her shoulders. Mine hadn't been this short since I was a toddler with no other option because my baby hair was still growing.

"How am I going to pull your hair now when we do what we do, Mrs Walker?"

At the sound of his voice, I stopped and waited until the others were out of earshot. "Do you like it?" I ran my fingers through my hair, my fringe touching the bottom of my left ear. Somewhere between a pixie cut and a short bob.

"I love it. It brings out your eyes and I can't wait to see you naked with that new style."

I shook my head and laughed. The three people ahead of me spun around to face me.

"Fin, are you okay?" Lizzie smiled, knowing only one person could get me to laugh like that.

"Yes, just saw a mother struggling to buckle her toddler into his car seat and realised soon our lives will be turned upside down. I don't think any of us realise what's in store for us and how it will affect us. Forever," I said to all three of them, my words directed at Gabriel.

The poor fool would never have a child of his own. If only he had stayed gone and never returned to Marcel hell-bent on destroying my life, and that of the man I love. His mere presence put my child in danger.

"Do you think it's a boy?" the fool asked.

We returned to the house, our stomachs full, my heart even fuller despite the circumstances. Eli and I had decided we would get to work as soon as we set foot in the house. In the bedroom's corner, several items waited to be used in my quest to answer the mystery which hung over Pepper Gorge like an impenetrable fog. Ironically, early in the evening, a fog crept over the mountain as Eli and I sat in the living room.

Eli leaned back on the couch, rubbing his temples. "That's

everything I found last night."

"I would say it's more than enough to order a missile strike against the ones responsible." With my index finger, I drew hearts on my growing belly.

How could anyone hurt their own child? It was a question I had pondered since I was a teenager and my mother founded Tabula Rasa – a safe house for victims of sexual abuse, domestic violence, and trafficking. One occupied bed is one too many. We might never stop the evil in this world, but we can and should do everything in our power to protect the innocent, and failing that, help them heal after we rescue them.

"You've been using a lot of military jargon today. What's up?"

I mimicked his posture and let out a heavy sigh. "Must be after everything I saw in the garage. Sorry, the arsenal, bunker, whatever you want to call it." *Evidence.*

"Is that where he did this?" Eli brushed his fingertips over the bruises on my right bicep. When Lizzie had seen it, she had marched up to Gabriel and punched him so hard he had to ice his jaw. Of course, I had given her a high five and then Eli wrapped a pack of peas in a dishcloth and held it against her knuckles. Her Krav Maga sessions had paid off.

"Yes."

Eli rolled his head towards me, his breath warm on my cheek. In a low voice he said, "For this alone I will kill him the first chance I get."

I matched his voice. "Get in line."

The sound of the kettle boiling in the kitchen broke the vengeful silence.

"What are we going to do about Pepper Gorge?" Eli asked.

"We need to look into Coopersville Police Department. I need to know everything about the detective assigned to the case as well as their captain. Captain Taylor in Marcel will be able to help, I need to speak to him."

"Fin, you can't do that. He might trace the call and tell Aidan where we are. The fact that he warned you of Aidan's arrest is proof enough his loyalties are with you and not with justice," he said, no longer whispering.

I wasn't going to tell a man I didn't know for a fact stood on our side that Captain Taylor is a friend of the family I had married into. Aidan had mentioned in passing how he and Captain Taylor had become acquainted as children. There were too many things we had to discuss on our last night and not enough hours. Never enough hours when it came to being with him.

"Give me the satellite phone you or Gabriel have, and I can use that. Or we can send him an email, routing it across the world; you can do it in a second." I brought the bottle of water to my mouth and returned it to the side table after quenching my thirst. "An email is perhaps best. As for Pepper Gorge, we need to go back there."

Gabriel cleared his throat from the doorway. "You're not going there again."

"You're the last person who gets to tell me what to do."

"As long as you're the mother of my child, I do." He crossed his arms over his chest, this time wearing a shirt. I had the cooler temperature, which moved in with the fog, to thank for sparing my eyes. The sight of him repulsed me, even more so after he laid his hands on me the previous night.

"Let's get something straight right now, and we will never discuss it again." I pushed to my feet and turned to face him, my fists clenched, my jaw tight. Heat spread to every part of me; my heartbeat in my ears.

"Step down." Aidan's voice kept my mouth shut. "You're turned on by me giving you orders, aren't you? The way you're licking your lips makes me want to do it."

I shut my eyes, no longer wanting to see Gabriel or have Aidan look at him. Aidan could see through my eyes and the surveillance cameras. *Double vision for someone with 20/20 vision?* Eli reached for my hand and pulled me down onto the couch.

"What were you going to say?" Gabriel sneered.

"You impregnated me without my consent, you have no

legal rights to this child, and believe me when I tell you I will hire the best team of lawyers in the world and ensure you spend the rest of your life behind bars for what you've done. My child will never know your name, will never hear as much as a whisper about the man who slithered into my life." I leaned forward. This position wasn't helping my poor bladder.

Leaning back again, I kept my eyes on his, my neck getting sore. "If you won't allow me to go to Pepper Gorge, then you will go. You will do everything I tell you to do, without asking questions, without as much as raising an eyebrow. When, not if, those responsible for whatever horrors are being committed there are either arrested or killed, I will reconsider your involvement in my child's life."

I pushed to my feet, Aidan not giving knee-weakening orders this time. With my arms extended towards Gabriel, I continued. "You need to atone for what you have done. Prove yourself, and we can discuss the possibility of you being a part of this child's life. Hear me, Gabriel, for I will only say this once. *My* child will not have your surname, your name will not be on the birth certificate, we will not live under the same roof, but more than anything, after you assaulted me last night, no way in hell will I let you touch my child. *If* I allow visitations, it will be in my presence and that of multiple armed bodyguards."

The carrot wasn't dangled in front of him as much as I threw it at his face, wanting to push it down his throat until he choked. I wondered if his body would turn orange in death. It was an idiotic idea. I was perhaps more exhausted than I had realised. Sleep wasn't an option, not until Eli and I had drafted a plan of attack on Pepper Gorge and the Originals.

"Whatever you need me to do I will do, without question. However, I want to be included in this investigation. I marvel at the way your mind works. These aren't the predators you're accustomed to hunting."

"That's your first mistake." I sat and gestured for him to take a seat in the chair next to the window.

Twelve

Location: Classified. Neither here nor there.

Heather Walker stepped around the dining room table, pressing her lips to the top of her husband's head, and glanced at her eldest and youngest sons. Aidan patted his brother on the back as they got to their feet.

"I wish your brothers were here. It's good to have you under the same roof." Heather rested her hands on Ryan's shoulders. She had come down for dinner dressed in jeans and a T-shirt, no shoes.

Aidan had always appreciated how she could keep her work persona separate from being their mother, their father's wife. As most young men do, he had vowed never to marry a woman like his mother, yet he had. The similarities between Finley and his mother scared him, specifically their lust for vengeance and their understanding of the workings of human predators' minds.

"I was supposed to have a few weeks off and then Aidan got himself in this mess," Rowan said as he bumped his shoulder against Aidan's.

"Aren't you glad it's my mess for a change and not yours or Liam's?" Aidan placed his arm around his brother and hugged him, releasing him just as quickly. The way manly men do.

"If it meant I could get your wife at the end of this, I'd take the worst mess imaginable."

Aidan turned his back to his family and walked towards the fireplace. He stabbed at the glowing logs with the poker. "It doesn't get much worse than this."

"It does. Remind me to tell you a story next time we are down in the shooting range at Wild Bay. We all need a week-long family holiday when this is over." Ryan shifted in his chair. His hip would never be the same after the first explosion he had survived.

"Will Quinn be joining us tonight?" Rowan asked.

Aidan turned to his brother and rolled his eyes. "You're wasting your time pining after her."

"Since when do you roll your eyes?" Rowan placed his hands at his sides, above the holstered SIGs.

"Since Fin started doing it, don't ask me why. It's irritating her more than anyone else." Aidan laughed, the sound pained.

Heather closed the distance between them and wrapped her arms around his waist. "It will be over soon, sweetie."

"I'm worried about her. She picked up their scent and she will not back down. She will go back to Pepper Gorge and I'm worried her level of frustration and not being in control will make her careless."

"You keep reminding her of who she is, now it's time *you* remember who your wife is. Who she was before you met."

Aidan rested his chin on his mother's head and stared at his father. "Do you think things would've turned out the same had she never enlisted?"

"For her, yes, and for Duncan and Victoria Williams. The fact that she is who she became, who she always was, with her military training and the skills she gained as The Hangwoman. All of it kept her alive. It's how she will survive this mess. The Originals are no match for her."

Ryan pushed to his feet and stepped closer to the fire. "Heather, you need to speak to our girl. She understands the individual criminal better than they do, but she doesn't have your experience with them as a collective."

Heather placed her hands on Aidan's face and stared up at him. "I watched when Eli told her. She's already figured them out." She pulled his head down to her mouth and released him with a predatory smile on her face. The same Finley gets when she hunts. "They will rue the day Finley Walker drove into their little community."

Thirteen

Eli had made me printouts of what he had found on Pepper Gorge the night before and walked me to my bedroom. He apologised for not allowing me to use his laptop to do my own research. I again tried to convince him to email Captain Taylor and ask for his help.

I settled on the king-size bed and spread the pages out around me. As I scanned through the documents, I realised the writer who identified him or herself in one post as Sevens Hunter hadn't once called Pepper Gorge what it is. A cult. The most interesting conclusion I came to while listening to Eli summarise what he had uncovered: they have multiple leaders and not just one, as most cults do.

The moment I had stepped through the restaurant's door, I had noticed strange things about the interior, the menu, and the people. The furniture – new a few decades ago. The menu – written on a blackboard. Only one meal option served for breakfast. The people – none over fifty, by my estimate. They had either found the fountain of youth on the farm or made their own anti-wrinkle cream and bathed in it twice a day. Not a mobile phone in sight. No television or radio blaring tunes which would make me contemplate sticking a fork in my ear.

The men and women wore neutral colours and all the women had long hair, their faces void of artificial beauty enhancers. Ones I appreciated after a late night.

Regardless of what Gabriel had said, I needed to go back. Perhaps when Aidan learned of my plans, he would give me more panty-dropping orders. Who would've guessed I, Finley D. Williams-Walker, like being told what to do? Perhaps it had more to do with the one giving the orders. I filed this new revelation for self-analysis at a later stage, when Aidan and I were back where we belong.

The duvet cover balled into my fists. Not having access to a laptop was infuriating. I couldn't wait until the following morning to ask Eli to conduct the search for me.

Two options presented themselves. One, I could ask Gabriel, as I didn't want to wake Lizzie by knocking on the door of her and Eli's bedroom. *In a world where tea is more delicious than coffee.* I focused on the second option. The only one which would allow me to sleep.

Quinn spoke as soon as I closed the bathroom door. "Do you need room service? A wake-up call tomorrow morning? How may I, the humble voice in your head, be of service to you tonight?"

"Tell me what the layout is of the compound. How many people do you estimate live there? Based on what I've seen, there's only one street, a dirt road, but they must sleep somewhere. Do they live further up into the mountain, in the woods, or are they living in the other buildings in that street?" I rubbed my hands over my belly and lowered myself onto the toilet, the lid closed.

"It's almost midnight, go to bed. Tomorrow morning, I will answer all your questions."

"Dammit, Quinn, you're a difficult person to work with."

She laughed, and the sound made me smile. "Touché. There are more buildings further into the woods, but the tree canopy blocked our view."

"I've always wanted to fly a micro drone. Any parting words as you aren't being all that helpful tonight?"

"I will give you a hint, we deleted it from the original posts, there's a book you need to find. Let's call it their manifesto for life."

"Why did you delete it?" I lifted the lid, pulled down my pants, and took up my earlier position.

"I didn't think we were that close yet." Quinn let out a deep breath.

"You don't have a lot of female friends, do you?" The

sound of my bladder emptying itself filled the ensuing silence. "Personal question aside, you're in my head, so I get to ask you whatever I want."

"Fair enough. I have a friend, but we work together, it's how we met. I'm not good with people."

"You're good with the Walkers, and you're good with me. There's more to you than you give yourself credit for, Quinn."

"You and Heather are too alike. With two of you in the family, I might ask to be emancipated."

"You're not a child, so you're stuck with us. You deleted it because you didn't want anyone to copy their beliefs or decide to join."

"Thanks for changing the subject. Well done, Mrs Walker."

"You advance to the next round of 'What the hell is going on at Pepper Gorge'." I mimicked a TV presenter.

"Bet you don't hear this a lot, but I like you."

The feeling was mutual, and I told her so. "I'm not going to enjoy the next round, am I?"

"No, ma'am. On the plus side, no 'get out of prison free' options in this game."

My kind of game. "How big is this web?" I squirted toothpaste onto the toothbrush, stifling a yawn.

"Sleep tonight, work tomorrow."

"That big?"

"Goodnight, Finley. The answers you seek will find you after your first cup of coffee tomorrow morning."

I told her decaf held no answers, but she didn't say another word. Sleep came after I realised why the investigation had been stopped before it had ever begun.

In that sweet, confusing time before I fell asleep, Aidan's voice filled my heart. My body ached for his, the warmth of his lips on my neck as I drift into sleep. His presence chasing away the nightmares...

The rising sun warmed my back; no longer did the grey fog lock us in. Still, I wasn't free to leave. I stretched my legs out towards the river and lifted my face to the sky. Somewhere in the distance, an eagle called. I wondered if it ordered breakfast. Perhaps my growling stomach the reason for another strange thought.

"Good morning, Mrs Walker. You need to head to the bathroom when you get back, I want to see you."

"Good morning, my love. I have something to show you now." Pushing to my feet, I lifted my shirt and gazed down at my belly. I placed my hands on my growing bump. Others might not have been able to tell I was pregnant and not just bloated, but to me it was a sign of life, of hope, a promise of a time when I would no longer be a prisoner.

"Lift your shirt higher." I could hear his boyish grin, feel the pull of the naughtiness in his eyes.

"I'll make you a deal, Dr Walker: you tell me the truth and I will strip for you tonight. What should we call it? Ear sex? Surveillance camera sex?"

"Wouldn't be the first time we have improvised when we couldn't be together."

"I needed the stress relief during the Sophia investigation." I shrugged. The weight of everything that had kept me up during the night slid off my shoulders. Aidan has an effect on me that I can't put into words; even now, having no part of him with me but his voice.

"As I recall, it was the photo I sent you during my lunch break."

"Yes, well, if any other man sent me a photo like that, I would've cut it off and pushed it up where nothing should ever go."

"In case Quinn is listening, I would like to state for the record it was a photo of my hand, and suppositories are a medical marvel in my and Lizzie's opinion."

"For the record, you and Lizzie came to that conclusion while you were drinking Tiger Beer in Vietnam, I think after your fifth. And for a year I was subjected to your hand and all the wonderful things you can do with one, or both."

"Subjected to? You make it sound like a bad thing."

I bit my bottom lip and took a deep breath. "I like bad, Mr Walker."

"You only call me Mr Walker when you want the one part of me which is yours alone."

"Come get me." My fists clenched and my spine straightened at the sound of Aidan sighing. "When will this be over? We can hunt together, we're stronger together. Aidan, I ache for you."

"I can't. The person responsible for all of this is much more powerful than you think. I wish it was someone else, someone not in his position. Finley, if I could, I would come for you right this second, but we would run for the rest of our lives, and neither of us runs from a fight. Do you trust me?"

"With my life." I blinked hard, clearing my vision. "If I need to stay here, you need to tell me the truth."

"I can't tell you his name."

I shook my head and reminded myself Aidan stood in my corner. He wouldn't keep anything from me if he didn't have the best reason. "Pepper Gorge. Quinn lied to me. Why?"

"I know nothing more than you do, but I know who does. Hold on."

The sounds of nature surrounded me. Aidan moved around without a sound in our house. Why would it be any different now? *Trained to be invisible.*

"Tell her the truth right now or I will get her and run for the rest of our lives if I must. I will not tolerate you lying to my wife."

"Who are you talking to?" I asked.

The voice of the person who answered caught me off guard. Similar to my mother's in many ways. "How is my girl doing?"

Every time Aidan's parents called me 'my girl' it made me feel safe, loved. I placed my hands on my tummy and hoped our child would know the same devotion, protection, and unconditional love Aidan and I did. My parents were long gone, yet their love remained a part of me and forever will.

"Mom." It had been easy to call Heather and Ryan Mom and Dad.

"I'm sorry, Finley, I broke your trust by analysing you and this situation."

My legs failed me; I sank onto the grass. My bum connected with a sharp rock and as I stared at it, clarity came to me. "I would've done the same."

Heather laughed. "Yes, yes you would have. Sometimes we lie to our children. Not always big, life-altering lies, but little white lies to protect them."

"To protect Gabriel from me. To protect me from myself." Shaking my head, I reached for the water bottle and drank a big gulp. "Tell me, is Pepper Gorge even real or did you construct it just to keep my mind focused on hunting my own enemy?"

"At your core, you will always be a protector. It's who you are, it's one of the many reasons why we love you. Finley, sweetie, Pepper Gorge is real. Something bad is happening in that place and we have only scratched the surface."

"The truth, not the sugar-coated version. I don't like sugar as much as you do."

Heather cleared her throat and confirmed what I had suspected, to an extent. It had been a little too easy, yet difficult enough for Eli the brilliant hacker to whom the dark web was nothing more than an eight-piece puzzle which came with the picture and step-by-step instructions.

The day I had activated the tracking device, the satellite was rerouted to get an aerial view of where Lizzie and I were. Quinn had noticed strange activity as the satellite moved away from our location. She had discovered Pepper Gorge and brought it to Ryan's attention. Part of their work includes identifying terrorist groups and bringing them to the relevant government's attention. They work without borders, without a single government or organisation to report to. At that point I didn't know much more about what they did with the information they gathered except that they conducted multiple

black-ops missions. Ryan would call it grey-ops because of
the number of recognised black-ops divisions and operatives
they took down when they crossed over to the enemy's side.
The power to dish out death and destruction is not something
everyone is made for. Some days I admit I shouldn't hold such
power. Every day, the need to protect rages within me. I hope
it never stops.

Ryan had approved Quinn's request to investigate Pepper
Gorge and determine whether it formed part of the group
Gabriel worked for.

The posts made by Sevens Hunter hadn't been fabricated.
However, Quinn had the dates changed to two weeks before
our arrival in the middle of nowhere. After reading what Sevens
Hunter had written, Ryan wanted to launch a full investigation
and an extraction team if needed. Heather had talked him out
of it, telling him 'Finley is drawn to evil'. They left me to find
it, and if not by the time Aidan had resolved our situation,
Ryan could do as he saw fit. *Resolved our situation? Internal eye roll.*

"The book Quinn mentioned, did Sevens Hunter say what
it contains?" I asked.

"Only that it's their guide to life. My apologies for not being
honest with you from the moment you pulled into their little
town."

"I noticed the word *seven* comes up often in the information
you left for me to read of the original posts. What else did you
delete?"

"Nothing. There wasn't much to go on other than the
writer's ramblings about how the people are brainwashed from
birth."

"From birth? So, no new people come in? Sevens Hunter
wrote of cars driving through town and further up into the
mountain to an area off-limits to the inhabitants. After a few
days, the cars leave. If no fresh blood comes into the mix,
why didn't I notice any of the deformities, characteristics, and
traits we would expect with this level of inbreeding? Seven
generations. If Sevens Hunter hunted people for the group,

what happened to those people?"

"That's a question only you can find the answer to."

"You're keeping me busy to keep me safe. To keep Aidan safe. When will this be over?"

"Aidan can answer that. Ryan and I will leave to give you privacy. Finley, we love you and we are proud of you. In case you were wondering, Aidan refuses to tell us the gender of your baby, he says it's something you have to do together. I've started buying white clothes and gender-neutral toys and whatever I can get my hands on."

"I love you, Mom, and tell Dad he needs to keep my husband safe."

"Rowan will keep Aidan safe. He has his brother's back, and yours."

The Walkers had lied to keep Gabriel unaware of their presence. Unaware of the eyes they had inside the house.

Aidan had identified the Puppet Master.

As I made my way back to the house, I contemplated why a person in a position of power would be set on destroying our lives. By the time I reached the back door, I didn't have an answer. Aidan knew, and for now I would breathe easily knowing that whoever the Puppet Master was, he stood in my husband's crosshairs. No one who had ever done so survived. Except me.

I longed to see Aidan in action, stalking his prey, squeezing the trigger. This time I suspected Aidan planned to take his mark alive. Only a breathing Puppet Master could answer our questions. *How is Tom involved?*

Heather was right. We do tell little lies to the ones we love, to protect. On the other side of the wooden door, Gabriel's voice sounded. The lies I would tell him wouldn't be little or for his protection. Half-way back to the house I had realised the time had come for me to change my plan of attack. I told Quinn I would find a way to get to Pepper Gorge later in the day and asked her to meet me in the bathroom.

Aidan had been listening and asked what I had planned.

I told him. As my husband, he didn't agree; as a warrior, he did. We both needed to focus on our enemy and keep sight of the war's end. The hours didn't pass fast enough, but I had a mystery to solve.

Fourteen

Gabriel carried the breakfast plates to the dishwasher; I turned my focus to the man sitting across the table. The father of my sister's unborn child. I still didn't know whether he would walk away at the end of this or get a bullet between his eyes. Not a decision for Aidan's coin to make.

"We're going out for lunch, back to Pepper Gorge."

"No, it's too dangerous." Eli lifted Lizzie's hand to his mouth.

"I'm not asking for permission, I'm telling you we are going back there. Today. Lizzie's coming with us."

For a moment, her eyes lit up. "You said they kill people. I don't even have my gun anymore." She turned to Eli. "Why did you have to take it? Don't you dare say for my protection, you trained me to use it."

Eli had, better than my father or I ever could. We tried. Hard. Lizzie just couldn't be bothered until a sexy, Israeli, ex-soldier bribed her with something he didn't want to mention to me. She had told me later – sex. My sister's easy. I don't judge. Aidan and I often bartered with the promise of a weekend locked inside the house, both of us naked. It's how we resolved the odd fight. More often than not, the fight started and continued for a weekend of resolving our differences. It's hard to fight when you're trying not to flirt or laugh because fighting about which curtain should be opened first is as ridiculous as it sounds. I will fight with him about the amount of sugar granules I put in his coffee if it meant a weekend of resolving.

Eli pressed his lips to her ear. Lizzie shook her head, letting out a laboured breath.

Time for me to present my case. "Hear me out. The three of us can go in, play the whole sister wives thing, use the fact that they're into polygamy to our advantage. While we're having lunch, Gabriel can do recon."

Gabriel pulled out a chair, spun it around, and straddled it. "I'm listening." *Ah, he promised no questions.*

"You're the best of the three of us in reconnaissance." I didn't know how well-versed Lizzie was in military terminology. She isn't built the way Gabriel, Eli, and I are. "Lizzie, you've read up on inbreeding and will know what to look out for. Eli, you know what you need to do. I need to build rapport with Nicol. She's our best bet of getting inside information."

Gabriel rested his arms on the back of the chair and turned to face me. "What makes you think a child will talk to you?"

"A teenager, not a child. At her age, we are programmed to be rebellious, ask questions, stand up to the man and all of that. The fact that she and Henry asked to be married shows her strength, and it's unheard of in their community. The Originals decide who marries whom." *Oh, to be sixteen again and not grow up in a cult.*

"We need to get aerial footage of their compound before we go in. I will head out there now. Do you want to come with me?" Gabriel asked me.

Did I want to spend time alone with him? No. Did I want to remain locked in this house? No. Did I have anything better to do? Maybe if I plucked all my lashes out with a pair of tweezers. Or read the printout Eli had made for me for a third time.

Eli shook his head. "If one of them drives past, we can't have them see Finley. There are at least five cars, so we know they leave the farm."

"Sevens Hunter wrote about the people they hunted and brought back to the farm. He or she didn't say why or how they choose their victims. How many other hunters are there? When did they start hunting, last year or centuries ago?"

Gabriel touched his fingertips to my face, I willed my butt to remain in the chair and my hand not to reach for the fork he had forgotten on the table.

"I love the way your mind works, Ley." He removed his hand from my face, but the feel of his skin against mine would linger until I washed my face for the second time.

"Is there more paper and duct tape lying around?" I doubted he would give me anything I could use to restrain him.

Gabriel left, returning minutes later with the items I requested and black permanent markers. He placed the items on the table and again straddled the chair. "Do you need help creating a board in your room?" he asked.

It struck me again. He, they, had invaded our privacy with their surveillance cameras strategically placed inside our home, hidden in the belongings we had moved from the penthouse. At the time I had found it odd that Aidan took it upon himself to redecorate our entire bedroom, not that I complained about the end product. I missed our bedroom, our home, our life.

Placing my hands on my belly, I realised it wasn't safe for me to climb up and down a chair, not with this being a high-risk pregnancy. Whatever happened in the next few days, the baby's safety would be my top priority. Nothing was more important. Not even ending whatever was going on at Pepper Gorge. My child's safety far more important than that of people I didn't know. Strange, as I never had to think of someone else's safety. Everyone in my world could take care of themselves. Even Lizzie.

My sister, the brilliant chemist. CEO of Williams Pharmaceuticals, the company our father had started from nothing. She had built it into an empire. The distributor Aidan had put her in contact with made it possible for her to take Williams Pharmaceuticals across the globe. For the time being, Nathan Walker steered the ship. There wasn't anyone I trusted more to look after Lizzie's company, my father's legacy.

The Walkers were as much a part of us as we are of them. Our child – proof of a connection Heather had once mentioned, went back to the start of Tabula Rasa. She and Ryan had been part of the original donors, and throughout the years remained the biggest contributors. They shared my mother's vision.

I turned to Gabriel. "I would appreciate your help." The wall clock indicated enough time for me to wash my face until I no longer felt his skin against mine and could get started on my board. Before I had called it a murder board, now no name seemed right. Not until I knew what the hunters did with the people they hunted. Perhaps the hunters didn't know either.

I made notes and ordered Gabriel where to stick them on the wall across from the bed. He had closed the door when we walked in; I had opened it and the window. My excuse – fresh air would help me think. Gabriel stepped back and stared up at the pieces of what had once been trees. A riddle on every page stuck to the wall. None of it made sense. If the hunters had been hunting people for centuries, where were all the people? The bodies? Why did the hunters need to first hunt each other? Death filled my bedroom. So did the number seven.

"Gabriel, please leave. I've got about two hours to make sense of all of this."

"Are you sure you don't want to talk it through?"

The realisation that they had watched me create a murder board in my home office sickened me. They had listened as Aidan and I discussed the victims and the case. If only Aidan could help me now. He sees answers where I don't even see a question. I needed him to talk it through with me.

"No. Thank you. We can discuss it on the way to Pepper Gorge."

Gabriel dropped his gaze to his bare feet. "I'm sorry, Ley."

"Stop calling me that. I *was* Ari's Ley, never Gabriel's. I don't have time to discuss this with you. Again."

"You were always my Ley and forever will be. Time is the one thing we have."

The tick-tock of a clock echoed in my mind, counting down the seconds until I would be back in my world, with Aidan, preparing for the birth of our child. The wedding ring weighed heavy on my left hand, not only for the weight of the diamond, but as a reminder that I couldn't wear it and the mask of deception. "Get whatever you need ready, I have work to do."

Gabriel left, closing the door behind him. I stepped into the bathroom and stared at myself in the mirror. "I need your brilliant mind, Dr Walker."

"Seven siblings arrived on the farm which the eldest had purchased. Five Originals. What happened to the other two? Back then women had no rights, so it's safe to assume the two sisters weren't given any rights, and it's possible the brothers took them as wives, or they left. Perhaps they were murdered. When you go to Pepper Gorge, look for the word or the letter seven. Where it's placed may be of importance." Aidan's voice forced my brain to work. The wheels turned, faster and faster. *Take that, pregnancy brain.*

"Seven days in a week. The number of completeness, perfection, and a holy number in the Bible. God created the world in six days and on the seventh day, He rested. It's considered lucky in Western culture." I rubbed my temples, desperate to get my brain functioning.

Aidan rambled on about what seven is mathematically. If someone placed a gun to my head, I wouldn't be able to recall what he had said. Something about it being the lowest natural number. At first, I had thought he swore in one of the many languages he speaks, which I don't. Then I smelled the smoke from my brain combusting, trying to follow the language he spoke fluently and my high school teachers had tried to teach me.

"Dude, you know I can do my own taxes and basic accounting but stop swearing at me. If whatever you're saying relates to the case, you need to explain it to me and draw me a picture. If not, hush."

His laughter filled my soul. If only the baby could hear his voice. At the same time, I was grateful that at seventeen weeks, the baby remained unaware of the outside world.

"Dude?" Aidan laughed louder.

"Yes. I'm good at many things, but maths isn't one of them."

"I'm sorry, *dude*, just trying to help."

"You are. Any way you can hurry things up on your end?"

"My new plan is hurrying it up. I'm sorry, Finley, but you will understand when I tell you who the Puppet Master is. Again, I'm not telling you for your own safety. You will march out of the bedroom and torture Gabriel until he tells you what only the Puppet Master can answer."

"I know. Doesn't make it any easier to sit on the sideline and wait."

"You're not waiting, Dr Williams-Walker, you're hunting an evil which might be centuries old. You've never hunted one like this before. And if you don't figure it out soon, you won't get the chance. Do you want someone else to take over and hunt what you're destined to bring down?"

"Are you trying to seduce me, Dr Walker?" I stared at my reflection in the mirror.

"Our entire relationship is one big seduction, Wife. Now, before we get side-tracked with long distance self-play, go hunt, my orca. Pregnant or not, *you* are the apex predator. If anything, I suspect your need to protect has already increased if I consider the level of constant vigilance and aggression you exude. Can you please tone it down? I get hard watching you move around the house. The way you're looking at yourself in the mirror right now..."

Quinn cleared her throat. "I might never be able to look either of you in the eye again or be in the same room as the two of you. It's constant verbal porn."

Aidan and I both laughed.

"Stop listening to our conversations. There should be a way for you to know when we aren't talking?"

"There is, and I didn't hear your entire conversation, only Aidan's last two sentences. Aidan, I'm sorry, time for you to leave."

My throat constricted as my heart stopped. "Where are you going?"

"In a matter of days, you will stare down at the person

responsible for all of this."

"Aidan, I have another idea. You won't be in Marcel, will you?"

"No, heading back to Europe, and no, I won't share my itinerary. What's your idea?"

"What has Tom been getting up to since we left Marcel?" I asked.

"Nothing. Work, home, the odd visit with Ashley and her family. Hope is getting big."

"Do you have eyes on their house?"

"Yes, operatives are set up in the house across the street. We're keeping them safe and monitoring Tom."

Deep inside me, the darkness flapped her majestic wings. Time to let her out, to do what she does best – play. A predatory sneer consumed my face.

"Can you stop doing that? Dammit, Fin, Quinn is listening in and my parents will walk through the door any second." Frustration replaced the normal calm in his voice. "I love your light, I met your dark in that parking structure, but you controlled it even through the Sophia case and all of Gabriel and Tom's stunts. What's your plan?"

"Get ready to see me play in the grey. Isn't that where us Walkers operate? Where we thrive?"

"I love you, Mrs Walker. Quinn, you need to give her a gun. If you do this, I need you armed."

"Thank you. Aidan, I love you. Tell Rowan if he doesn't keep you safe, I will come for him."

"Finley, for this to end, your worst nightmare will become your reality. Remember what I always tell you."

Fifteen

A knock on the bedroom door pulled me from my thoughts where I lay on the bed staring at the notes Gabriel had taped to the wall. I had realised what else there are seven of. "Come in," I said with my back to the door.

"Are you ready?"

I turned to face my sister. Lizzie stood in the door cradling her stomach between her hands. Strange how often pregnant women touch their bellies, perhaps to bond with their unborn child. I did it to feel connected, but touch is also how I show love and affection. I held my hand out to her and as soon as she lay down next to me, I placed my hand on her stomach.

"Fizzie-Lizzie, I love you, and your baby. Has Eli mentioned where Tom is in all of this? He helped them set this up. I heard when he told Gabriel it was time to initiate Operation Alphas." I rolled my eyes. Could they not have thought of a name less of a cliché?

"No, he hasn't spoken about him at all since we left Marcel." She covered my hand with her own.

"Aidan left a note saying he would kill whoever stood in the way of us being together. It's why we left, to keep you and me safe from him. Tom had been vocal about his hatred for Aidan on so many occasions, why hasn't Aidan taken him out? He's our godfather. He stepped in to be our parent after Dad and Mom died. Why hasn't Aidan gone after the one person who we would turn to when we needed help?"

The darkness soared and lifted with it the notion from the pit where she had returned to after I stopped being The Hangwoman. *Hello, old friend. Welcome home.* In her own way she had guided me in my hunt of the depraved who have their own darkness. Had, as they all died in front of me. It's what

93

happens to those set on hurting innocent people, too often children. I realised she was a part of my subconscious, my imagination, the part of me who understood. Some might say a symptom of PTSD.

For too long I had fought to live in the light, to follow the law and hunt within the restrictions thereof. Now I didn't see black and white, light and dark, only grey.

Lizzie lifted herself up on her elbows and stared at my board. "Why is seven written on almost every page?"

I pushed myself up on the bed and leaned back against the headboard. Lizzie did the same. "I suspect seven refers to the deadly sins."

"Lust, gluttony, greed. I can't remember the other four." She still stared at the notes covering half of the wall.

"Sloth, wrath, envy, and pride."

"What is the significance?"

"I'm not sure yet. The name Sevens Hunter might be a clue. The people they hunt on the outside world may represent the seven deadly sins. Could be that they're trying to purge the outside world to be as holy as they believe themselves to be. Maybe once the world is eradicated of these seven sins, they can leave the farm. Then again, they would need an army unrivalled by any power in the world and start the Third World War for that to happen. What about all the other sins?"

"How do you understand them?" She stared at me as if I was a stranger.

"At this point I don't know if I do. I'm speculating. I don't have enough to draw up a profile. The best option right now is to gain Nicol's trust."

"How are you going to do that?"

"Play it by ear."

From the front door, Gabriel called us. Eli mumbled as he strode past the open bedroom door. I turned to Lizzie and smiled. "It will be okay. Eli and I won't let anything happen to you."

Lizzie wrapped her arms around my neck, leaving me

gasping for air. She released her hold and grabbed my face between her palms. "You, Finley Duncan Williams-Walker, aren't bulletproof." She grabbed my arm, tracing the scar underneath the orca tattoo with her fingertips. "You're flesh and blood. And pregnant." Lizzie touched the bruises Gabriel had left on my upper arms. They had begun to turn purple. I've been through this rainbow dance before.

With my forehead against hers, I whispered, "So are those I hunt. Minus the pregnant part, as far as I know. Gabriel won't let anything happen to the child he believes will justify his existence."

"You're turning into the person you were when you came back, after you were rescued."

I shrugged.

"She scares me, Finley. You didn't go there after the serial killers abducted you."

"It's not you who should be afraid, Liz." I rubbed my forehead against hers. "This is who I am, I've been fighting it for too long." The notion stretched. Goosebumps rippled across my body. *Time to play.*

I drew her closer, pressing my lips to her ear. "No matter what happens in the next few days, just go with it. Question, argue, but accept this is what I have to do. I love you, our children, and Aidan. I'm fighting for my family, and I will keep fighting until there's nothing but carcasses in my wake."

Gabriel had loaded all the items I kept stored in my bedroom in the back of his SUV before we left for Pepper Gorge. Lizzie had grabbed my hand as soon as I closed the passenger side door and held on until we stopped in front of the restaurant. Bringing a civilian along might have been a mistake. Strange how I still saw myself as separate from the general population. I'm not made for a nine-to-five, to sit behind a desk and push buttons on a keyboard all day. The age of paper long gone.

We left Gabriel 500 metres from the turnoff to the farm. I hoped he wouldn't get himself killed before finding the answers I needed. Once he did, his life would be free for the taking.

Eli opened Lizzie's door and stared daggers at me. "You're being reckless by dragging your sister into this. I don't like it."

"She's armed and neither of us will leave her side. So be a good future brother-in-law and play your part. Two hours max and then we will pick up your buddy and head back to the house."

I had checked the Glock 24 Gen 4's they had given Lizzie and me, and ensured the magazines were loaded and both had firing pins. Lizzie had stared at me again. Something she had done for weeks after I had returned to Marcel. Then she had stared at the scar on my face, a keepsake from the horrors I had endured in that hot, dusty bunker. The scars on my soul I had learned to live with, and hide. No plastic surgery to correct that. Long-term therapy isn't something offered to the soul-battered ex-soldier, but I found my ways to cope.

The five vehicles stood where they had been days before. I had scanned every available surface and hadn't noticed the word or the number seven anywhere except above the door of every building. Eli drove as far as he could down the street and made a U-turn where a tree lay across the road. The road led further up into the mountain; someone had recently used it. We stepped into the restaurant and again were met with surprised stares.

Nicol hurried over, fear visible in her eyes. "We aren't serving lunch anymore, you missed it by half an hour. Sorry." She stepped forward, gesturing towards the door behind us.

"We're on our way home and I wanted to show my other wife your darling little town. Can we at least have something to drink before we leave?" Eli placed his hands on my and Lizzie's lower backs.

Nicol glanced to her right where the same man we had seen the first time Eli and I had been there sat. He nodded with a smile. Not quite a smile as much as a change in the position of the corners of his mouth.

"Thank you, Nicol. We appreciate your hospitality. It's such a long drive back and we want her to see your town. There's just something special about this place that we couldn't describe." I stepped past her and made my way to the same table, the same chair. The silence in the room was deafening, so I broke it with a sporadic 'hello' at the other patrons.

The menu hung next to the door I believed to be that of the kitchen. They had served tomato soup and bread for lunch. I don't eat soup unless it contains some kind of meat. Nicol took our order and disappeared behind the door next to the menu. The same hand had written today's menu. I wondered if anything ever changed around here.

Eli reached for Lizzie and my hands at the same time. It took me a second to remember we were supposed to be married. I never did drama or any kind of stage production in school, I never had the time because my father always had some kind of car for me to build or take apart.

I excused myself and headed to the bathroom. Nicol remained in the kitchen. As soon as I stepped through the door, I checked to ensure I was alone, and placed the listening devices behind the toilet cisterns in both cubicles and one at the back of the only washbasin. Quinn stood behind me as I came to my full length. She winked, closing her brown eye, and watched me with the blue one. This woman an odd mixture of mischief, secretiveness, lethalness, and warmth. I sensed in her a great deal of sadness, anger, and confusion. Not that I'm by any means psychic, but I do consider myself an empath.

"I'm learning a thing or two listening to you and Aidan."

"The only thing I hope you learn is that anyone can find love; a life partner who accepts you no matter your past, your present, or your future."

Again, she held her hand out towards me, a Glock 24 Gen 4 on her palm. I took the baby Glock and holstered it close to my groin. Nowhere else to hide it. A bullet already chambered. No person in my world wouldn't carry one up.

"I believe you have something for me."

I placed the ring in her hand. "Where will you keep it?"

Quinn shook her head. "I won't lose it. Promise."

"Not like the one I dropped in the drain. Woops." She smiled with me.

"Are you sure about this?"

My turn to shake my head. "It's just a ring. The commitment Aidan and I made to each other is more than a metal circle with a gorgeous blue diamond or a piece of paper."

"Something will go down in Marcel. Soon. There has been chatter on the networks that someone is looking for a person with a very specific skill set."

"Ah, yes, I expected this to happen."

"I enjoy seeing this look on your face. It makes sense why Aidan reacts the way he does."

I turned to the mirror. This face I have never seen, but I have felt it. Darkness played in my eyes. The notion shook with excitement. It's been a long time since the two of us hunted together.

"You need to leave, Quinn. I guess I won't see you again, not until this is over."

She moved into my personal space and wrapped her arms around me. "I'm always with you, and if things go wrong, I'm closer than you think. Remember that." She released me, taking with her the comfort she offered. "And if Gabriel touches you again, I have a direct order from Aidan to take him out."

"It won't be necessary. Gabriel is about to learn how much this apex predator likes to play with her prey."

"What are you going to do to him?"

A sneer consumed my face as rage clawed into every muscle fibre of my body. "Patience, my dear, Quinn, I don't want to spoil the surprise. Please feel free to comment on my progress. My gut tells me you and I are alike." I hugged her and returned to the table where Lizzie and Eli sat in deep conversation. Eli's focus was on the man at the door, but his eyes remained on his fiancé.

Nicol carried out a tray with our drinks, dread radiating

off her every step. I thanked her and asked her to join us. She declined, heading to the bathroom instead.

I sighed; it was time for me to use the loo again. And not just as a ruse.

Nicol spun around as I closed the door.

"Have there been more deaths?" No point in wasting time. She shook her head.

"Nicol, I can help. I told you last time." I stepped forward. She stepped back. We were conducting our two-step again.

"We take care of our own problems. Besides, this is no place for a pregnant woman." She glanced at my stomach.

I smirked and removed the Glock. "It's a gun, not a baby."

"Oh, your shirt is hanging loose. I thought..."

"I've gained some weight since we got married. Thank you for reminding me it's time I hit the gym, hard, when we get back home."

"Are all three of you married?"

I returned the Glock to the holster, careful not to flash her some protruding belly. "Yes, bet you don't see that every day. Polygamy is frowned upon, but who is to say we can't love each other and be happy? Besides, my sister became my fellow wife, we shared our mother's womb, not at the same time, why not then a husband?"

"The people where you live, do they treat you differently because you're living the way we should?"

I shrugged and checked my reflection in the mirror behind her. "Of course, but people are more accepting of one another these days. At the end of the day, *we* need to be happy. They need to be happy with their life choices, and I will not judge unless their choices hurt others. Then I will do what I do best."

"What's that?"

"Protect. I keep people safe for a living, it's my life's mission. Protect and put away the abusers, the murderers, the rapists, the people whom the victims trusted to protect them against evil." I held up my hands. "I shouldn't be saying this, I'm too passionate and you're still a child."

Nicol pursed her lips. "I'm sixteen, old enough to get married, to have children. You don't need to treat me like a child. Nobody around here does, I don't care for your outside world ways."

I lowered my hands. "Hey, I get it. I was your age once, got this tattoo, moved out of my parents' house, and made my own way in the world. Saw some stuff, did some stuff, and here I stand. Loud and proud." *Is it a sin to lie to someone if you're trying to help?*

"Leave. Forget about this place. We don't need your help." She stepped past me. I grabbed her arm.

"You've got my help whether you want it or not. Nicol, you're either with me or against me. But hear me when I tell you I will find out what's going on here. If you decide to run to the Originals and warn them, it would be a pity if they heard about the secrets you spilled to the outside world. What the hunters do. How you're eradicating the world of the seven deadly sins. All of it."

"I never told you anything!"

The tears I expected, but the hot rage flashing in her eyes I did not. *Good girl.* "Who do you think they'll believe? A stranger who drove into this place by accident, or a child who goes to the waterfall to do what you do up there? Let's not forget you convinced Henry Bailey to approach his father and ask for permission to marry you. It's not the way of your people, Nicol. What will happen when the other four learn that you're manipulating the rules, breaking your sacred laws?"

"You have no idea what I've done, what I'm capable of." She lifted her head and met my stare.

"Sevens Hunter isn't working alone; who is he? Your lover, your brother, or isn't that the same thing around here?" I smiled at a child who had never truly been a child. Not growing up in this place. "The second I walk out of here you lose my protection. If you want to beat them, you need me. If you don't, you'll end up like all the people the hunters bring here. Stop playing a game you can't win. The Coopersville police are hunting him down, Nicol. This will not end with the two of you riding off into the sunset."

Tears filled her eyes. "No one can beat the Originals, they're too powerful. As long as the preacher lives, not even you can stop them."

"Tell me where the preacher is, and I will end it. Today."

Nicol blinked, sending tears down her flawless, youthful face. "He's everywhere."

Sixteen

Current Location: Classified. Final Destination: Classified.

Rowan returned from the bar, a Jameson in each hand. He held a tumbler towards Aidan and took a seat next to his brother. "Do you remember the last time we were on a plane together?" Rowan asked.

Aidan nodded; the memory of the day so vivid he still felt the warmth of Nathan's blood on his hands.

"You saved my life that day."

"You've gotten better at taking orders since then. It's best none of us work together." In the silent moments when sleep evaded him, Aidan longed for the thrill of working for his father's organisation, for the difference they made. A difference few people even knew about. None of them were in it for recognition, praise, or money. Wrongs have to be righted, no matter the cost. Even when it means walking with one foot in the light and the other in the dark.

"I was young, tried to prove myself worthy of being out in the field with Aidan the Great and Liam the Conqueror."

Aidan laughed, turning to his brother. "Aidan the Great? If I had been great, my wife wouldn't be on the other side of the world, doing what she has to do." He clenched his fist around the crystal tumbler, not hearing the crack or feeling the liquid spill onto his jeans.

"You're bleeding." Rowan stood and grabbed a cloth from the bar counter. He handed it to Aidan and went in search of the first-aid kit. Blood oozed from the cut, the whiskey disinfecting it. Aidan removed the pieces of crystal from his hand and bit back a curse despite the cut not being deep enough to require stitches.

Rowan returned and opened the kit, leaving it to Aidan to take what he needed. Only when Aidan leaned back in his seat did Rowan speak. "You need to stop watching her. It can't be easy to see, and your head needs to be in your end of the game."

"My head, heart, all of me will always be with Finley. And don't give me any of that sanctimonious crap about her needing me back alive. I know. It's the reason I formulated this strategy." Aidan pushed to his feet and rolled his shoulders. "Don't you dare say I'm taking the coward's way here. If I could, I would storm in there and rip him to pieces with my bare hands. You know as well as I do that's not the safest option, not for me, but least of all for the rest of this team. I won't have more deaths on my conscience."

"Your biggest problem is you can't handle making mistakes. What happened to Nathan isn't your fault."

Aidan balled his fists and pushed them into the front pockets of his jeans, ignoring the pain in his hand. As a child, his mother had told him even he could make mistakes, that making a mistake was nothing to be ashamed of. Heather told him he couldn't anticipate another person's every move and in war, nothing is a given. No matter how often she told him, he couldn't accept his mistakes, or flaws. Finley took it in her stride when he forgot to buy milk or bread on his way home. The days when the thought of being home with her consumed his mind. Days when he had to tell a patient she had miscarried, or her pap smear results came back positive for cancer. Finley simply requested he make it up to her any way he saw fit. With every passing hour, his longing for her intensified to the point where he thought of nothing but ending this war.

Finley grounds him as much as he does her. Not being together, not hunting together, was wrong. They both felt it. His heart clenched, he ached to scream, shoot something, someone, anything to unleash the frustration bubbling inside him. "I need to go get her, there has to be another way."

Rowan placed his hands on Aidan's shoulders. "There isn't,

you've considered every scenario. This is the only one in which Fin and Lizzie can survive, and there won't be any casualties on our end. You created this strategy years ago, and it hasn't once let us down. Think about all the times we've done this."

Aidan did; Rowan was right. It had worked the first time, and every other time. Nothing was more important than keeping Finley, Lizzie, and the babies alive. At least Finley wouldn't be going back to Pepper Gorge.

"How old were you when you came up with this strategy?" Rowan kept his hands on Aidan's shoulders, his grip firm.

"Thirteen."

"Did it fail then, or any of the dozen times we've done it since?"

Aidan shook his head.

"What happened to Nathan wasn't your fault. It will never be the same as this. You were in a hot zone, in the middle of a drug war. Shit hit the fan, Aidan. It happens. Nathan has never blamed you. He chose civilian life, even after Dad offered him a fantastic position in the intelligence gathering division. Nate decided to no longer work with us."

No matter how many times his family had said the same, Aidan never took it to heart. When he had told Finley, she had held him, listened, and when he stopped talking, she kissed him. The sweetest kiss he had ever experienced. It had pushed the weight off his shoulders. She hadn't said it wasn't his fault; Finley never judged his need for perfection within himself.

Rowan released Aidan's shoulders and picked up the laptop. Finley's focus fixed on the back of Gabriel's head. "Are you going to tell her?"

"No." Not because he didn't trust her to keep up her act, Aidan didn't have the words.

Seventeen

Gabriel glanced at Eli for the third time since we had picked him up. Neither said a word. Nicol had drained the last drop of my patience. I was born with a blinking emergency light. The scar under my left eyebrow proof of this; I tried to run before I could walk. "Out with it, what's going on?"

"You were right." Gabriel handed me his mobile phone without taking his eyes off the road.

Male. Approximate age between fifteen and eighteen. Time of death would have to be calculated, taking into consideration the heat of the past few days. I wasn't familiar with the rate of decomposition at this altitude. Educated guess – seven to ten days, based on the red discolouring of the body and bloat. The body? Staged. At one time he had been positioned with his back against the tree. If my conclusion proved correct, the seven carved into the tree would've been right above the boy's head.

"Did you find any other bodies?" I asked, still staring down at the child for whom the Grim Reaper had come too early. *Death is never late.*

"Yes, but swipe left, I found other areas with signs of decomp. Hard to tell whether it's human. The carving makes me think it might have been."

"Or dry runs. Did you start your ritual with animals, including this much detail when you practised? Your signature didn't evolve, you perfected it before your first kill."

Lizzie whipped her head in my direction. "I hate when you talk to them."

"Sorry," I lied. It's my way of getting inside their frame of mind. By asking the air around me for answers. *Maybe I was born with it, maybe it's me.* "Gabriel, can you print these out for

105

me and help me put them up?"

"You want to sleep with that in your room?" Lizzie gagged. *Is she even my biological sister?*

"A young boy was butchered. Death isn't pretty, Liz, certainly not the way he died." The carving in his torso happened while blood still flowed in his veins; another educated guess. "I don't relish in his death, but if not for people like me, who would bring those responsible to justice? Like you write formulations on a whiteboard, I, too, work on sight. I guess we got it from Dad. Do you remember how mad he would get whenever we left pictures for him on one of his boards when we started to draw?" Joy filled my voice. "I would drag chairs closer while you carried the crayons or whatever we could lay our hands on. He ended up installing two little boards just for us to *work* on."

I took her hand in mine and continued. "We owe it to this young man to find the answers. To everyone else robbed of a lifetime of what we had and will have. We're the voice of the voiceless. If I don't ask, who will?"

She scooted closer and placed an arm around my shoulder. "I get it. I always have, it doesn't mean I like it. Thank you for sacrificing your sleep, and all the other sacrifices I don't even know about. I'm proud of you. Mom and Dad would be, too."

Lizzie rubbed her right hand over my left and stilled. "Where's your ring?"

"When I washed my hands, I dropped it in the sink. No drain cover. It's gone."

"Gabriel, turn around, we need to go back for Fin's ring."

I grabbed her hand and squeezed. "No, we don't. Aidan chose death and destruction over our life, over me. He wasn't who I thought he was." I closed my eyes and drew a deep, shaky breath. "Aidan Walker is a cold-blooded killer. I'm no longer his wife." The tears weren't fake; it shattered my heart to utter such horrid lies.

"I love you, Mrs Walker," Aidan whispered.

Aidan Walker is strength, courage, righteousness, compassion, and brilliance down to his core. It courses through him like lava waiting to be spewed into the air. He's my husband, and will be as long as we can evade death's clutches. Before he came for me, I would rip Pepper Gorge to shreds and find the truth of that dark place. For the boy whose last moments I clutched in my hand, for every person the hunters had brought there. *Where are you? What did they do to you?*

The four of us had a late lunch, seeing as we had received no sustenance from the unwelcoming folks at Pepper Gorge. Gabriel had printed the photos and stuck them to the wall where I requested him to. Staring at it, I grabbed my stomach and prayed my child would never be on the receiving end of evil. To my dying breath I will protect my child and raise him or her to fight for those who can't fight for themselves. Aidan and I will be there to remind our child to cling to the light.

No parent should ever lose a child, least of all at another human's hand. This is where it becomes grey. What if someone's child is a rapist, murderer, or paedophile in a country which supports the death penalty? Grey to some; black and white to others like me.

Movement behind me. I didn't need to turn around to know who it was. "Did you forget something?"

"Finley, Eli and I need to speak to you and Liz. Do you mind coming with me to the kitchen?" Gabriel left without waiting for my answer.

"I'll be right there; the baby is bouncing on my bladder." I felt guilty for blaming the baby. *Mommy's sorry.*

With the bathroom door locked, I hurried to the washbasin and lifted my eyes to the mirror. "Aidan? Quinn?"

"Right here, babe," Quinn said.

"No. You and I will not be the kind of girl friends who call each other *babe*. Come on, Quinn, I expected more from you."

"Why not? I saw women in a reality show call each other babe. I thought it's what friends do."

I rolled my eyes. "No friend of mine watches reality television. And if you have time to watch television, you're not doing your job by helping Aidan and monitoring the situation here."

"Just because you're my boss's daughter-in-law, it doesn't give you the right to take that tone with me. I'm bored. Surveillance isn't my forte. Either you do something exciting which will force me to binge watch the boring episodes of your current life, or I will continue frying my brain with reality television. Really, Fin, why are we trying to keep these dumbasses safe? They're too thick and full of Botox and fillers to even suspect we exist."

"I will take whatever tone I want with you; *you* live inside *my* head. How I speak to my inner voice is up to me. To top it all off, you see what I see. In the shower. In the mirror. I'm never alone. The only person I have ever allowed to be this close to me is Aidan."

Memories of my squad scratched at my soul. Powerless, I had watched as they were murdered. Their screams still echoed in the darkness when sleep evaded me. War is brutal and cruel. No one wins. Least of all the survivors.

"I get it, but I'm bored. You're not making any headway with Pepper Gorge, and you haven't stabbed Gabriel to death. I was told you're a force to be reckoned with."

I knew she tried to bait me, and for that I liked her even more. Few people have the guts to say what they think. Quinn's one of the rare few I want in my circle. "Get the popcorn ready, things are going to change around here real soon."

A heavy sigh bounced off the top-to-floor white tiles. Whoever did the interior decorating of this specific bathroom had gone for an abattoir look. Or an autopsy room. If only I had luminol to test for blood. Then again, sleeping with photos of a murder victim watching over me was one thing. Sleeping next to a murder room? No, thank you. Not if I'm not the one utilising it.

"Quinn, what happened?"

"I believe Gabriel is about to tell you."

"It's because I said you live in my head, isn't it?" Silence answered me. "You just rolled your eyes."

"Your bad habits are infectious."

"Suck it up, it's what happens when you get close to someone. Say it, Quinn. Say you're my friend."

"I admit I don't despise you and might sit next to you at Christmas dinner."

"Good enough for now. You, my dear armadillo, have started to shed your hard exterior around me. You're one weird woman, Quinn, all hugs and compassion when we're face to face, but when you're only in my head, you're all shields-up."

"Enough with the nerd talk. Go find out what your big mouth has done."

That's what I did. *Oh, what a big mouth I have. All the better to rip them to pieces with.*

Eighteen

Lizzie and I had handed the Glocks back to Gabriel upon our return to the house. I kept the one Quinn had given me holstered in my bra; pregnancy boobs and the craftsmanship of Dr Schmidt offered cover to the slight bulge.

Lizzie sat next to Eli on the two-seater couch. I sat alone on the three-seater which doubled as Gabriel's bed. He stood at the window to my left, his back to the room.

"Eli, I think it's best if you tell them." Gabriel focused on something in the woods.

Eli kept Lizzie's hands in his and stared at the coffee table.

The thin thread by which the last drop of my patience hung snapped. "I have work to do, so either tell us who died or I'm leaving."

Gabriel spun around, sending the lamp on the table next to him tumbling towards the hardwood floor. Cat-like reflexes saved it from smashing into pieces. "What makes you think someone died?"

"We've been here for over two weeks, but this is the first time you've summoned us for a meeting. Is this a meeting? It sure feels like one, as I'm bored, and there's a ton of work waiting for me. Eli and I need to set up so we can put the listening devices to use."

Lizzie had placed a device underneath her chair as well as Eli's and the table. Eli had done the same as me, only in the men's bathroom.

"I'm hungry. Lizzie?" She shook her head. I headed to the kitchen and returned with a tub of strawberry yoghurt. It wouldn't surprise me if this baby was born with red hair considering my sudden craving for strawberries. Juice, yoghurt, the fruit itself.

Gabriel settled on the windowsill, glancing between Lizzie and me. I gestured for him to get to the point between mouthfuls of delicious, sweet, full-fat yoghurt. *No fat-free garbage depleted of all its nutrients for this baby.*

"While we were in Pepper Gorge, Aidan placed bombs inside your houses, and I'm sorry to tell you, there's very little left."

Wordless, Lizzie and I stared at him. She was mute because of shock, but I wanted to hear the rest.

"Not only did he destroy your homes, but also Tom's. Luckily for Tom, he stopped at Ashley's to see Hope. Had he not, he would be dead. Your godfather could've been murdered by the man you swore to love until death parted you. Is it going to take another death before you realise what he is?"

I licked the spoon, placed it inside the tub, and lifted my left hand towards Gabriel's face. "I'm glad I lost my ring. He's dead to me. I'm glad he destroyed our home, but I'm furious he destroyed Lizzie's." I stood and walked over to her. Sitting on the arm rest, I stroked her golden hair. "We will rebuild, stronger than before." I pressed my lips to her hair. "I'm sorry, Lizzie." I meant it.

"You're sorry?" She pulled away from me and buried her face in Eli's chest. Over her head he stared at me, his expression unreadable.

"Yes, I'm sorry. For bringing this evil into our lives, for us needing to hide out here in this thin-air hell. Most of all, I'm sorry for being powerless to stop this, to stop *him*."

"As long as Aidan's alive, no one is safe. Tomorrow I will pick Tom up at the airport, he'll stay with us until this is over," Gabriel said.

I covered my face with my hands to hide the victory my eyes couldn't mask. *One more fish in the barrel; time to shoot, Mr Walker.*

Later, when Lizzie and I went for our afternoon walk, she told me she was happy her house had been destroyed. Time for her and Eli to start anew. Build a home of their own and not have him living with her in her house. I asked why they had kept postponing the wedding.

"Eli didn't want to get married before he righted a wrong." Lizzie shrugged and linked her arm through mine.

What wrong?

A two-bedroom cabin, or mountain house – I couldn't put my finger on what I should call a brick building with a garage converted into an arsenal. Five adults living in a two-bedroom house with only one couch almost big enough for a man half Gabriel's size, spelled trouble. Where would Tom sleep? For all I cared, he could sleep hanging upside down in a tree. He had been central to this mess, still was, I couldn't figure out why. His animosity towards Aidan, his hand in framing my husband for murder; why would my godfather, a man who had been my father's best friend, be involved in destroying my life?

I sat on the edge of the corner bath and waited for Aidan to answer me. He didn't, but Quinn did. "We don't quite know the extent of his involvement in this yet. Fact is, he gave Gabriel a place to stay when Gabriel came back to Marcel. Not even Eli was aware Gabriel had returned and they go back twenty years."

"I've told you this before, but when I found out Gabriel and Tom are acquainted, Tom acted concerned but never told me to stay away from him. Not the way he did with Aidan. Why not? He did background checks on all my ex-boyfriends, if he did one on Gabriel, he would've discovered what Gabriel had done."

"To disappear in the middle of an operation isn't unheard of. It will surprise you how often we end up taking these guys out."

"Because they cross over and join the enemy, whatever form that enemy might take. Who did Gabriel join? You must have the intel?"

"We do."

"But you won't tell me."

"Above my clearance level."

"Quinn." I rubbed my hands over my face and stared at my palms. "Why did he disappear? Something happened, something he did."

"You're getting warmer, but I'm under explicit instruction not to disclose any aspect of this to you."

"This has been fun, we should do it again sometime. I ask questions. You refuse to answer. I get it, Aidan's waging this war, but it's my life, too. Gabriel came into my life long before Aidan did. This comes back to me, and yes, I adore Aidan for trying to protect me, but I won't stop asking questions."

"As long as you ask me and not Gabriel."

I slid off the side of the bath and pulled my knees to my chest. "Nothing is more important than Aidan surviving this, and our baby. I'll stop."

"How did you know Aidan was the person you want to spend your life with?" The emotion in her voice caught me off guard.

"Because I want to spend my *life* with him, something I never even contemplated with anyone else. Not until I met Aidan did I even consider that another human being could infatuate me this much. For the first time in my life, I wanted to understand his mind, him, like I want to get inside that of a serial killer. Or other criminals, seeing as I'm branching out these days into cults. Aidan intrigues me, keeps me on my toes in the best way, and more than anything, he accepts my darkness and my light. We can talk about death and destruction and minutes later laugh about something else, of course."

Despite the smile, I wiped at the wetness under my eyes. "Aidan's the first person who saw both sides of me and still he accepts *me*, wants me. With Lizzie, I need to hide my understanding of criminals. To this day she doesn't know I killed the trafficker who attacked my mother and me outside Tabula Rasa. My parents ensured the police never filed charges against me. They attributed it to shock and my need to protect, in this case my mother. Gabriel always saw Finley the soldier, a fellow warrior. Tom saw someone who would one day grow up and become a profiler, someone in law enforcement like him. But with Aidan, I can be every side of me, who I am at my core."

Over the years I came to realise how few people ever find a single person with whom they can be who they are. Someone they can voice their every thought and desire to. Aidan found the same in me.

Darkness descended on the mountain. I waited for the stars to appear, hoping to see the satellite, hoping it still watched over us and Pepper Gorge.

"Will you be awake when I get back?" Gabriel asked as he sat down next to me at the top of the stairs.

"Where is Tom going to sleep? He sure as hell won't sleep in my bed with you while I end up on the couch." I swatted at a bug, wishing I could stomp on the larger-than-life cockroach sitting next to me.

Gabriel laid his hand on my lower back. I closed my eyes and forced myself to breathe. "I'll never expect you to sleep on that thing, pregnant or not."

"Where do you think I slept during my deployments? In a comfy bed? I slept in foxholes, on sand, once in a tree, in buildings reduced to rubble."

"You're pregnant, and this isn't war."

I turned my head to where the sun had retreated to hide the smirk. *But this is war.*

Gabriel rubbed his hand up my back and the hairs on my neck stood up. "I've slept in far worse places than you; I'll sleep on the floor and still get a good night's rest in. Some nights I still expect rockets or gunfire to wake me up."

"Why did you leave?"

"I had to leave you to infiltrate the human trafficking ring. Why are you asking again?"

"No. Why did you leave Sayeret Matkal? After everything you had to go through to get in, the good they do, why did you leave?" I stared at him, not seeing his dark eyes.

"When would you have left had things not turned out the way they did?"

I wasn't getting anywhere, so I played the one card that would always win. "If you want us to raise this child together, we need to get back to a good place. I won't raise this child surrounded by hatred."

Gabriel moved his hand up to the back of my neck. My shoulders didn't sag from enjoyment. "I love you enough for the both of us."

The mother of all mental face-palms. "Why did you leave, Gabriel?"

"Stop this, right now. You know the reason, he doesn't need to tell you. Think."

I hated every second of not being in control. For a control freak, this is a dangerous situation to be in. Aidan knew it.

"I'm sorry," I said to Aidan. "Let's focus on the here and now and forget everything that happened before this moment. Clean slate?" I extended my right hand to Gabriel, hearing the sugar drip from my words.

He took my hand, lifting it to his mouth. Against my skin he whispered, "Deal. I will do anything for you. One day you will understand how much I have loved you since the first time I laid eyes on you. The fire in you spoke to my own." He pressed his lips to my hand and took a deep breath through this nose.

Pulling my hand from his, I forced my lips to pull back and show my teeth. Pointless in the dark, but I tried. "I'm going with you tonight."

Gabriel cupped my face before I could scoot back and out of his reach. "Fitting, us hunting together again. Like the night we play-hunted each other in the woods at your lake house. The night we made love for the first time. If I remember correctly, it was three times we became one that night and twice the following morning, even before we got out of bed. I've missed you, Ley."

I'm sorry, Aidan. There wasn't an ex-boyfriend or lover Aidan didn't know about, but to hear one of them talking like this... bile rose in my throat. If they didn't destroy the lake house, I would put it on the market the first chance I got. Even though I had donated the bed and ripped out every surface Gabriel and I had done what we had on when I refurbished the entire house, I couldn't expect Aidan to go back there.

As if reading my mind, Aidan whispered, "I don't care. He had a small part of you for a brief moment of your life. I have *all* of you, and you of me."

The light above our heads came on. I squinted, waiting for my vision to adjust to the brightness. Gabriel stood and held out his hand. I couldn't move, desperate to stay in the safe space Aidan's words had created.

"Go, my wife. Hunt them. End them. Soon I will lay our enemy at your feet."

"Was the lake house also destroyed?"

"I'm sorry, Ley." His hand still extended towards me. "I will buy you a new house, we can make better memories there. With our child."

Conflicted, I reached for Gabriel's hand. With the lake house destroyed, there was one less thing for me to do upon my return home. I laughed without showing it. Home? Both of mine had been reduced to rubble. My parents had left me the lake house in their will; I loved it for more reasons than I have fingers to count.

"He's lying. The lake house remains the way you left it. It might not be standing at the end of this, they gave me an idea. Remember what I tell you about your nightmares."

Gabriel pulled me to my feet. I said to Aidan, "It's just a house. I think a new one, a place to make new memories, *our* memories, is precisely what we need."

The smile on Gabriel's face I knew didn't match my husband's.

Nineteen

A whisper woke me at 0300 hours. I had fallen asleep staring at the young boy who had been brutally murdered. I wish I could say he was the first victim whose photos I had seen, or that this was the first time I hunted a killer. It never gets easier.

The deep slashes across his abdomen had bombarded my brain. I had witnessed the horrors humans can inflict on one another more times than I care to remember. The dark web is a macabre photo album. Not to mention the evidence and case files kept by the police. In two and a half years, I had seen more than any person ever should. And the realities of war will forever play like a slideshow in my mind.

Gabriel pulled off the main road and drove as far as possible down the dirt road leading to a private mountain lodge. The owners, Eli had said, were in Europe. It seemed to be where all the action was. I wondered where in Europe Aidan found himself as well as the identity of the one we called the Puppet Master.

"Are you ready?" Gabriel asked, returning his travel mug filled with caffeinated coffee to the cup holder. It mocked my decaf-filled travel mug next to it.

I nodded and slid out of the SUV, pulling my raincoat close to my face. The storm had moved on, leaving a faint, constant drizzle to soak the earth.

Gabriel opened the back door and removed what he needed, but I didn't see what, as the interior lights offered no help. "You can wait in the car and watch on the screen, I don't want you to get sick."

"Rain won't make me sick. I want to see how you fly this thing."

He asked me to extend my hand, palm up; the pressure of

the drone was minimal, by the feel of it, not weighing more than a 9mm bullet. Why do the bad guys always have the best toys? *Our team has a satellite.* If my in-laws owned a satellite, I wondered what else they have in their arsenal? I couldn't wait to ask them all the questions I had made a mental list of and continued to add more to every day.

Minutes passed before the drone took off, heading for Pepper Gorge. With a range of fifteen kilometres, we were well within the perimeter as we stood eight kilometres to the east of the farm's border. It was another two from there to the town.

I headed back inside the SUV and opened the laptop to see the world through something else's perspective for a change. I could never hunt for the truth like this before. *This I can get used to.*

Under the cover of darkness, the footage the drone captured gave us a clear indication of the layout of the buildings. Once we got what I needed, the drone flew further up the mountain, towards where the tree canopy obstructed the satellite's roaming eye.

Five buildings stood separate from each other, but close enough that the neighbours could hear you sneeze. Or kill. This, I deduced, is where the Originals lived. Again, I wondered why we hadn't seen any of the deformities one would expect from generations of inbreeding.

"Welcome to my world," Quinn said. "You're enjoying this, aren't you?"

Yes, I wanted to scream, but I opted for a nod. I craved this without knowing it. A voyeur, seeing into the enemy's world. A looking glass. Anonymity. A way to hunt without being in the firing line. My senses were overloaded by the realisation of what this meant.

The taste of righteousness; evil shouldn't be allowed to operate unseen. To study them in their habitat. I considered nothing about Pepper Gorge natural, except the fauna and flora. A fairy tale setting for horror.

I stood a breath away from touching their depravity, from understanding it. This moment revolutionised my hunting strategy. Much like taking that first hit of an illegal substance or getting your first tattoo. I needed more.

The drone returned to the SUV while I waited for Gabriel to deploy the other drones to position the surveillance cameras in the areas I had identified during the first drone's recon. In less than thirty minutes, we completed the mission and headed back to the house. This day I would come face to face with my godfather, the man who betrayed Lizzie and me. The person who had been fundamental in framing my husband for two murders. But first, I needed sleep.

The scent of coffee pulled me from a deep, restful sleep. I reached for the warm body next to me and moved closer to snuggle against to him. A cold emptiness greeted me. I opened my mouth to tell him I longed to wake up to his beautiful face, his sleepy smile which kick starts my blood circulation and sends my hormones into overdrive. Aidan, not there. I wondered if I could still remember his scent. Not the smell of his cologne or body wash, the smell of his skin, the lines of his muscles, every groove I had explored with my eyes, hands, and tongue.

The scent of coffee remained. I didn't want to open my eyes in that place one more day. Or spend another day wearing a mask I could feel slipping with every passing hour. Rage grew into an unknown, uncontrollable beast.

I rubbed my hand over my stomach. "I love you."

"What does it feel like?"

My eyes shot open, my heartbeat in my ears. "I would appreciate it if you don't enter my room and watch me sleep. It's creepy."

Behind me, the tell-tale sound of a coffee mug being placed on a wooden surface. I drink a lot of coffee, I know the sound a paper or plastic cup, or a ceramic mug, makes on any surface.

Rolling onto my back, I stared up at him, his eyes fixed on

the bruises on my arms. I clutched the duvet to my chest and positioned my back against the headboard, drawing my knees to my chest. He considered it an invitation and sat down at the foot of the bed.

"Do you need anything from town? I'm on my way to pick up Tom." Gabriel smiled.

For the first time since I fell pregnant, I felt nauseous. The sight of him so comfortable in my space made me sick. I didn't need anything from town, but I needed so many things in that moment that the notion spun as the words kept forming. Freedom. Aidan. A new home. Your blood on my hands. My child safe. Answers. The Originals brought to justice. Their co-conspirators in prison. The truth. Days not filled with fear. Sleep without nightmares. Eggs Benedict. Aidan's arms around me. His love. Our life. A world without monsters. No child being hurt. Justice for every victim. Aidan.

"No, thank you. I need your laptop."

Gabriel gestured towards the mug on the nightstand to my right. "I made you coffee, decaf. Inside the fridge is a bowl of overnight oats, I added extra strawberries for you and made it with strawberry yoghurt. Will bring you more of everything when I get back. I'll get all the usual items, but if you want anything specific, I can add it to the list."

Gabriel, the domesticated hyena. Was this his attempt at being considerate, trying even harder to get back on my good side? For photographs, it's my left.

He pushed to his feet and turned to face me once he reached the doorway. "We won't be here much longer. The police have launched a nationwide manhunt for him after he bombed three homes in Marcel."

"Four."

A deep groove appeared between his eyebrows. "Four?"

"Mine, Lizzie's, and Tom's houses in Marcel. Plus my lake house. Four." *Look at me counting, Aidan will be proud.*

"Yes. Four. I will see you later." Gabriel showed his teeth. "Maybe you and I can have dessert tonight on the back porch.

I'm in the mood for something sweet."

"If you don't have it on your grocery list, please add salted crackers. I'm craving salt."

"Of course. Lizzie loves sweet, you love salt. Which of your parents preferred which?"

The question about my parents caught me off guard. He never asked about them. I shrugged. "I can't remember. It's funny the things you forget and what you never will."

My parents both loved dark chocolate with a glass of gluhwein in winter, or a scoop of vanilla ice cream with melted dark chocolate drizzled over in summer. No Sunday lunch was ever complete without the Baklava they had made together.

"Will you tell me about them? Tonight?"

The hairs on the back of my neck reached for the sky. In all the years I had known them, neither he nor Eli had asked specifics about my parents. Lizzie and I preferred not to talk about them. The wound forever raw. She had told Eli this when he had asked while we were in Wild Bay the weekend of Ashley and Kyle's wedding. The weekend Aidan had found me.

"If you don't mind closing the door, I need to shower and get to work. The mystery of Pepper Gorge won't solve itself. Eli said there haven't been any new postings by Sevens Hunter."

Gabriel nodded. "Okay, see you later. Tonight, you and me, and I want to know everything about the woman you were before we met."

Either the file they had on me was incomplete or he had turned into a fisherman. Why ask the questions now that he should've when we had met? "Who I was back then isn't who I am now. Sure, bits of her are still in here somewhere, but why would you want to hear about someone who doesn't exist?"

"Our son is half you, half me, a quarter of each of our parents. I want to know about your family to better understand our child when he's born."

"Gabriel, this child is a hundred percent unique. And I need to use the bathroom."

Again, he showed his teeth. "I enjoy watching you wake up.

Later, Ley."

A putrid taste filled my mouth, but not because of morning breath or the coffee I had taken a sip of. Gabriel thought us waking up in the same house, him bringing me coffee, that this was his future. I almost felt sorry for him, but I knew what he is. A murderer. A man who takes a life with one hand and money for it with the other. A man not above physical violence towards a woman. One he claimed to love, one he thought carried his child.

I hurried to the bathroom. My stomach growled, and I wondered whether it would be safe to eat the breakfast Gabriel had prepared. I realised once he had his hands on this child that there would be no need for me. Why his sudden interest in my past, and my parents?

"Good morning, you could've done with another hour or eight. You look like something the cat refused to drag in." Quinn laughed.

I needed a double shot of espresso to have even the slightest chance of feeling like my energetic self. "Do you have to be so chirpy? I woke up to that man's face. And he will return later with the man in the middle of this mess. How are things going on Aidan's end?"

"Good. A word of advice. You might want to put all your energy into uncovering the truth about what's going on at Pepper Gorge. The mess, as you call it, might be cleaned up sooner than you expect."

"Might be or will be?" Not even the cold water I splashed on my face revived my tired cells.

"Do you believe you know Aidan Walker better than anyone else, including his parents?"

"Yes."

"Then what do you think?"

"That you're full of riddles again today and that Aidan is much closer to ending this than what he lets on." Energy and clarity struck me at the same time. "Gabriel went AWOL because he had to, he did something he would've been arrested for. What is it?"

"There she is. Good morning, Dr Finley Williams-Walker, glad to see you picked up the scent."

"I'm not going to like the answer, am I? If you tell me 'what do you think', I will reach through this earpiece and pull your hair."

Quinn's laughter filled my ear. It brought a smile to my lips. "Pull my hair?"

"I'm opposed to women slapping or punching each other unless it's a matter of life and death."

"Fair enough. I won't say it, you already did."

"Is there a point to you interrupting my morning routine or did you just miss me?"

"Neither. I wanted to tell you it's midday and you've lost valuable hours hunting the Originals."

I placed my hands on my belly. "The baby needs me well rested. Nothing is more important than little Walker's safety and growth."

"You're a good mother, Finley. Baby Walker is lucky to have you and Aidan as parents. You realise I was there when you found out the baby's gender?"

"Force of habit, as we can't share our news with the family yet." I wondered what had happened to Quinn's parents; she had been legally adopted by a man who worked for my father-in-law. The Walkers see her as one of their own. But now was not the time to ask. "May I please shower and get dressed without being watched? I need to get to work. As much as I would love to sit back and let someone else go after the Originals, I can't."

"Hurry, Finley."

I did, wondering where in the world Aidan found himself.

Twenty

Somewhere in Europe. Location: Classified.

The entire time Gabriel had watched Finley sleep, Aidan's stomach had been in a knot. He knew the look in Gabriel's eyes. Any man would react the same if another man looked at his wife with such raw and savage lust. Rage trickled over his skin like the feet of a million spiders. If not for his mother's assurance that Gabriel's obsession with Finley kept her alive, he would never have allowed her to leave Marcel with him. It had, after all, been Aidan's idea. *Divide and conquer.*

Aidan stared at a man's face, not unlike any other. A man with ambition, charisma, and a face people liked. A man with a family, a home, a country.

"Are you ready?" Ryan placed his hand on Aidan's shoulder.

"Yes. Gabriel asked about her parents."

"There was movement at the lake house last night, they're still trying to find the room."

"Why haven't they taken down walls? He told Finley I destroyed the house. They could tear the place apart and cover up their handiwork." Aidan turned, lifting his eyes to Ryan's face.

"What they're searching for can be anywhere. Nathan's keeping a close eye on movement at Williams Pharmaceuticals. They know Duncan wouldn't have kept it at the office."

"Why would he have left it at the lake house? Anyone could go there and get their hands on it."

"He didn't. Duncan was too smart to leave something that valuable where anyone could find it."

"Dad, I should tell her." Aidan rubbed his hands over his face and switched to the feed from the camera imbedded in the contact lens in Finley's eye. With his father next to him, Aidan, for the first time, hoped she wasn't in the shower. She was religious in putting in the lens as soon as she awoke, only taking it out before going to bed. The night before, she had fallen asleep with it still in her eye, when she had lain looking at the victim whose body remained in the forest at Pepper Gorge.

Finley wasn't in the shower. Relief and regret washed over him. Watching her shower reminded him of the mornings they had showered together before they left for the day, set on making the world a better place in their own ways. Now Aidan realised being a doctor had been an escape. A temporary one. Once this was over, he would talk to Finley about their future.

"Son, we've been over this. If you tell her the truth, you know how she will react. Finley's unarmed, outmanned, and pregnant. There's no scenario that ends with her walking out alive."

Aidan rolled his eyes. "I did the math, remember?"

Ryan laughed, patting Aidan on the back. "Tomorrow night, are you ready?"

"Rhetorical question?"

"No. Are you ready to face the man responsible for the deaths of the father- and mother-in-law you never got to meet? It's a shame you never will. They were remarkable people. Both in their own right."

"I'm ready to be home with my wife, not that we have one anymore. I don't have a choice, I have to destroy the lake house." Aidan kept his eyes on the monitor; Finley made her way through the house and opened the refrigerator door. She reached over the container of overnight oats Gabriel had prepared and retrieved two eggs. The overnight oats contained no poison or glass splinters. He had watched Gabriel make it.

"You don't *have* to destroy the lake house, you want to."

Quinn must have told his father what Gabriel had said about the time he spent there with Finley. "Am I jealous they were intimate once? No. Finley had past lovers and so did I.

From a strategic point of view, it's a solid plan and you can't disagree."

"Consider the fact that her parents left it to her. It's where she feels closest to them."

Aidan hadn't thought about it. His EQ never matched his IQ. "What do you propose I do?"

"Let her sell it if she wants, after she learns the truth. What they did..." Ryan shook his head, placing an arm around Aidan's shoulder. "There's nothing a parent won't do, or sacrifice, to keep their children safe."

"There's another way. Can you get me a fresh corpse?"

His father laughed and so did he, both remembering the first time Aidan had made this same request. He had been six years old and wanted to learn about the human body, but pictures in textbooks just didn't cut it. Aidan attended his first autopsy before the Tooth Fairy came for his first tooth.

"I'll take care of it. The team is waiting for you to run through another simulation."

Not a single member of this team was fresh; they had all done this before, this exact operation. Aidan trusted them each with his life, with Finley's and their child's. No room for error. No one questioned him when he ordered another simulation. Every person on this team knew what losing Kate and their son had done to him. They were his former colleagues, and some even his blood.

Ryan watched his son leave, pride filling his heart. Aidan had grown up to be a remarkable human being, doctor, and husband. A fire had ignited inside his son the day he had met Finley Williams. Similar to the fire Aidan had while he worked for the organisation. Ryan stood and closed the door before returning to the desk. "How is my girl doing today?" He laughed as Finley dropped the fork mid-bite.

Twenty-one

I marched to the dishwasher and placed my plate and cutlery inside. Next stop, the bathroom, to have a chat with my father-in-law. I spent an inordinate amount of time in bathrooms talking to the voices inside my head. The stiffness in my shoulders lessened as I closed the bathroom door. "I love you, old man, but not so much when you give me a heart attack."

"I couldn't help it," Ryan said.

"You just like sneaking up on people, and I'm beginning to understand why."

"Ah, your recon of Pepper Gorge this morning. You enjoyed it."

"It cuts out so much wasted time. No red tape. Just answers."

"And, which questions were answered?" Ryan asked.

"They have armed guards patrolling the farm's borders. There are nine cars in town now, four are visitors', I assume. I'm waiting for Eli to tell me who the cars are registered to. I bet you can tell me, but you won't."

"You have a knack for gambling. Let Eli tell you, no big surprises there. One might, but I need your reaction to be authentic. You're not the best at this acting thing."

"I'm rather theatrical when I'm torturing someone." I pursed my lips. Why did I always tell him things I didn't tell anyone except Aidan?

"You don't need to hide things I already know from me, my girl. Alas, now is not the time to compare hunting stories or whose body count is higher."

I nodded. "What can I do for you, Dad?" I loved calling Ryan Dad.

"Today, I can do something for you. Two things. First, hurry your investigation into Pepper Gorge, time isn't on your side. There's a reason for the four cars you saw. Second thing, there's a book inside their church building. You need to get hold of it. That book holds answers to questions we haven't even thought of."

"Who on your team has seen this book?" I ran my fingers through my hair, still liking the shorter style.

"Quinn has many skills, not unlike yourself. Get the book, and Finley, you better send Gabriel to retrieve it. It's a bit of a suicide mission and I need you and the baby as far away from that place as possible."

He, too, had told me to hurry as Quinn had earlier. "Is Aidan close to getting his hands around the Puppet Master's neck?"

"Yes. Aidan will go ballistic if he knows I told you, but you won't be able to turn your back on the innocent people of Pepper Gorge."

"Are there any innocent people other than the children?"

"Yes. Remember one thing, our ideas of what classifies someone as a child aren't the same as theirs."

"Dad, if you know so much, why didn't you tell me everything when I first heard you had launched an investigation into Pepper Gorge?"

"For Aidan's sake, Quinn kept investigating. I can't put you or my grandchild in danger."

"Am I not in danger being in this house with an assassin and a man I'm still not convinced is on our side? And don't forget Tom will arrive at any moment."

"The assassin believes he's in love with you, he won't hurt you more than he already has. You can handle Tom with your hands tied behind your back. Eli's on your side. He has been since he fell in love with Lizzie. Finley, keep your sister safe. Wherever you go, she goes."

"Of course, I've always been Lizzie's protector. I can't see myself leaving this place again, not until Aidan comes for us. Where is he?"

"Ensuring this is over soon. So, my darling girl, get to

work. Finley, I love you."

I swallowed the lump in my throat. "I love you too, Dad."

Eli sat at the dining room table pounding away at the laptop's keys. Lizzie stood behind him, rubbing her hands over his back. *If he hurts her, I will strangle him with his intestines.* The last person who hurt my sister isn't alive to tell the tale; he had only posted it on the dark web for the depraved to see. My future brother-in-law had embedded a virus in the file. A virus which alerted law enforcement agencies across the world when it's downloaded. Nine out of ten times, the culprit has a cache of violent pornography. We should call it what it is – video footage of men, women, and children being raped. Rape will always be rape, no matter how people try to sugar-coat it.

"Lizzie?"

She turned to me and held out her hand. I stepped forward, and she pulled me into her arms. "You miss him, don't you?"

"Who?"

"The one we will not name."

"Who?" I sounded like an owl.

Lizzie pressed her mouth to my ear. "Aidan."

I held her tighter. My longing for him had increased when Ryan had said I needed to hurry. I struggled to breathe. "Always."

She kept her ear to my mouth. "I'll cut back on the touchy-feely stuff in front of you."

"No, don't; you and Eli are together and soon you will be able to enjoy the start of this new chapter with your baby. Put a ring on him."

Lizzie pulled back, mischief in her emerald eyes.

"No, not what I meant. Although I should tell you about the new model I purchased online a while ago."

"What?" She dug her nails into my shoulders. "You? I would never have thought."

"Lizzie, my dear, you're gullible. To be honest, there's a bunch of things you don't know about me."

Whatever Lizzie was into, it couldn't be anything I hadn't seen during my time as a dominatrix. The things a student won't do for money to fix her father's prized recent addition to his muscle car collection.

"Like your sudden infatuation with strawberries? Or the fact that you still blush whenever I say the name Griffin Stark?"

"The baby wants strawberries, and the increase in blood production makes me blush. I want milk, do you want a glass?" I glanced past her. "Eli, can I get you anything from the kitchen?"

"No, thank you," he said over his shoulder. "Liz, drink the milk. The baby needs it."

Lizzie shook her head. "You can't keep telling me to eat just because the medication the doctor prescribed is helping with my morning sickness. I'll eat when I'm hungry, otherwise we'll need a bigger bed."

I wondered what she would say if she learned the doctor who she had seen in Coopersville wasn't an actual doctor. Lizzie would learn the truth; at Christmas, when we all sat around the Walkers' dining room table with Doctor Duvall. The truth about my past with Griffin Stark only Aidan knows.

After finishing the glass of milk, I stared at the tray of strawberries, but returned to the dining room empty-handed. Quinn and Ryan had advised me to hurry the investigation. No time to eat. "Eli, as we're operating without the strict rules of the law, let's make this interesting."

He stopped his assault on the laptop's keys and turned to me. "I'm listening."

"If we put our heads together, I bet we can uncover the truth about Pepper Gorge within the next twenty-four hours."

"No rules?" Eli held out his right hand to me, I shook it.

"No rules." I liked this, more than any sane, hormonal, being-held-captive-by-your-ex-the-assassin, pregnant woman ever should.

"What do we get if we succeed?"

"What more do you want than righting wrongs and saving

innocent people?"

Eli switched on the monitors he had positioned on the dining room table. "Fair enough."

I scanned the live feeds streaming from the cameras the drones had placed across Pepper Gorge. A familiar voice filled my head, his words my heart. "What you get is me."

I lowered my eyes to my belly. "You're more than I ever hoped for. I love you."

"The baby can't hear you, not yet," Eli said.

I wished he hadn't read the pregnancy book Lizzie had bought the first time they went grocery shopping in Coopersville. "Does it matter? This child needs to know he or she's loved and wanted."

Lizzie placed her hand on my stomach, I covered it with mine.

Twenty-two

Seven. The number stared back at me from the laptop's screen. Someone had carved it into the tree where the body of a young boy lay. This is where he died, judging by the amount of dried blood surrounding his body. Was the seven carved before or after the killer used the boy's abdomen as a piece of paper?

Another word mocked me – Truth. Gabriel had taken photos before and after he had rinsed and wiped the flesh of this boy who had stood on the verge of manhood. Ryan's words came to me. Did they consider teenagers adults? Of an age to marry and bare children, as Nicol had said? If only I could talk to her again.

"Can we kidnap Nicol? Seeing as we're playing outside the rules." It wouldn't be my first time, and the adrenalin coursing through me told me it wouldn't be my last.

Right there in the dining room, our current ops room, I listened to the inhabitants discuss the celebration planned for the following night. This took hunting to a whole new level. From my eavesdropping I learned that the inhabitants of Pepper Gorge ate every meal in what we had thought was a restaurant. They ate in shifts, all the same food. Which made sense when you cook for a family; of how many, we didn't know.

"I need eyes in every building. The cameras we positioned last night work great for tracking their outside movement, but I need to see and hear what's happening inside. Does Gabriel have any more of the mosquito-sized drone thingies? The proverbial fly on the wall."

Eli chuckled. "Of all the things I expected from you, being a voyeur never even made the list."

"Yes, well, desperate times." I shrugged, shifting my gaze

to the screen furthest to my left. Nicol carried a basket with what appeared to be linen towards a building. Its use? I didn't know. *So many questions.*

"Not that I'm not enjoying seeing this side of you, but why the sudden urgency?" Eli leaned back and rolled his head from side to side.

Lizzie left us to indulge in an afternoon nap. I envied that she saw this as a mini vacation. Then again, with her workload and commitment to growing Williams Pharmaceuticals, I couldn't fault her for making the best of it. Perhaps for the first time she could process everything that had happened since I had been taken prisoner, the deaths of our parents, my return to Marcel, and the horrific assault she didn't remember, other than what I had shown her out of desperation to know whether I had killed an innocent man. Few things I regretted more than showing her that recording. I had been selfish; I could've killed him and lived with the guilt had their encounter been consensual. *Lie.*

"For the past 209 years, something has been going on at that farm, and it's time someone exposes it."

Eli crossed his arms over his chest. "Okay, what do you think it is?"

Pushing to my feet, I stepped to the wall where we had moved the pages constituting my murder board. Lizzie hadn't liked it, even after I promised to take it down in twenty-four hours. "Sevens Hunter referred to hunting on the farm and in the outside world. He or she mentioned that being a hunter is an honour, as this means the survival of the community." I turned and strode to the other side of the dining room table. The best way for me to make sense of the little information available to us, to walk it out, talk it through. "Could there be enough deer and other wild animals to feed their community?"

"Doubt it. This is farmland, with only one reserve, which is next to their property."

"How many cows and sheep did you count on the drive in? I counted twenty cows, milk cows for the record, and about thirty sheep. Perhaps they keep pigs and poultry somewhere out of view. If they need to buy food, where would they get the money?"

"Can we focus on the murder for now and worry about their finances later?" Eli smiled.

Pregnancy brain scattered my thoughts all over. *Focus.* I shut my eyes and chanted the first word that came to mind. "Seven."

"Do you still think seven refers to the deadly sins?"

"Yes."

Eli shifted in his chair. "Why?"

I smiled. "We've never worked together like this."

"Maybe this won't be the last time either. Who knows what the future holds." He cleared his throat. "Once Aidan's captured, or killed, a new life awaits us all. We can go wherever we want, be whoever we want."

"Lizzie won't leave Marcel, and she will never move or sell Williams Pharmaceuticals."

"Not what I meant. Less than twenty-three hours to your deadline. Focus, Finley."

I rolled my eyes before lifting my palms to cover them. *Consider what you know.* "Their meals are dished for them, no one asks for seconds. That covers gluttony. As you may recall, there are no overweight people."

"The other six?" He gestured for me to continue.

"They all wear similar clothes, no one stands out. No make-up or special hairstyles for the women. Pride. Although, Nicol's friend is the daughter of an Original. Nicol mentioned she doesn't have the extra language lessons her friend has."

I returned to my chair, fatigue barrelling towards me. "Two down, five to go. If everyone eats the same, lives and dresses the same, there's no place for greed. I suspect the Originals might be above this as we saw five cars, all registered to men. If they all live the same, they can't be envious of each other." I tapped a forefinger to my mouth. "Nicol wasn't happy about the fact that she won't be Henry's first wife."

"Would you say envious?"

"Yes. Since we sat down to monitor the activity on the farm, have you seen a single person not working?"

Eli closed his eyes and yawned. "No."

"No sloths in Pepper Gorge. Work, work, work. Keep people busy and they won't have time to think." Truth be told, I do some of my best thinking when I'm busy with something mundane like cooking, driving, or doing the dishes. I've even had a mental breakthrough in the shower.

If you lived in a world without access to the internet, television, mobile phones, or any outside stimulus, what would you think about? How would you draw your own conclusions? I wondered as to the syllabus taught at their school, a building one down from the restaurant. The drone had captured footage of the tables, chairs, and blackboard. All appeared farm-made.

"Where does wrath and lust fit into their way of life?" Eli stood and returned from the kitchen with two bottles of water. He handed me one.

"If the Originals control marriages, there isn't any room for lust. Unless they're lucky enough to end up with someone they're attracted to." Six down, one to go. The last one I understood. "Wrath. I don't understand how this plays into their status quo unless you're not allowed to provoke the Originals. Or take matters into your own hands."

"Okay, all of what you said makes sense. Why are the hunters allowed to hunt then?"

"They bring people from the outside world to be cleansed by the community. Sevens Hunter mentioned a ceremony, but no one except the Originals attend." I scratched my chin without thinking. "What happens to their prey? For lack of a better word." Victims might be a better description, but exhaustion diminished my vocabulary. Night after night of sleeping only a few hours at most, the night before playing spy with a man I despised. Not forgetting the little person growing inside me.

"You're the profiler." Eli lifted his arms, palms to the ceiling. "If this was one individual you were hunting, what would your conclusion be?"

"This isn't a single offender, but at least five who might be equally involved. And the hunters."

"Sevens Hunter stated it was his destiny to be a hunter. A *birthright* is the exact word used."

I dropped my head to my arms resting on the wooden table's surface. "Let's assume Sevens Hunter is a man. Men patrolling the borders – the soldiers, protectors, whatever they want to call them. And the hunters, I can't see them allowing women to roam the outside world on their own."

"That's sexist, you're the last person I would ever expect to say something like women aren't capable of taking care of themselves in an unfamiliar setting."

"I haven't been brainwashed since birth." To be honest, my father naming me after himself and raising me like the son he never had, and my mother being allowed to work outside the home and not expected to be pregnant and barefoot in the kitchen may have been the biggest influences in my life. The hardwood floor was cool underneath my feet as I rubbed my hands over my belly. At least I wasn't in the kitchen. I made a mental note to wear shoes the next time it was my turn to cook. *Feminists unite.*

Eli rolled his eyes. I hated that this was catching on. Without uttering a word, I berated my eye muscles and ordered them to stop. Time would tell whether they would follow my direct order. I missed Aidan with his panty-dropping commands.

"Why are you sighing?" Eli asked.

I yanked my mind from the memory of Aidan's authoritarian voice, the lingering anticipation of seeing him again. *Soon.* "The male to female ratio seems off to me, considering we have seen none of the textbook signs of inbreeding." My hand reached for Eli's arm. "What if they bring in fresh blood, fresh DNA? The women the hunters are sent out to abduct."

"I see where you're going with this, but you would still have five men impregnating these women."

"Raping them, not only impregnating." Sevens Hunter had

mentioned more than once that the hunters were to remain celibate until their dying day. I wondered whether the soldiers were also cursed with celibacy? Were they eunuchs? Could any man smother his primal urges, basic human needs? Perhaps, if given no alternative.

I jerked my head towards the screen displaying an unobstructed view of the town's only street. "Who do the four cars belong to?"

"Three are rentals, signed out at the airport in Douglasdale. The other is a vehicle recently impounded by the Coopersville police."

"We already concluded that someone high up in the Coopersville police is involved." I tapped my right foot against the wooden surface below. Eli placed his hand on my knee and shook his head. "The airport in Douglasdale is an international one. Nicol and her unnamed friend mentioned foreign visitors. Is there any way you can search the despicable directory and see if the folks of Pepper Gorge are perhaps listing items for sale?"

Eli ran his fingers through his black hair, the wristwatch not catching a single hair. He cursed under his breath.

"I will do it if you aren't up to it." If I was to step back into the abyss, I needed a bucket. Not my first rodeo with darkness.

"No. I just need to step outside and prepare myself."

I watched him go, understanding his need to steel his stomach and his soul.

Eli didn't have to do it. He had tangoed with the abyss often enough, for the same reasons I had. The outcome of his dance never the same as mine. I took his chair, breathed through my nose, and clenched my teeth. He didn't need to do this. No one ever should.

Twenty-three

Lizzie ran down the passage. "Finley, what's wrong? Are you sick?"

Eli caught her mid-stride and pulled her back towards their bedroom. "Baby, trust me, you don't want to see this."

Liz held her ground. "Oh, come on, like I haven't held her hair back before."

I stared at them. Miserable. A putrid taste lingered in my mouth, my soul. I could wash my mouth. My soul? Never.

"Finley, what's going on? Are you sick? Do you have cramps? When last did you go to the bathroom? Any spotting? What did you eat for lunch?" Lizzie tried to yank free of Eli's hold.

He placed his hand on her face and his forehead against hers. "Finley isn't sick. This is the part of our world we don't want you to be exposed to. Ever. Please go back to the room. I didn't realise—"

"What? What didn't you realise?" Lizzie searched his face, then mine. I shook my head.

Eli pressed his lips to her forehead. "That she would search without me, that she would look at all." He turned his focus to me, his hands still holding on to Lizzie. "You did it for me, didn't you? More than you wanted answers."

Despite the tears trickling down my face, I smiled. "You told me."

"Told you what? What's going on?" Lizzie stepped back, staring at both Eli and I as if we were strangers. "Why are you both crying?"

My shoulders sagged. I wiped my eyes; pointless as the tears kept coming. "I'm sorry."

He shook his head. "I should've told her a long time ago."

"Told me what?" Lizzie pulled her hair away from her neck and tied it at the back of her head. Her face was red. Never a good sign.

I closed the laptop and left them to talk. Fresh air called my name.

Unpolluted air greeted me as I stepped onto the back porch. I longed for the salty breeze which greeted me every morning when Aidan opened our bedroom's sliding doors.

I kept walking, fighting off fatigue, nausea, and the pain I knew Eli felt as he told Lizzie the only thing I knew about him she didn't. To my knowledge.

While I had been in hospital, after the incident with the Scarecrows, an incident which saw me dying twice and Aidan saving my life twice, Eli had taught me the art of hacking. More a case of me bullying him into it than him waking up one morning and deciding that that would be his greatest accomplishment of the day. I had played the 'I'm so bored, I'm getting up and walking out of here' card. Fact – I had been bored to the point of questioning my sanity. Fact – I couldn't sit without help, let alone walk.

With my newly acquired skill, I set out to test it, and hacked the Marcel Police Department's records. Curiosity is more of a challenge to me than a death sentence. I'm no cat. I read the files the police had compiled on The Hangman. *And Eli calls me sexist?*

A separate file on each of The Hang*wo*man's victims, victims the police had realised were predators within hours of their bodies being found. Sometimes even before the body had been found hanging from the spot I chose.

The taped confessions, wallets, and other personal items I had delivered to the police lead them to, in some cases, locating the predators' victims. Some alive. One of the victims who hadn't survived had been a friend of Eli's. His name had been in her file. Eli had identified her body.

A few days after he had tutored me in the art of cyber digging, he again visited me in hospital. I had asked him about her and confessed why I had accessed the case files.

For years, Eli had roamed the abyss looking for her. She had vanished after clearing customs at Marcel International Airport. Her family had said she had come over on a work visa after securing a position at a resort outside Wild Bay. The resort had no record of being in contact with her. The email address used to contact her, send her an employment contract and a flight itinerary, hadn't been used in years. Gregory Mitchell had never worked for them, or even stayed at the resort as a guest. After he committed suicide and I sent his belongings to the police, they uncovered the truth about Gregory Mitchell. The real Gregory Mitchell I had met while I hunted him, and those like him, in the abyss.

Daddy#Princess, as I had known him, until I opened his wallet and found his driver's license, wasn't a trafficker. That was beneath a man who hid behind a mask as the principal of one of the most prestigious private schools in Marcel. If I hadn't gotten to him, the police would have for fraud. He had stolen money from the school to feed his depravity.

Eli's friend hadn't been his only victim, but his last. I had been too late. Eli never forgave himself, and I shared his guilt. So many 'what ifs' came to me, it made me sick. The nurse had thought the antibiotics were too strong. I couldn't tell her that my self-loathing was the reason. If only I hadn't set up a meeting with another predator as vile as Daddy#Princess instead of leaving Gregory Mitchell for the following night. If only I had known Eli spent his every available hour scouring the corners of the abyss, hoping to find her and pay whatever price to give her freedom. If only the dark web didn't exist. If only monsters didn't walk amongst us, living in our own homes, sharing our blood.

"You need to let it go."

I wiped my eyes and rubbed the moisture on the back of my jeans. At my feet, the river raged. I shook my head.

"If you didn't get to him, he would've continued to kill. You stopped him, Finley. You."

"None of it brought any of the victims back." My voice broke. "Some families got broken, hollow people back. Others, bodies to bury. What about the ones who got nothing back?"

"It's not on you, my love. You stopped vile men and women from destroying the lives of more families. Of raping and killing more children, men, women, and animals. Focus on the ones who were saved. The people you rescued and took to Tabula Rasa. Look how well they're adjusting."

"It's all Ashley." A survivor of trafficking herself, she understands every aspect of their brokenness and what they need to heal as best as any person can who survived what they did.

"You, Finley Duncan Williams-Walker, stopped evil. You saved the lives of countless people who would've fallen victim to those monsters."

I smiled through the tears. "You're brave to call me the D-name when you're not standing in front of me."

"I'm proud of you. For what you did, for who you are, and the good you will still do in this world. Thank you for sharing your life with me."

I sobered. "This sounds like a goodbye. Aidan, you promised we will be together when this is over. Don't do anything stupid. Without you, the darkness will swallow me, and I can't go back there. Our child needs both of us."

"Hormones – 1. My darling wife, the love of my life – 0." Aidan laughed.

I fought the urge to roll my eyes. "Not a goodbye?"

"Of sorts. I will be radio silent until this is over. Things are moving along at a rapid speed on my end."

"How will I know when it's over?"

"When the world implodes around you. Remember what I always tell you about your nightmares. Finley, this isn't a goodbye, but I do love you. You're my life, Mrs Walker."

"It sounds stupid, but I'm not good with words. I love you, Aidan Walker, more with each passing day. Hurry, my love. It feels good to say it to someone else for a change."

Aidan's laughter made me laugh. "Heads up, Wife. Game face on. Tom just arrived. Thanks for setting it up without even trying."

"I aim to please, Dr Walker."

"Oh, that you do, and then some."

My once beloved godfather stood with his back to the door. Lizzie glanced in my direction, her eyes red and swollen. Tom turned to me; the elated expression on his face I had once looked forward to upon returning from a deployment. Now I saw the mask. Much like the one I used to smile back at him.

Tom stepped closer, covering my shoulders with his hands. I forced my body to neither retreat nor lunge. "I missed you." He wrapped his arms around me; every muscle in my body contracted. "You and I will mend our relationship and be closer than ever."

Heat spread to every part of me; the notion stretched, unleashing a rage so consuming it choked me.

Tom released me. "How are you, and how is your baby?" He placed a hand against my belly.

I stepped back, the door blocking my retreat. The betrayer had no right to lay a hand on my child, not even while safe inside my womb. Not a word constructed in my mind made it past my lips. Rage rendered me mute.

"After dinner you and I should catch up. Gabriel mentioned you came to see the light."

The light I craved? To see it leave his body when he took his last breath. The line between love and hate so fragile, a single lie can break it. This man had destroyed too much of my life, hounding my husband, being involved in all of this. I needed answers. "Did your friend tell you he did this to me?" I stretched out my arms.

Tom stared at the bruises. A muscle twitched in his jaw. He spun around so fast, Gabriel had no time to respond. Tom's fist met skin; Gabriel stumbled backwards.

Not bad, you snake; well played. This act was nothing more than a sugar-coated olive branch for my benefit. One I will never accept. No one frames my husband for murder, sets up this farce, and escapes my wrath. It bubbled inside me, or perhaps I needed the loo again. Unsure which, I headed to the bathroom.

Lizzie followed me and closed the bathroom door behind her. My sister had seen me do far worse things over the years, so I relieved my bladder, as did she.

"What's Aidan doing about this?" she asked, rinsing her hands at the basin as I did the same.

"What he does best." I smiled at my reflection. It would take all of my mental faculties to keep the mask from slipping. Not yet time for the dark rage festering inside me to come out to play.

"Where are we going to live, seeing as we're both homeless? I don't want to stay in an Airbnb or a hotel. House-hunting sucks. I liked my house, it was my home, Fin. Mine. I bought it with my money. And your house was perfect. Good beachfront properties the size of a castle are so hard to find these days." Lizzie bumped me with her shoulder.

Mansion perhaps, but not a castle. I rested my head on her shoulder, uncomfortable as it was, as we're the same height. In this moment, I belonged. As long as I have my sister, my Aidan, and the babies growing inside Liz and I, anywhere can be home. "We can go stay at your house in Wild Bay until we figure it out. For now, I need to get to the bottom of what's going on at Pepper Gorge. But first, I need to eat. I'm tired, Lizzie, I'm so tired."

She pressed her lips to my hair as I resumed my normal standing position, my hands covering my belly. "You've been tired since you got back to Marcel. Something else happened during the war. It changed you."

Four months of being held prisoner, tortured, and raped on an almost daily basis would do it. I kept my mouth shut. Lizzie knew about the torture, not the rest.

"Thank you for being there for Eli when he needed someone

to confide in about his friend. I get why he didn't talk to me about her. We had just started dating and you understand. Why, Finley? Why do you understand evil people? How can you put yourself in their minds and comprehend the reasons they do the terrible things they do?"

All I could do was hug her. I couldn't tell her I understood because a part of me was as dark as their entire beings, or that I fought against it every single day. The difference being I ached to use my darkness on them, never on innocent people. The deaths of the soldiers I had killed during combat still haunt me. A weight I will carry for the rest of my life. The deaths of predators who preyed on innocent children, women, men, and animals? I have never lost a single moment of rest.

"I don't know what to tell you. I'm an empath."

Laughter filled the bathroom. "I call bullshit. How does it feel to kill someone?"

I pressed our bodies together as tight as I could. "Please don't make me tell you. You're my safe place, a place where I'm still who I was when we were children, students, young and carefree. Don't tarnish all of those memories for yourself. Please. I can't have you look at me the way I look at myself." Tears dripped onto her shoulder.

"You've always been different, Fin. Even when we were children. You're strong, beautiful, compassionate, always a warrior. No matter what you've done, or what you've lived through, none of it will ever change how much I love you. I'm proud of you, because you survived. How you survived all those days with two serial killers is beyond me."

We sank down on the floor. Relief washed over me, spilled out of me. Lizzie held me and stroked my hair, just like she had done when we were little girls. For the first time, we broached the subject of what I had lived through.

"Thank you," she murmured, as I dried my eyes on a piece of toilet paper she pressed into my hand. I didn't even realise one of her arms no longer enveloped me.

"For what?"

"Avenging me."

The implication struck me so hard I gasped for air. *She knows.*

"I told you I'm proud of you. Thank you for darkening your soul for me."

Tired of lies and masks, I said the last thing I expected to say. "I've never lost a single night's sleep because of what I did. He raped you, and at least five other women. There's nothing I won't do to keep you safe, Fizzie-Lizzie."

"You're a protector. So, dry your eyes, rinse your face, and get back in that dining room and protect the innocent people of Pepper Gorge. Then we wait for Aidan to end this nightmare. Until then, we play nice with Gabriel and Tom. Eli won't let anything happen to either of us."

I eased back to find compassion and love in her eyes. She reminded me so much of our mother, my stomach turned on itself. Why did both our parents have to die in the same accident? "Did you ever read the police report on Mom and Dad's accident?"

Lizzie shook her head. "I couldn't make myself, and why would I after I saw them on those cold tables. They were dead, and you were in a hospital halfway across the world. Why are you asking about it now?"

"The question should be why didn't I before. Next month it's three years since they died. I never questioned it; accepted they died in a car accident. Don't you think it's strange that they died the night I was rescued? Mere hours after."

"Why are you asking about this now? I didn't at the time, and since then I've been too happy to have you back. Too busy keeping Williams Pharmaceuticals afloat."

"Think about it. Mom and Dad died the same night I was rescued. Gabriel slithers into my life, and he doesn't kill Tony Andretti, aka The Angel Taker. Takes his arm instead of his life." *Some assassin he is.* "Gabriel leaves, and you and Eli fall in love and get engaged. Then Aidan comes into my life and Gabriel returns. Tom picks up his torch and shotgun and hounds Aidan. Gabriel doesn't make any attempt to move out of your house after you graciously took him in, considering a serial killer tried to kill him, and she was still on the prowl. Aidan gets framed for two murders and Gabriel tries to impregnate me. You get pregnant while on the pill. Here we are."

"Where is here?" Confusion filled her eyes.

"A clusterfuck." I shook my head and pushed to my feet. "My husband is out there hunting down the person responsible for us being in this elevated hell. What am I missing?" A headache started building at the base of my skull. I ignored it and held my hand out to Lizzie. "Are you sure Eli is on our side?"

"Yes," Lizzie and Quinn said. It took me a moment to realise they had spoken at the same time.

"Liz, I need a moment on my own. Think I need to take a shower before I get back to work."

"Okay, I'll ask Eli to make dinner. I need to go lay down for a bit."

"I'm sorry for voicing all of this to you. All these questions have been nagging me, and sitting here with you like this, it just took shape."

"Never stop being who you are. I will never again say you give me the creeps when you talk to killers and criminals like they're in the room with us. If only there were more people like you. Fin, a part of me knew since I heard the news that he had been murdered. Thank you."

"Don't thank me for taking a life, even though he deserved far worse."

"He got what he deserved. Must say, you left quite a mess." Something flashed in her eyes I had felt in my own as I had stood over his body, intestines spilling onto the sheet, his weapon shoved down his gaping throat.

"What do you know about messes?"

"Eli showed me the crime scene photos."

I covered my mouth with my hand and took a big step backwards. Bile rose in my throat, I swallowed hard.

"I had nightmares. To this day I can't remember anything, just what you showed me. Perhaps not knowing makes it worse. Eli showed me that someone had slain my monster, and I didn't have to live in fear anymore. At first, I thought Eli had done it, but at the time, he didn't love me yet. Only someone who loves me could do what you did. You're *The Hangman*."

Rage scooted over, allowing shock to press the mute button in my brain.

"Doesn't take a rocket scientist, Finley. You return to Marcel, and soon after, bad people get what they deserve. The Angel Taker and Scarecrows didn't just happen to cross your path."

I shook my head, dropping it forward, regretting the move as the headache shot to my frontal lobe.

"The Hangman avenged the innocent and righted wrongs by bringing those responsible to justice. *Her* own kind of justice. People were saved because of what you did. People can sleep because you slay their demons. Like I said, you're a protector. I'm sorry I can't kill the men who kept you in that bunker during the war."

"They're dead."

A single question formed in her eyes, but I shook my head. "Not me, I couldn't even walk out of there. The team who rescued me took them out."

"Good. So, there are more people like you in this world."

Not enough.

Twenty-four

After a two-hour nap, I showered and spoke to Quinn. Again, she said I should ask Eli how he came to be on our side.

The chair scathed across the wooden floor as I pulled it closer to the dining table. I might have slept, but fatigue lingered. My eyes darted between the screens, following the activity on the farm. To no one in particular, I said, "I need eyes and ears in every building. The book, I need that, too."

"What book?" Gabriel asked from the kitchen.

Eli placed a hand on my shoulder. "Sevens Hunter spoke of their rules, their laws being written down. No visuals of a plaque or something similar, and when I went through the footage earlier, I noticed something in one building which might be a big book. In my opinion, that building is their church, which would be the perfect place to keep it."

Inaudibly, I sighed; relief had me reaching for Eli's hand and give it a squeeze. Pregnancy brain, fatigue, longing, no matter what, it wreaked havoc on my brain. I had to be more careful about what came out of my mouth. Not the first time I realised this, but for the first time, my life, and the lives of those I love, depended on it.

Movement caught my eye on a screen which had shown none before. The surveillance camera was mounted in a tree close to where Gabriel had found the boy's body.

A young male darted between the trees. He pressed his back against the pine tree's trunk, peered around, and ran off, out of view. Moments later two hooded figures appeared, heading in the same direction. Their strides big, one's bigger, as they ran over the terrain. The gleam of a blade in one's hands unmistakable.

"They're hunting him. We need to get out there. Now!" I

pushed to my feet; the chair fell to the floor behind me.

"We won't make it in time." Eli placed a hand on my shoulder.

"You don't know that. We can save him." I yanked free of his hold, rushing to the front door.

"Finley. Stop." Quinn ordered. "Eli's right, they caught up with him. I'm sorry."

I shook my head, pursed my lips, and willed the tears to remain unspent. No such luck.

"I've got more cameras on the farm and in that forest than Gabriel has ever seen in one storeroom. What you didn't notice, and I suspect Eli did, is that victim left a blood trail. They've already started carving into him."

I covered my face with my hands and sank down to my knees. Another child was being murdered, and I took a nap. Not even during my first trimester had I been this tired.

"Not your fault, Finley." Quinn again.

Eli sat down next to me and pulled me into his arms. "I saw the blood, he would've bled out before we got to the SUV. I'm sorry."

I jerked my head up, unshed tears in my friend's eyes. "This has to end."

He nodded. "We will do this together. Think about what you just witnessed. What does it tell you?"

"I need to see it again."

Eli stood and pulled me to my feet. In silence, we watched the recording. Twice. Both times gut-wrenching. The last moments of a young man, a boy. Moments of sheer terror, being hunted like an animal. I've never been fond of hunting and despised it even more after seeing this adolescent run for his life.

I wiped the moisture from my face and dried my palms on my pants. "At least two hunters. Daylight. No one around who could hear his screams, or the laughter of the hunters." Except us. "Again."

Next to me, Eli swallowed hard. "We've seen it enough."

"Again. This time zoom in on the hunters." One much taller than the other.

Eli complied, and then I saw it. "There." I pointed at the object in the smaller hunter's hand. "Isn't that a GoPro?"

"It looks like it, but if I zoom in any more, the image will get distorted. These cameras aren't made for high-definition recordings this close up."

Eyes shut, I leaned back in my chair, distancing myself from the victim, seeing him as his murderers had. One carried the weapon, one a camera to record the hunt. The kill. Why? To relive it? As a souvenir? Their community was devoid of electronics and communication with the outside world. Could the killers be from out of town? Was this a human hunting farm, similar to how canned lions are hunted, without escape or a way to defend themselves? If you can't kill something with your bare hands, you have no right to kill it with any other weapon. Sevens Hunter had mentioned they're forced to hunt each other, as practise.

Was this their version of target practice? If this cult had hunted people for years, why have their leaders not been arrested? I clenched my fists and stood up. "These questions are driving me mad."

"What questions?" Tom asked, pulling out a chair.

At the sight of him, my hands cramped from the sheer force of the rage coursing through me. Behind the mask, I reminded myself, he had been a police officer, was currently still a state prosecutor, and into some black-ops something. Which was just another maddening question.

After Eli told him about the murder we had witnessed, not the actual murder but the build up to it, I listed all of my questions. The victim's last moments. I shook my head, desperate to suppress the emotions I knew that child had experienced during his last minutes. To an extent I've been there more than once; not running for my survival, but not being in control of my next breath.

Tom rubbed his right knee; the familiar sound the only

indication that his leg was artificial from the hip down. A bionic leg my father had gifted his best friend after a gang-banger had shot off most of Tom's leg with a sawed-off shotgun. His artificial leg was top of the range, only available as a prototype to this day. My father had pulled some very thin strings to get his hands on one. He had done it for his best friend, to give him a chance to continue his life being as oblivious to the missing limb as he could. My father had called him BionicCop. Tom had laughed. That day, the dark cloud had left Tom for good.

"Tonight, Eli and Gabriel will go to Pepper Gorge and get you all the answers you seek. At the very least they will get you eyes and ears in every house and building on that farm. I will stay here with you and Lizzie."

Without a second vehicle, I didn't know where he thought Liz and I would go. I couldn't walk to Coopersville, not with this being a high-risk pregnancy. Walking to the ravine was already pushing it. Aidan had reminded me to rest when he had said goodbye. Not a forever goodbye, just a 'I'm-going-hunting' goodbye.

Eli turned to me, a concerned expression on his face. "These chairs aren't very comfortable, why don't we move to the living room and discuss this further?"

"No, I need to monitor the screens. If my butt goes numb, I'll get a pillow."

From the kitchen, Gabriel spoke; I had forgotten he haunted the house, despite the sound of him cooking dinner. "Eli, push the table closer to the window, Ley can pace somewhere else."

He walked down the passage, his footsteps louder on his return. Gabriel carried in one of the recliner chairs which stood next to the fireplace and asked me to get up. I complied, and Eli carried the chair I vacated to the living room. The house far too small for five adults.

"Now you can be comfortable, monitor the activity on the screens, see your murder board, and put your feet up."

Thank you would've been the appropriate thing to say, but

I rarely say the appropriate thing in any situation. "I can't work on the laptop from here. It's not a good idea to have it on my lap, pregnant or not."

Gabriel stared at me, tilting his head to the right. "I forgot how demanding you can be. You're becoming yourself again."

Never in my life has anyone called me demanding. Control freak, weird, perfectionist, dark-humoured, short-tempered, all of those too often to count. If I were to create an online dating profile, those were the things I would list in my bio. Thank goodness I have Aidan and he accepts me for who I am, flawed personality traits, questionable youth, and all.

"When have I ever been demanding?" It felt like the appropriate response. My hands at my sides and the death stare I gave him probably not.

"You don't want me to answer in front of company." Gabriel drew his bottom lip between his teeth. I fought the urge to give him an uppercut to see if he could bite through it. "Wait, I have an idea. Remember, I'm always at your beck and call, Ley. Always will be."

Going to be hard to do when you're in hell. "Is that the reason for these bruises? Your way of taking care of me?"

"Low blow, Ley. I apologised for it, and Tom and Lizzie both punched me. What more do you want?"

Tom cleared his throat. "How the hell are you two going to raise a child together? Ari, after what you did, I will never give you my blessing for her hand in marriage. You have a long way to go in redeeming yourself, not only with me, but also with Finley. Not to mention Liz."

A slew of swear words thrashed in my mind. I pursed my lips trying for *appropriate*. "Let's get one thing straight – I will *never* marry Gabriel. The next person who calls him Ari will sleep outside on the porch tonight, and every other night we spend in this hellhole. His name is Gabriel." My left thumb rubbed against the bare spot where my wedding ring used to be. "Just because I've come to see the light, as you called it Tom, it doesn't mean I'm on the market to be discussed like livestock or that I will ever marry a man capable of physical violence towards a woman. I posed no threat to him; merely said something he didn't want to hear. Which again shows he has no idea who I am, because I always say the first thing that comes to mind." Minus swear words, it would seem.

"As I told you when Aidan and I got married, you're not my father, Tom. I don't need your blessing, and to be honest, I don't want it. The day will come when you will tell me how the two of you met. Today is not that day. Gabriel has to finish making dinner, and Eli and I need to discuss what I found earlier. So, everyone not needed in this room, right this minute, get out. *Now.*"

Three men stared at me with readable expressions. Eli looked proud. Tom shocked, which I suspected was forced. Gabriel's eyes held nothing but fury. Did he think I would throw myself at his feet after he had hurt me? As my anger settled, I realised something Tom had said. "Did you know of his plan to switch Aidan's sperm with his own?"

"What's done is done, Fin. You couldn't carry a serial killer's child."

"*Alleged* serial killer. To this day you have found no evidence. Two murders does not a serial killer make. Last I checked, it took three for a killer to be classified as serial." Not the time to lecture them on cooling-off periods in between kills.

Instead, I turned to Eli. "We need to discuss what I found, and you need to do another search because you're faster than I am. If Sevens Hunter wrote about the cult with such enthusiastic hatred, perhaps he's one of our killers."

"Who is his accomplice?"

"I don't know, but I'm looking at this all wrong. Our focus should be on the individuals, not the group."

Almost an hour later, Eli found what I had suspected. He turned to me, rubbing his fingertips over his eyelids. Exhaustion came for him as well. I stared at my future brother-in-law, my eyes burning. His exhaustion mirrored my own. Not from a lack of sleep, or irregular sleep patterns, but from vigilance. We both had to worry about Lizzie and the child growing inside her; Eli also worried about my safety.

I reached for his hand and placed it on my belly. "One day this child will know about the sacrifices you made to keep us safe. Thank you," I whispered.

"There's nothing I won't do for my family. You and this baby are as much my family as Lizzie and our child. You're my chosen family, and to me our bond is stronger than blood," Eli said in a hushed tone, his wristwatch covered by his other hand.

"What did you find?" I had other questions for Eli, but with the Puppet Master's constant watchful, hidden eyes and ears, I couldn't risk them learning the truth. That would come when Aidan decided it should.

"For a change, the dark web held no answers, but I found footage deleted by someone located inside the Coopersville Police Office. The IP address is registered to their building. Three recordings have been deleted."

Nothing is ever lost, except the loved one's death claims. Their memories linger, but they don't. "Are you going to show it to me, or tell me and leave it up to my imagination?"

"Which would you prefer, definite bucket, or possible bucket?"

The question every student should ask themselves before a night of binge drinking. "Just show me." I scanned the room, trying to locate a bucket, or anything close by if my stomach processed what my mind couldn't.

Eli showed me the first recording. Before starting the next video, he asked whether I needed a bucket. I did, but the baby growing inside me needed the nutrition more than I had to process the vileness humans are capable of. After the last video, I butt-shuffled off the recliner and headed to the kitchen, and returned with two bottles of water. The first sip one of the hardest I had ever taken, considering my stomach had lodged in my throat.

"Tell me what you found earlier, when you didn't want me to search the directories?"

I realised we could've used facial recognition to search the databases of the dark web, using stills from the videos of the inhabitants of Pepper Gorge. This search would've spared me seeing unrelated victims. People who needed to be saved, who deserved to be free, to not be sold to predators as if they mean nothing more than an inanimate object. To the predators, they are just that. *I forgot to pack my A-game for this captivating retreat.*

"The body Gabriel found, the date the file was uploaded and deleted, is the same day we arrived here. Another video was uploaded the day before, and also the day we stumbled upon Pepper Gorge."

Eli waited for me to continue while alternating the bottle between his hands.

"Based on the dates, they kill every five days, followed by a cooling-off period of two weeks, killing again five days apart."

The first murder happened on the day we arrived, the second on the sixth day. Murders three and four were on days fourteen and nineteen. I counted the days Aidan and I had been apart, losing track of which day of the week it was, but never the number of days since I had last seen my husband.

Could there have been more murders that Sevens Hunter didn't upload? Why was he uploading them on a website called – Pepper Gorge Truth? Every time the website went live, someone shut it down in a matter of hours, according to Eli.

If Sevens Hunter had uploaded the snuff films to the dark web, they would've remained there, undetected by the Coopersville police. Sevens Hunter wanted the public to know about Pepper Gorge. Murdering teenage boys to shed light on the cult was a tad extreme, in my opinion. But people often turn a blind eye on atrocities unless they shock, appal, or sicken them. Even when they take note, they discuss it once or twice and then carry on with their lives. Unless something terrible affects us, or a loved one, who cares? On their merry way they continue, let the poor people, most often children, fend for themselves.

"I found Nicol. Her photo is up on a site for the 'discerned international traveller'. Travellers who will fly across the world to take the virginity of a sixteen-year-old girl. A jet-setting rapist."

The victims were listed from every imaginable holiday destination, and like Pepper Gorge, destinations no one in their right mind would ever pay to visit. Unless the drawing card made up for what it lacked in scenery. No tans for the tourists flocking to Pepper Gorge, only memories of destroying a child's life. An opportunity to kill in another country and get away with it? Virginity can only be sold once. I hated to think of what happened to these girls after they had made the Originals their money. Virginity doesn't come cheap, and sometimes rape even less so. The rate of exchange and lower possibility of prosecution not the biggest factors in deciding your next international holiday, unless you're a predator who takes to the sky.

"How is Sevens Hunter making money if he has no formal training which he can fall back on in the outside world?"

"These videos are pay-per-view. He's making a killing in a matter of hours. He has to somehow inform people ahead of time for him to get the number of downloads he does in the couple of hours the site is live."

"A killing? Eli, no." I love a good pun but draw the line when someone else uses it in inappropriate situations.

"I'm sorry." He dropped his head in his hands. "I need to distance myself from the victims. If I don't, I might request an aerial strike on Pepper Gorge and write the innocent people off as collateral damage."

"You won't, you have a compassionate heart, and the victims aren't faceless to you. You've broken bread with them, sort of." Not that we had anything to eat during our second visit.

"Can you see if there are any birth records for Pepper Gorge? They have to register births, even if they are farm births. Home births just don't sound right, that place is no home, and it sure isn't an autonomous state."

Eli searched the national birth registry and came up empty-handed. On paper, the people we had watched for hours didn't exist. No wonder Sevens Hunter had to resort to snuff films to earn his bread and butter. My stomach growled, and I headed to the kitchen. Gabriel told me dinner would be ready in five minutes, but I ignored him and grabbed a tub of strawberry yoghurt from the fridge. I forced each spoonful down.

"Are we sure Sevens Hunter made those recordings?" I placed the empty container on the table and leaned back in the more comfortable chair. A part of me hated Gabriel even more.

"The last victim is the boy Gabriel found in the woods. No footage yet of the murder we witnessed earlier."

I ran my fingers through my hair, tugging on the ends, trying to pull my thoughts together to bring forth clarity. *Where are you now, notion?*

"Let me think." A sigh escaped. "They tortured the victims in a room or some kind of structure. Four males; the victim we saw earlier will make it five. How is the killer getting to them unless he's still part of the community? Then again, Sevens Hunter posted the footage." Brand consistency, both in the supposed normal and darkness.

"Eli, perhaps Sevens Hunter is living on the farm."

"He would need a laptop or phone with an internet connection to upload the footage and the posts he did to the dark web."

"Okay, fair point, but that doesn't mean cell signal isn't strong enough higher up the mountain. What if he works with someone in the community? The shorter hunter may be a woman or a younger boy." Accomplice or apprentice? Another question to add to my ever-growing list. Time to start writing them down; I didn't trust my hormone-infused brain to keep track.

With a sneer, I called Gabriel and asked him for more paper and a pen and got started on my list. I couldn't write down the questions I had for Eli or Tom and Gabriel. The ones Aidan could answer, he would, without me having to ask.

Twenty-five

Quinn answered as soon as I said her name. She had eyes all over the farm; visuals give answers. "Did you witness the murders of the other four?"

No response from the woman living inside my head.

"I need answers. Now. Another child will not be murdered on my watch."

"Passive-aggressive much?"

"When our other matter has been resolved, you and I can discuss your reluctance to save innocent lives. Right now, you need to tell me what you know about the murders that we don't."

"Not much. I installed my cameras on Sunday night, the day you first went there. I didn't know about the murders. You have to take my word for it."

"For now. What do you know that we don't?"

"Based on the footage you saw, are the victims held for hours or days?"

"Quinn, I don't have the energy for guessing games. Tell me what you know or at the very least say you won't help, then I can continue this frivolous exercise without holding on to the hope that you might shed some light on it."

"Why do you say it's frivolous?" She exhaled hard. "I'm asking legitimate questions, not yanking your chain."

I slid down the side of the claw-footed bath and stretched my legs out, my hands on my belly, eyes closed, in part because I didn't want to be reminded my toenails needed to be painted. I forgot to pack my black nail polish, and none of Lizzie's bright colours suit me.

Are baby clothes available in different colours, or can I dress the baby in black? We can be twinning, whatever that means. Focus, unprepared

159

mommy. "What were the questions?"

"The victims, were they held for hours or days?" Quinn failed to hide the amusement in her voice. "What were you thinking about? You were lost in thought or asleep, out for a full minute?"

"One question at a time, please." Not the time to tell an almost complete stranger I hoped my child's favourite colour would be black because I know nothing about colour matching, and black would be more practical considering stains. I had a lot to learn about milk stains and the projectile vomit little stomachs are capable of. I rubbed my hand over my belly and smiled. We would figure this parenting thing out together. Aidan and me. Our child and me. Instinct should kick in at some stage, I believed, semi-naïve.

"It's hard to say whether they keep the victims for hours or days. A medical examiner could comment on dehydration and malnourishment. If I had to guess – hours. A community that small, if someone from the outside abducted their own, they would leave no stone unturned on that farm and mountain. That's if they are fond of their own, and if they're not hunting their own. This might be the practise hunting Sevens Hunter referred to."

"You don't think it is?"

I forced my eyes not to roll behind my eyelids. "No, I don't. The fact that the woman was shocked and then the man immediately made it off as nothing. They removed the body Gabriel came across, but no talk of the discovery or even mention of the victim's name in the restaurant. Murder is news no matter where in the world you are."

"Why do you say it's frivolous to expose what has been going on there, perhaps for centuries?"

"Exposing them isn't the frivolous part. As much as I want to go in there guns blazing, I can't; we are outmanned, but not outgunned." My eyes opened so fast I had to blink against the harshness of the soft, yellow light. "Perhaps I can. Gabriel has more than one long range rifle in the garage, there are all kinds of grenades and assault rifles. We can take handguns for the fun of it."

"Hold on, Mrs Walker. What will your husband do when he finds out you put yourself and the baby in the line of fire?"

Spank me? Not that Aidan would, seeing as I was pregnant, and he never wanted to do anything more than joke about it. He did, however, love to do a whole range of other captivating things to me and for me. I missed my husband, my lover. Even with my past, I still enjoyed certain things, more so with Aidan. I trust him with every part of me, but most importantly, my life.

"You fell asleep again, this time with a strange smile on your face and your eyes open. Have I told you today you're one weird woman?"

"You will not be the first or last person to call me weird. You made my point for me. I can't go in there and arrest, better yet kill, those responsible. We can't call our friendly neighbourhood police department, not when someone high up is involved. So, who are we going to call?"

Quinn laughed. I waited. She didn't stop.

"I need some privacy real soon, so unless you want more girl-time and listen in on it, stop laughing. We've got a problem, Quinn. Are you going to send in one of your teams, and then what?" My bladder posed no issue, I just needed her to stop laughing. It had turned into the sound I assume pigs make when they fall in love.

"Not a lot of people can slip movie references into conversation, I might like you even more."

"Calm down, future best friend, I wasn't referring to any movie. What are we going to do once the truth comes to light? Can you contact Captain Taylor in Marcel? He might know of a colleague we can trust around here."

"I'll speak to Oliver and will get back to you."

"You know him?"

"Of course. It's a story with long and short versions, depending on who tells it."

"Your version will be a riddle. I need to go eat dinner and get back to work."

"Please try to sleep tonight. Your concealer isn't doing its job anymore."

I couldn't disagree with her. The dark circles were so prominent, they could be used as evidence in court. "Talk to you later, Quinn. Let me know as soon as you've spoken to our dear friend back in Marcel. Tell Oliver I send my regards and wish we could be working together on this case."

Captain Taylor and I had become close during the Sophia investigation. He had taken it upon himself to play bodyguard and keep Gabriel away. Oliver knew about my past intimate relationship with Sophia Blake's first victim. Not once did he judge me or bring it up in conversation. Another question on the ever-growing list – how did Oliver Taylor's life intersect with my in-laws'? This was one of the few questions I didn't need answered. Now.

During dinner Tom tried his best to create an atmosphere of jovial kinship. Except for Lizzie, none of them were my kin, and their deceit sucked the jovial out of the house. I carried my plate to the dishwasher and walked straight to the dining room. The image of the murdered teenage boy greeted me. I felt more at peace staring at him than I had listening to Tom tell tales of Lizzie and I as children.

He had been there for all of it. Our birthdays, graduations, my send-off on my first deployment. He had stood next to Lizzie at our parents' funeral. They hadn't waited for me to be released from hospital before they lowered my parents into the ground. I never got to say goodbye. For me there had been only the reading of the will, and my sister's pained stare the night she fetched me from the airport. Those were my last memories of my parents. No matter how hard I try to remember the last thing they both said to me, I can't. You never think it will be the last conversation.

Another 'what if'. What if I had left the army, as they had

both asked me to do? Closure would never come, but I could bring this child's murderers to justice. If not my kind, that of the law.

"Ley, do you need anything before I head out with Eli to prepare for tonight? I will come check on you before we leave. You can go to bed, Tom will monitor the surveillance cameras. He said it will keep his mind preoccupied from the devastation of losing his home, the last place he had which reminded him of Kelly."

An imaginary wheel spoke jabbed into my side, but I refused to take the bait. "He still has his house at the lake, the one he and Aunt Kelly bought for their retirement."

Cancer had devoured her in a matter of months. At the time of her diagnosis, the doctor informed her it was terminal.

"Would you return to the place where the love of your life died in your arms?"

I kept my back to him. "Correction. She died while being cared for by Ashley. Tom chose to work rather than take care of his dying wife."

"He couldn't bear to see her fade away; the constant pain which broke her bit by bit."

"Did you know him back then?"

He stepped closer. His breath stirred my hair. My fists clenched at my sides. "The worst pain I've ever endured was losing you."

"*You* never had me, *Gabriel.*" A step forward placed my legs against the dining table.

"When I close my eyes, I can still taste you, feel the way your body moved on top of mine. Not a day goes by that I don't remember the way it felt to be inside you."

An unknown calm came over me. A serenity in knowing soon he would bleed, plead for his life. Beg for my non-existent mercy. No matter the cost, I would get the truth from him. The darkness rolled its shoulders and settled. Patient. Anticipating. "Distorted memories. Ari's memories. You've been a ghost for the past twenty years, Gabriel."

"What we shared was real." He moved closer.

My heartbeat remained steady, my focus on the endgame. "Ari and I had sex a couple of times. Not one second of it compared to a kiss with Aidan. He messed me up for the rest of mankind. I've never settled for anything in my life, why would I settle now knowing what a real man can do to me? A man unafraid of who and what he is. A man who doesn't lie, deceive, and con his way into my life, my bed."

Gabriel placed his moist hands on my shoulders, rubbing his thumbs up the length of my neck. Goosebumps didn't appear. "You said you're done with him."

"Touch me again and you will lose your hands." He heeded my warning. "I did say that, doesn't mean I will ever be foolish or desperate enough to be with a man capable of hurting a woman."

I stepped away from him and headed for the door. He reached for me but dropped his arm to his side. I sighed with a smile. "Spare your breath with empty promises of it never happening again. I don't care for you, or your lies. You had close to three years to be the man you're delusional enough to believe you are. Inside you, there is *nothing*. Tell me, how does one love nothing? Nothing doesn't keep you warm, share your hopes and dreams. Nothing doesn't turn you on. No matter how appealing I once found the shell. Broken Finley had been too desperate for human contact to see you for what you are. Look in the mirror, Gabriel. Whoever you were died the day you became Ari."

Without another word, I left him standing there. His tears were not my responsibility to wipe away.

Gabriel, evading my question, answered it. He and Tom had known each other much longer than they had claimed to during dinner. Their answers were too rehearsed, scripted even. The truth – Aunt Kelly had died in Tom's arms at their lake house. Ashley and a nurse had taken care of her during the day, Tom at night. She had died the night before my parents' fatal car accident. Tom had held her funeral the morning of the night I returned to Marcel. In twenty-four hours, three of the people I had loved most in my life were gone.

I refuse to lose anyone else.

Tom would never, or have someone else, place explosives inside the place where he had told me more than once he could still feel Aunt Kelly's presence. The house Lizzie had inherited in Wild Bay stood, so did the lake house I inherited.

The places we called home – destroyed.

Twenty-six

The sound of the coffee grinder drowned out the silence I had grown to hate. Solitude isn't my friend. I craved the sound of an aeroplane passing overhead. Seagulls giving each other directions to a school of fish while I enjoy my morning coffee. The sound of the trees surrounding the lake house as the wind dances through them. The sound of Aidan in the shower while I lay pretending to sleep until he brought me my morning coffee. Perhaps I missed caffeine more than the sounds. I longed for a sip of my beloved liquid Walker at the end of a dark day. A day I made a difference in this sick, twisted, and dying world.

This night I could be part of the difference. Hunt a truth perhaps centuries old, two murderers, a potential group of virtual pimps who sold the virginities of teenage girls in the abyss. All of this from the comfort of a recliner, bottle of sparkling water in hand. The bubbles tricked me into believing this was different from all the other nights I had spent locked in this place.

It was. We had taken a big step forward in obliterating the cloak of incestuous secrets which hung over Pepper Gorge. The murders, rapes, whatever else we had not yet uncovered, it had to end. *Tonight.*

Tom pulled out a chair next to me and waited for me to speak. He grew tired of waiting. "Ari said they're almost done, they should leave within the next fifteen minutes."

"His name is Gabriel. Do you want me to tell you his surname, place of birth, his father's occupation, the reason he deserted his team in the middle of an operation?" The last I didn't know, but I'm always in the mood for a good bluff.

"What did you say to him to make him hurt you like that?"

He lowered his gaze to my uncovered arms.

"Tom, as a former police officer, a current state prosecutor, does a man ever have the right to leave these kinds of bruises on a woman? Or a woman on a man, to be inclusive?"

"If you weren't pregnant, it wouldn't have looked so bad."

I stared down at the dark blue finger marks, the edges beginning to change colour. "Should a man lay his hands on the woman who is carrying his child, or shake her until she's on the verge of blacking out?"

Tom slurped his coffee, the sound stirring the hairs on my arms. I stared at the screens; the two-dimensional activity on the farm.

"He's many things, but he will be a good father. He loves you to a fault. It has been his only mistake." Tom blew on his coffee. Same habits, different person. I couldn't pinpoint the exact moment he had changed. The instant he stopped being the man I had been proud to call my godfather. *Did he ever exist?*

"What do you mean, Gabriel's only mistake was loving me?"

"If he hadn't fallen in love with you, as hard as he did, he could've been married by now, raising children of his own, instead of being reminded of one lapse in judgement. You won't allow him to be a part of his child's life."

I leaned back and placed my feet flat on the extended leg rest. There's only one way I would allow Gabriel close to my child – if his body fertilised a tree in our new garden. Offering nourishment to the earth might be the one good thing he does in his life. Death wouldn't be too late for him to redeem himself, for as long as he decomposed.

"He made a mistake, get over it. *Gabriel* isn't a serial killer. You promised forever to one of those."

Till death, I did. Through the good times and the bad. I wondered whether our current situation was good or bad. Of course, I hated being separated from Aidan because of circumstances beyond our control. Our immediate control. Good he did on his end, and good I hoped to do on mine. We don't have to be joined at the hip to better the world. Aidan's a doctor who brings new life into the world, and I hunt those who take it upon themselves to end the lives of others. What would wait for us at the end of this?

In my gut, I knew neither of us could go back to the lives we had lived before. Fire filled Aidan's voice every time he spoke of his mission, to locate and end the Puppet Master.

"Finley, you need to speak soon. You're being weird again. I've created a temporary glitch on the live feed of their surveillance cameras. You have five minutes. We can only do this once. Can I just say, before you get a swing at Tom, I want first dibs? Five, four, three, two, one, and go."

"Be my guest." I toyed with the bottle of water in my right hand, my no-longer-ring-bearing hand tracing circles over my belly.

"What?"

Woops, I had answered Quinn. I rolled with it. "Will you be a guest at my next wedding? I'm not saying I will marry Gabriel, but I'm still young, and I have needs. Needs a battery-operated replica won't satisfy. Nothing beats a warm body, capable hands, a mouth so skilled at kissing you think a kiss alone will make you orgasm. Perhaps you even do."

"Finley Duncan Williams, I'm still your godfather, and not your sister or one of your friends. You will treat me with the respect your parents expect of you."

"They aren't here. And let's be honest, I haven't needed a godfather since I turned twenty-one. Therefore, I put it to you, using my age as exhibit A, from this moment forward, we cease referring to you as anything other than an old friend of my parents. Lizzie told me it was your idea to bury them before I got home. You robbed me of the chance to say goodbye to my parents."

"I've been waiting three years for you to bring this up. Three years you haven't mourned your parents, not a single day. You got back and carried on with your life as if they never existed. You remained enlisted even after they had begged you to get out. You're nothing but a spoiled little girl who got everything she ever asked for on a gold platter."

I prefer titanium. "You've been holding that in much longer than three years. Kudos to you for finally growing the balls to tell me what you think of me. Strange for someone who had watched me grow up, who stood next to my parents at my graduation, the very person who had scrubbed the trafficker's blood off my hands when I had done at sixteen what most people never have the guts to do."

"You're a murderer, Finley. I knew it then, I know it now. What I did was for your parents, not for you."

I prefer the term killer, as I never set out to end anyone's life, except for the thing that touched my sister. "You came to me, a *killer*. You begged for my help. I found them, the Scarecrows, and where did that get me?" Tortured for days. Dying twice. I had Eli to thank for my rescue, Aidan for my life.

"It takes one to know one." He drained the mug and placed it on the table.

"Like you and Gabriel know each other?"

He answered me with silence.

"Why are you here, Tom?"

"Hiding from your husband, the Marcel Sniper."

"Oh, Tom, you poor, foolish old man. If Aidan wanted you dead, you would've been dead a long time ago. He told you, you had access to his military records. What was his furthest kill?"

Tom shrugged as I pushed myself to my feet.

"Now might be a good time to close the curtains, before that tiny dot appears on your forehead. See, the thing is, Tom, you won't even know he's in the same city as you before his bullet rips through your skull." I quoted Tom word for word.

He twisted his neck and stared up at me, his expression so readable I almost laughed.

"Remember the night Gabriel phoned you after he saw Aidan and I making love at the lake house?" I laughed; the sound similar to the first time I had tortured a predator in my wine cellar.

The information regarding the conversation between Gabriel and Tom, Aidan had shared with me on our last night together. For nineteen days I had chewed on it.

I bent forward and placed my hands on Tom's shoulders. My right thumb found the lump of skin under his clavicle; another reminder he wasn't bullet proof, just hard to kill. For some. As my thumb pressed deeper under the bone, pain covered his face, and his mask slipped.

With my mouth against his ear, I said, "There comes a time when it's too late to tell the truth. Truth will not hide in the darkness of those who try to obliterate it. Tick. Tock. Tommy-boy. Your worst nightmares are unicorn, bunny, and rainbow filled dreams compared to what I'm about to do to you."

I eased my head back and patted his left cheek. "Go to bed, old man, you need the rest. Oh, and, Tom, put your mask back on. If you tell Gabriel I'm on to you..." I winked, knowing my face resembled an apex predator ready to launch her attack.

"Time's up," Quinn said.

The same victorious sound bubbled out of me as I came to my full length. "I can't believe I forgot that joke, it must be your smell. Your scent is engrained in my best memories. You said some things tonight, Tom, that I hope we can put behind us. You're the closest thing to a grandfather this child has, seeing as Gabriel's father is playing chess with the devil. Go to bed, I've got tonight covered. Tomorrow morning, we carry on as if the hurtful things you said left no scar on my heart. Abuse is never acceptable. Once you have a good night's rest you will remember you live to serve and protect women in my situation, and men." I pressed my lips to his clammy forehead and left him.

Motionless, Lizzie stood in the kitchen. Her cheeks red. In her eyes, rage twirled to the rhythm of my darkness' flapping wings.

Twenty-seven

Eli and Gabriel parked in the same spot Gabriel and I had the night we sent the drones on their nocturnal flight. I rubbed my eyes, my temples, and pushed my fingers through my hair. Too much screen time, too much two-dimensional same-scene sightseeing. The people of Pepper Gorge were not made for reality television. Poor Quinn, watching us, listening to me snore at night, according to her. I refused to believe her.

On the farm, the Originals slept; unbothered by the laws of the outside world, with their armed guards patrolling the borders of their perverse land.

Before Eli and Gabriel had left, I instructed them to wear body cameras. What they saw, I wanted to see as well. What they heard, I needed to hear. To be honest, I didn't trust Gabriel alone with Eli. I didn't trust him alone with anyone.

Down the passage, Tom rolled on the stretcher Gabriel had set up for him. Such good friends they are. Tom taking Gabriel's side, Gabriel ensuring Tom slept as comfortably as possible on that rickety thing. Where was their bond forged? In the fires of hell? It didn't matter; it existed. Bent on the destruction of my family. The rage I had seen in Lizzie's eyes was as much for the things Tom had said as for the lies she, too, had believed about him. What someone did to one of us, they did to the other. This is our way.

I turned my focus to the bottom right-hand corner of the laptop's screen. 02:15 a.m.

"I'm sorry, baby. You sleep tight, tomorrow morning I will sleep in, and when the people of Pepper Gorge can sleep as free members of the world, you and I can rest as much as we need to. One day you will understand why Mommy did this. One day you will know what it is to fight for those who can't fight for themselves. I hope righteousness courses through you no matter who you are when you're grown up. No matter who you will become, I will love you. You will be enough for me, but most importantly, for yourself. Just never be in a hurry to grow up, my love; the world is not what we want it to be. I promise to keep fighting to make it a safe and wonderful place for you, and as many other children as I can. This is my promise to you. You will be safe, no matter what I need to do to ensure it." My hands splayed over my stomach, and I prayed in silence for this child, for Aidan, and for myself.

Movement caught my eye. Half of the laptop's screen showed Eli's view, the other half his companion's. They're the same height, give or take a centimetre or two for Gabriel, but their builds are so different. Gabriel had indulged in steroids for a good part of his adult life, even more so after we were involved.

Contrary to Gabriel's laboratory-created inflated muscles, Eli is lean, his muscles rock hard. The perfect soldier, like Aidan. My sister had told me in great detail, despite my vehement vocal protests, many things about Eli that I didn't want to know about my friend, my future brother. He and Aidan have much more in common than their body composition. The Williams sisters sure are lucky.

Night sounds filled my ears as I activated the two-way communication. If either of them farted, I would know. These puppies picked up everything, or so Eli had said when he set up my command centre. Command centre? I liked this – being in charge, calling the proverbial shots. The other screens showed no movement; the farm folk had turned in hours before.

"Are the two of you sure you can do this? It has been a long time since you were on a mission together. When was the last time? Does it start with – It was a dark and stormy night?"

Eli laughed, the sound faint. "No time for old stories, let's get this over and done with. I want to get back to my woman and snuggle up to her warm body."

"Will I have a warm body to snuggle up to when we get

back?" Gabriel asked.

Down the passage the television's screen flickered in the quiet living room slash bedroom of two grown men.

"It appears Tom is still awake. You might be in luck."

Gabriel huffed and turned on the night vision of the body camera fastened to his jacket. I had begged Eli to wear the vest I had seen in the garage, the only time I set foot in there. The tactical armour vest was light and easy to conceal. I never got to play with the toys the special-ops guys did. My squad had access to the standard military-issued items, which were more than capable of doing what was needed, until the day they weren't.

Outmanned. Outgunned. Mission failed. A part of me had died that day, and every day after that when one of my squad members was murdered in front of my eyes. Civilians will never understand the bond forged in war. The only one who survived – me. Some days I wonder if any part of me prior to those four months had survived. Once I returned to Marcel, I never had time to ponder over it. I had a serial killer to track down, then a paedophile, then a rapist. On and on it went. It never stops. For me, it never will.

"Fin, we're ready if you are?" Eli turned my field of vision through his body camera a strange green. I never got used to wearing night-vision goggles.

"Just like we talked it through. Head to the church building first, find that book. Then head to the five houses. I need that book more than I need to know what's being said and done inside their homes. Be safe." I drew a deep breath. "Eli, come back to your home."

"Yes, ma'am."

With the footrest up, I shifted my bum until I found the comfortable sweet spot. I could get used to this; hunting without being in the line of fire. This way, I kept my child and myself safe and saw more than I would've if I was there running through a cornfield. Laughter bubbled inside me, but I kept it contained. Many horror movies have scenes with cornfields. Only the scene in front of me, not fiction.

For most of their jog towards the town, I kept my attention focused on the screens monitoring the inhabitants. The men who guarded the property slept, as they had the night of the drones. *If that isn't a name for a horror movie, then I don't know what is.*

The abrupt stop in movement on the laptop's screen caught my attention. Ahead lay the buildings which made up the town. Perhaps a better description would be the main or communal buildings, but this place operated like a town. They even had tourists. Not the kind we had been, but anyone who drove in there would've thought it a place time forgot.

A place where evil stops the pendulum's swing.

Soundless, they moved closer to the church building, shadows providing safe passage further into the darkness. Eli and Gabriel's movements were choreographed, a dance they had done before.

It never crossed my mind to ask Eli what it had been like for him when Gabriel deserted him along with the rest of their team. Here they were, side by side, doing what they do best. This had been Aidan's world once, and still was that of his parents and two of his brothers.

Was someone watching him like I watched Eli and Gabriel? Did Aidan watch, like me? I hoped for the latter, knowing better. I've never doubted his capabilities in the field, but I needed him back unharmed. Without him, I wouldn't have a home. Neither would our child.

Gabriel ran ahead and slipped through the door when he reached the building, Eli on his six. Every few seconds the barrels of the Colt M4's came into view as they moved through the church, towards the back door.

Eli dropped to his knee, neither of them giving me an unobstructed view before the door opened. Good thing Eli is a master lock picker, with the frequency Lizzie locked herself out of the house. The very house which no longer stood.

Inside the room, an office or conference room by the look

of it, the first drop of truth splashed in my face. Five kings ruled over Pepper Gorge, none higher than the others. This I concluded from the hand-sketched faces of five men hanging on the opposite wall in a perfect horizontal line. On either sides, and above the door, hung more faces, hand drawn. Frozen in time.

Strange that they wouldn't have actual photos taken but made use of technology to orchestrate the rapes of teenage girls.

I kept my eyes focused on the footage being captured by Eli's body camera. He did a three-sixty, giving me a clear view of the room and its contents. There was a wall safe on one end which might take him longer to crack. No windows.

In the middle of the room stood a wooden table, farm-carved. The shape too extraordinary for it to be store-bought: a pentagon, surrounded by five identical chairs. In front of each chair, a single number carved into the table's surface.

Eli walked closer to the table and bent forward. "Fin, do you want me to take photos of the sevens carved into the table?" He moved around the table to give me a better view of each carving.

"No. Whoever did those isn't our murderer. It appears those were all carved by the same hand."

"How do you know it's not the same person?" Gabriel joined Eli and bent over the table.

I lifted my hands in the air and shook my head. Who would've guessed that an assassin doesn't need an eye for detail? "Look at where the seven starts. The murderer didn't carve a straight line, the seven he carved looks more like the seven on playing cards, with the slight down line." Words didn't form fast enough at this time of the morning, but they would get the just of it.

"I don't see the book." Gabriel walked around the room, pressing his hands to the walls. He stopped and rapped his knuckles against a wooden wall panel.

The book had to be there, hidden out of sight, kept for

the eyes of the Originals alone. "Eli, look under the table."
It's what I would've done as the leader of a cult, or one of
five in this case. Strange dynamic – five ruling as one. Pride is
something we all deal with to a certain extent. Could these five
men have overcome a primal need to be dominant? Generation
after generation?

Eli complied, pulled a chair away from the table, dropped
to his knees and rolled onto his back. Again, the number I
once never thought twice about stared back at me. Eli slid the
box out of the brackets and placed it on top of the table. Inside
it held what I hoped to be answers.

The book was much smaller than I expected it to be; a
perfect fit for the rucksack on Eli's back.

"Okay, time to plant my eyes and ears."

Gabriel mumbled under his breath, in Hebrew, forgetting
I understand well enough to follow a conversation. Unlike
Aidan, I can't read or write in Hebrew or any of the other
languages he speaks fluently without a hint of an accent. I
hoped he passed this on to our child.

Gabriel slipped the book into Eli's rucksack, and together
they made their way out of the building. Once outside, darkness
enveloped them as they headed up the mountain to where five
houses stood, side by side, none bigger than the other.

"Three down," Eli whispered as he leopard-crawled to the
next house. This might have seemed drastic, but even with the
guards asleep, if someone woke up, spotted them, and sounded
the alarm, they would be too far in on the property to get out
unharmed. Eli needed to return to Lizzie. No one could hurt
Gabriel but me. If Aidan asked, I would oblige and step back,
but I doubted he had it in him to torture. Unlike me, he prefers
to kill from a far.

I realised none of the victims the hunters had brought there
ever left. The people who paid to be there secured their way
out.

Sevens Hunter had found a way out, yet he didn't break
free, perhaps unable to put this place behind him.

It had been easy for Eli to slip into the houses and plant the surveillance cameras and listening devices. Just like the rest of the town, the interiors of the houses were from a different era. One the rest of the world might never have entered.

When you're on the frontline, there is no time to appreciate the precision with which your teammates move, or their skills. Watching these two men ignited a need in me to tell them how good they were. Despite who and what Gabriel became over the years, I couldn't fault him for his precision, sure-footedness, and stealth. Too bad he played for the enemy.

Eli stepped out of the house and I watched him approach Gabriel through the body camera mounted to Gabriel's chest. My head jerked to the other screens. Movement; heading in their direction.

"You've got company. Eli, three o'clock."

Gabriel spun around and jogged into the dark tree line.

"What the hell are you doing? Wait for Eli, you get out together."

He covered the camera with his hand, half of the laptop's screen turning black. The instant he removed his hand, I covered my mouth with mine.

The back of a man's head came into view. Both the assassin's hands reached forward. *Hand to temple, hand to jaw.* This I was trained to do. As a soldier; as the assassin's student.

Eyes shut, I waited for the snap.

Twenty-eight

The ability to improvise is a gift. This ability had turned into a curse in Gabriel's DNA. I dropped my head into my hands and breathed. *Inhale. Exhale.* A desperate attempt not to hyperventilate because of the rage consuming me. Eli wouldn't appreciate it if I smashed another of the screens on the dining room floor. Soon it would be dusk; sleep avoids the enraged. Uncaffeinated Finley isn't a pleasant site, not at any hour.

Gabriel shrugged as my eyes met his. Eli had left us to fight it out with *our words* as his parting orders. Fists would be more fun had I not been with child.

"How could you do this?"

"I saw an opportunity and took it. You want answers, I bring you answers. A thank you would be nice. Do you want coffee?" Gabriel left me to stew.

At the sound of his footsteps behind me, I spun around. "Hey, dipshit, one of their guests is the Captain of the Coopersville's Police Department. How long before they start a search? They will go from property to property until they find him."

"Ley, calm down."

"Never in the history of rage did the words 'calm down' ever calm a person down." Too tired to stand, I slumped down on the recliner and pulled my legs to my chest.

Gabriel pulled a chair closer and handed me a mug. "Decaf for Mommy."

"Just because you didn't get hurt in Pepper Gorge doesn't mean you won't bleed here." I sipped the coffee, appreciating the taste, missing the kick.

"Ley, there's a killer on the loose, one they haven't tried to stop. For all they know, that young man was murdered by the same person who killed the others. They're not sending out a search party. Look at the screens, they don't even realise anything has happened."

The assassin made a valid point. I refused to verbalise my agreement. It didn't make the position he put me in any easier. "Give me the book, I need to work. Today is my and Eli's deadline to uncover all the mysteries which enshroud that farm."

"You need sleep; your body needs the rest, and so does your mind. Our child needs you rested." He placed his hand on my shoulder, but I shook it off.

"How do you want me to sleep after what you did?" The yawn caught me off guard.

He smiled; it reached his black eyes. "Let me take you to bed, tuck you in nice and tight, and after you've slept, you can have all the answers your beautiful little heart can handle."

"If you want to take me to bed, you better knock me over the head and drag me by my hair."

"It's too short. I prefer you with long hair."

"My hair and my sleep deprivation are not your concern."

"Yes, but my child is. You heard Doctor Duvall, this is a high-risk pregnancy, you have no choice but to get adequate rest, and by rest I mean actual REM sleep."

The early morning hours turned into the attack of the yawns. They kept coming for me and winning. The last time I checked the laptop's time display, it read 04:19 a.m.

"I will stay here and monitor their activities. If anything happens, I will wake you up, but for now, go to bed. What's done is done. Get up, I want the comfy chair."

I obeyed the assassin's orders. As I reached the doorway, I turned to him. "Why didn't you kill him?"

Without looking at me, he replied, "You need answers. He's the son of an Original. Who better to give you the answers you seek? Henry isn't going anywhere. I'll take him breakfast later. Go to bed, Ley, dream of me."

Oh, I will, of you begging for my non-existent mercy. One humane deed didn't undo years of lies and deceit. While Gabriel held that young man's life in his hands, he had no idea who he was. For the second time, he could've killed but didn't. First the Angel Taker, now the son of an Original. Another question to add to my ever-growing list.

Six hours later I opened my eyes, but his side of the bed remained empty. Cold. I placed my hand on a pillow he had never laid his head on and shut my eyes. My pillow absorbed the moisture dripping from my eyes. The ache in my heart grew with each passing day. Each day brought us closer to being together, back home, wherever that would be.

The tears could stop now. I had never cried so much; it had to be the hormones. For the first time in my life, I felt genuine fear. Fear of this not ending. Afraid we would never learn the reason all this had begun. Fear for my child's life, Aidan's, Lizzie's, and my own. Aidan gave me a reason to live, reminding me of the good we can do in this world. My baby; cocooned in my womb and my love. How I had prayed for this child. I smiled. My mother had once said you never stop praying for your children, and I realised it starts long before they even take their first breath. More so for children whom we beg for from God.

I pulled the duvet over my head and kept my voice low. "Quinn?"

"Good morning, thunder cloud, you sure aren't a ray of sunshine today. You look like you need more sleep."

"I need Aidan. Where is he?" Quinn drew a deep breath; I had learned her tells. "He's not in a position to talk to me, is he?"

"No."

"If you're here and he is wherever he is, how do you know?"

"Heather is with me, she spoke to Ryan a while back."

"Why is Heather here? Shouldn't she rather be with Aidan?" I fought the urge to lift the duvet off my head.

"She's here to monitor Gabriel. After the night in the

garage, she's worried she profiled him wrong. Do you want to talk to her?"

To hear my mother-in-law's voice would bring more tears; she would say the words a mother would, and at that moment I didn't need comfort or compassion. I needed my husband. "No. I want to speak to Aidan. Please arrange it."

"Finley..." Another deep breath in my ear. "He's preparing to execute his plan."

My stomach lifted into my throat. "I can't lose him." I buried my face in the pillow. I had to get up, go to the garage, and make a young man tell me all of his peoples' secrets. But before I set foot in that place again, I needed to hear Aidan's voice, for him to centre and calm me. "Quinn, tell him I love him, and he has to come back to me." I wrapped my arms around my waist and curled into a fetal position. "He has to come back to us."

"He will, no matter what happens, remember that. What can I do for you today?"

"Coffee, scrambled eggs and rye toast with avocado, followed by a bowl of strawberries. I wish you were with Aidan to keep him safe."

"Don't worry about Aidan, Liam and Rowan are with him and you know how much they love you. They won't let anything happen to Aidan. Ryan didn't brief me on the details, but Aidan has taken every potential variable into account. There's very little chance of error, not when it's one of his strategies. Your husband has been our chief strategist for years, even after he stopped working with us."

Aidan, like almost every other person, kept forgetting he was only human. He hates making mistakes, just like the rest of us average intelligence folk. "If you can get a message to him, I would appreciate it. Tell him I love him."

"Will do, Mrs Walker. Now tell me, what are you going to do about the child locked in the cage?"

"Not torture the truth out of him; he didn't choose to be born there."

"Finley, sometimes we need to do whatever it takes."

Images played in my mind, of men and women chained to a bolted down chair in my wine cellar at the lake house. My torture room. A place where they had made the decision they should've made before they had hurt innocent people. Children. Life is full of choices and I have seen enough death to last me a million lifetimes. No longer would I heed the darkness' call. There had to be another, better way.

My stomach growled. Shower, food, and then I would ask Eli to go with me to talk to Henry Bailey. The son of one of the current Originals, whatever that meant. None of the original five brothers still lived, unless vampires and zombies are real.

Twenty-nine

Somewhere in Europe. Location: Classified.

All of her emotions he could handle, but one. Anger – take her
to the shooting range. Frustrated – let her spar with Eli. Aidan
couldn't spar with her, he had tried a few times, and it always
ended the same way – them naked in the first place they could
find.

Of the seven basic emotions, he had seen her experience
them all, but one he had seen only for the second time the night
Gabriel had grabbed her. She had told him everything she had
endured during the war. The wounds he had stitched told the
story of her time with the Scarecrows, so did her dislocated
shoulders. The first time he had seen her decimated by fear had
been the night he found her on their bathroom floor holding
their embryo in her hands. Powerless. Fearful. Broken.

"Your mother cried just as much when she was pregnant
with Nathan." Ryan placed his hand on Aidan's shoulder.
"Hormones."

Aidan stared at the monitor; Finley pushed herself off the
bed and headed to the en suite bathroom. "Not hormones,
she's frustrated."

Ryan pulled the tray closer and poured coffee for them
both. "Why didn't you talk to her?"

"I learned the truth over days, she will hear all of it in one
sitting. I'm beyond livid. What will she be? This is her family,
her parents, her and Lizzie's lives. Dad, when she learns what
Tom did, I'm afraid of what she'll do."

"She's killed before, and him dying won't be a tragic loss to
humanity." Ryan brought the mug to his lips and eyed his son
over the rim. "What's bugging you?"

183

"I don't want her to live with more death on her conscience. I see the toll it has taken on her over the years. She's crying because she can't use any of her normal coping mechanisms, it's her body's way of trying to process all the contained rage." Aidan stood and walked to the window. This was not the Puppet Master's country, but he was close enough to shoot. The Puppet Master would breathe as long as Finley allowed it, or she might decide on a punishment far worse than death. Leave him to rot in a black site, built by Ryan Walker in his quest to better the world.

"How do you cope?"

"I train with Eli, or I surf. I will miss living next to the ocean, Finley and I loved that house. If it rains, I go to the shooting range. The only thing Finley does differently to cope is that she doesn't surf, she runs; when she's upset or frustrated, it's always a run and never a jog. I doubt she's jogged once in her entire life." Aidan smiled. His wife kept pushing her own limits, a quality he loved. Now he realised the strain she had been under. Unable to empty magazine after magazine, as she, to everyone's knowledge, didn't carry a concealed weapon. With a high-risk pregnancy, running wasn't an option. So, Finley cried. The sight broke his heart and enraged him at the same time.

"It might help if you tell her it will be over in a matter of hours. Tomorrow this time you will hold your wife in your arms."

"If everything goes according to plan." Through the faint rain, Aidan saw the parliament building, the reason the Puppet Master came to this very city.

"This strategy of yours has never failed us. Sergio has been waiting for this opportunity for three years." Ryan laughed. "He's a tad peeved that our friend ended his relationship with the supermodel. Sergio saw her as a job perk."

Aidan shook his head. "Are you sure he's the right person for this if his primary objective is having sex with a beautiful woman? He needs to focus on the big picture, marry someone the people will adore and can be a role model to the youth.

I hope he doesn't try to rekindle the relationship with the supermodel, it might derail the entire operation if he does."

"I doubt he will make that mistake. In her defence, she's much more intelligent than she lets on, I met her a year ago at a gala. She's using her international platform to raise awareness for the plight of her people."

"Ironic, considering *he* is the reason there is a plight."

"Let's not talk politics. Sergio is ready, he has been ready for years. I have the utmost confidence in him, he has proven himself and he considers this a working retirement compared to the operations he and I ran over the years. If an attractive woman on his arm, in his bed, is a bonus to him, good for him. He never had time to have a lasting relationship and he's still young enough to have a family of his own."

"Dad, he's forty-eight. Can't see him getting up to help with nappy changes in the middle of the night."

"In his new role he can hire all the help he needs to raise a soccer team if he wants. Whatever his future holds, Sergio's focus is on righting *his* wrongs. The people suffered long enough, it's time for change and the time is right for bold moves forward, without drawing unnecessary attention to Ruastan. The country has progressed under his leadership, albeit for his own agenda. If not for us intervening now, he would've ended up in The Hague."

"How many are there in his position we can't touch?" Aidan drained the last of the coffee and returned the mug to the tray.

"Again, not the time for politics. It's been one long chess game since I founded this organisation. One at a time, that's how we'll win the countless unseen wars raging at this very minute. For now, focus on freeing the people of Ruastan, but most importantly, bring the man behind the reason you're here to justice while Finley is preparing to question a young man, who for the first time in his life, set foot off that farm. Against his will, but still. Can you imagine what it must be like for him? The very people he was warned against his entire life are now the ones holding him prisoner."

"You don't know that he hasn't been off the farm, and he might not consider Finley the enemy."

"She wears no wedding ring, yet she's pregnant. Didn't Quinn tell you what she read in that book your wife got hold of?"

"Must have slipped her mind, when did she read it?"

"Quinn isn't the green operative she was when you worked with us. A lot has changed in the past ten years. You should stop by my office, let me catch you up on a few things."

Aidan laughed. Ryan's smile softened his chiselled features. Except for having his father's eyes, Aidan took after Heather.

"Why do I suspect I will walk into your office and walk out back on the payroll?"

"Because you're my son. As much as I love your brothers, and how proud I am of the men they've become, they're not the natural leaders you are. When I retire, I need to know someone capable will call the shots and take the shots when needed. You see the entire picture, beyond it even, into the next frame. You have a gift, Aidan, think of the good you can do. The difference you can make in the world. The opportunity this will offer Finley." Ryan joined Aidan at the window.

If not for the bullet-resistant glass, neither of them would stand there in open view. A safe house, a place Aidan and Finley can call home if they decide to raise their child in Europe.

"Finley needs to be part of this conversation." Aidan stared down at his wedding band.

Finley had chosen a black Damascus ring for their second wedding; he hadn't chosen a ring for himself for their first surprise wedding. Something as personal as a wedding ring he had wanted to leave up to her to choose. Finley had chosen this ring for the physical aspects more than the beauty, the way the metals mould together to create a unique swirl effect. Long-lasting and scratch resistant – words she had incorporated into her vows, words only he understood. Every time he looked at the ring it reminded him of how he and Finley were forged together in their life, their love, their unconditional acceptance of each other. Nothing can break their bond. Nothing except death.

"I need to be there for her when this goes down, Dad. He knows who I am, he needs to understand this is the end for him. I don't want him to suspect for a second that it's one of his many other enemies. Finley needs me to be there even though she has no knowledge of him, apart from seeing his name on television and in the newspaper."

Ryan nodded and placed his arm around Aidan's shoulder. "I've waited years for this moment. Since the night Victoria Williams confided in your mother that her youngest daughter was being held hostage."

Thirty

With my stomach filled with scrambled eggs, avocado on rye toast, and a handful of strawberries, I headed to the garage. The place Gabriel had shown me his true colours. While I had stilled my hunger, we played another round of our game. He refused to not be present while I speak to his captive. I refused to be in that confined space with him. On and on it went, ending with me contemplating using my fork as a projectile, but stopped by Eli's kind offer to accompany me to a place I never wanted to set foot in again.

Lizzie had watched our heated debate, her expression unreadable. I have always been able to tell what played in her mind. The first chance I had alone with her, I wrapped my arms around her and reminded her that this would soon be over, even though I couldn't tell her when. I asked her whether she worked on a poison all the hours she had spent in their bedroom; she assured me she wasn't, as there weren't any natural poisons in the surrounding fauna. Lizzie had searched. Perhaps we shared more than blood, or she tired of hiding with the enemy. Before I had released my hold on her, she had whispered, "I miss Aidan. He's to me what Eli is to you." *A brother.*

Eli and I shared war and vengeance. Lizzie and Aidan shared healing and bettering the lives of others through medicine.

To keep Lizzie from continuing to contemplate murder, I had asked Gabriel to go to Coopersville while Eli and I spoke with our restrained guest. Gabriel's mission was simple – buy me bigger clothes. Only three of my shirts fitted loose enough to conceal the Baby Glock above my slight baby-bump. Lizzie added her own items to the list. Gabriel Berkowitz – assassin and personal shopper.

As I reached the garage's only usable door, the main door nothing but an illusion, Eli grabbed my arm. "Are you ready for this?"

To find answers? Yes. To uncover the truth about Pepper Gorge and bring an end to whatever darkness roamed that piece of earth? Of course. Leaving this hell and returning to my Aidan? There are no words in my vocabulary to say how ready I was. Perhaps an expletive followed by yes. This wouldn't have been very ladylike, as my mother would've told me, as she always had when I brought my soldier's mouth home with me. Even before my parents had died, I longed for them.

For four months I had ached to return to them, even if it meant fragments of the person they had known returned to them. Covered in dirt and blood, I had dreamed of hearing their voices. To be home with them, at the lake house. In my dream, my dad and I smoked cigars and drank Johnny Walker Blue Label to our hearts' content. My mother prepared my favourite meal and scolded my father and I for our smoking and the bottles of Walker we emptied over the weekend. Lizzie held my hand and listened as I gave no details of the horrors I saw, caused, and survived. Our weekends together were filled with laughter, joy, and love. The way families should spend time together celebrating life. We never took the little, or big, things for granted.

I shook my head and focused my attention on the young man waiting on the other side of the door, locked in a cage. It didn't surprise me that Gabriel owned a cage.

"Talk, you weirdo. You need to schedule a session with Heather. Soon. This zoning out can't be normal. Just an observation, don't put glass in my food." Quinn laughed.

I fought the urge to roll my eyes as I stared at Eli. His frown lines reminding me I hadn't answered him and had in fact zoned out yet again. *Damn, Quinn.*

"No. But I don't have a choice, as your friend brought me this gift like a freaking cat bringing a mouse to its owner."

"Gabriel wishes you owned him."

Ah, but his last breath I do.

Eli lifted his wristwatch to his face, his eyes on mine. "He has to redeem himself for the way he treated you the other night before I will refer to him as my friend again."

This time I rolled my eyes. "You must continue hosting the self-defence classes at Tabula Rasa when we return to Marcel. The women trust you, and it's important they learn to protect themselves in the future." Too many of our guests ran from abusive partners. "But we need to consider teaching them to use weapons and giving them each a K-bar or something smaller for Christmas. With all my training, I couldn't protect myself. What chance do they have?"

"You walked out, didn't you?"

"Duh." I gestured with my hands over my body. We were stalling, but why, I didn't know.

"Then you live to fight another day, sometimes that's the win. Now, this food is getting cold and you want to impress your guest, or so you said."

"What's the time?"

"1300 hours."

I smiled; the exact time Henry ate every afternoon. Reaching for the door handle, I froze – to knock or not to knock? I chose the latter. Henry wasn't our guest, and for all I knew he had posted the photos of the young women on the dark web. Including that of his future wife, Nicol.

Eli and I burst through the door, I felt a tad whimsical, and even more mischievous than I had in a long time. Interrogations – interviews would be the more socially acceptable word – stir an anticipation in me which climaxes in a signed confession. I preferred the taped confessions of the ones who found themselves in my wine cellar. But this time there wouldn't be any pen and paper, or voice recorder, and no corpse dangling from a building.

I stood in the grey. Uncharted waters; the notion paced. Neither of us knew what to expect, or if I could keep fighting the darkness' call. It danced between the back of my mind and my only thought. Vengeance became my nemesis. I became soft, or so I thought.

"Good afternoon, Henry, I brought you lunch." I dragged a chair closer while Eli slid the plate through the hole in the bars.

"*He* brought me lunch."

Tough little nut you're going to be. "If you're into technicalities then, yes, but Eli is a gentleman. Much like they raised you to be. Were you not taught to treat your elders with respect?"

Henry huffed and dragged the plate closer. "You're too young to be my elder."

I almost blushed at his unintentional compliment. I had at least two dog years on him, but this wasn't the time to correct him.

"Besides, you're a woman. *You* must serve." He lost all his brownie points in a single breath.

"Is that what you expect from Nicol once you're married?" I settled on the wooden chair. It looked similar to the ones in the church's back office.

"All my wives will serve me."

"All but one. A fellow Original, your first wife, she's exempt from chores, yet she won't be considered a sloth. Why not?"

"You're familiar with our ways." He dug into the beef lasagne and I waited for him to clear his plate. As he slid the plate through the bars, he lifted his eyes to mine. "The meat tastes off."

"Why did you eat it then? We could've made you something else."

"I was hungry and didn't want to be a rude guest."

Elbows on my knees, I leaned forward. "A guest? You're locked in a cage."

"For now." Henry moved back until the back of his head rested against the steel bars, his eyes focused on mine. *Ah, the ignorance of youth.*

"Five young men have been murdered. It's not hunting season. That's not until next year. What changed?" I had scanned through enough of the pages of the book before Gabriel had started up with his antics to ask a couple of questions before leaving this young man to ponder the sins of his people.

"He knows enough about our ways. He won't ask questions which have nothing to do with him." Eyes shut, a condescending smile on his face.

To ask who would put me ten steps back, and I needed to create rapport. "He isn't here."

Henry laughed until he coughed. "By now he's aware of my abduction. He will look for me, wouldn't risk his secrets coming out."

"The thing is, Henry, no one has contacted him. Your father and the other Originals believe you're the latest victim of the person who murdered the other five young men. They're searching the woods for your body as we speak." Eli dragged a crate closer and positioned it next to me.

While I had slept, Eli had monitored the activity on the farm. "They don't have a clue that their precious guide to life is missing. What will happen if it isn't returned before tonight's celebration?"

"They will contact him. He will send his people. They will kill you. The chair you're sitting on, where do you suppose it came from? How do you think it came to be here?"

"He doesn't know we're here, and your family thinks you're dead." I leaned back in the chair in question and crossed my arms over my stomach. Time to try a different approach. "If we feared him, would you be here?"

"Oh, but he does, he knows everything. He's your world's version of me." He stretched out his leg, his teeth still on display. "You have no idea who I am. Fools."

Brainwashed? Too big for your size eight men's shoes? "Has it occurred to you we are working for him?"

Henry shrugged; the sneer no longer as pungent.

"Enlighten us as to whom we have the honour of meeting then. As you won't become a true Original until the current have left to become the guardians of Pepper Gorge," Eli said.

"I'm born who I am."

"You're the preacher's prodigy." I almost applauded myself when the smile slid from his face.

"Not a prodigy, I am who I am."

Tired, and with a corner of my stomach not filled, I pushed to my feet. "Look, Henry, this is how it works in the real world and not your backwoods, your parents are cousins or siblings, little farm. You learn what you need to learn from the Originals before you, and the one who follows you will learn from you." I had read more than I gave myself credit for. "It's what we, in the real world, call a prodigy. A student, if you will. As long as the current preacher leads your little DNA sharing group, you, my friend, are not the preacher."

Eli placed his hand on my back and tapped a finger against my spine. It irritated me more than it calmed me, but I sat down.

"This is the problem with your world. Women aren't allowed to speak to men like this. How dare you?"

"A man?" I laughed at his fluff-covered face. "How old are you?"

"Eighteen." The confidence in his voice made me choke on another laugh.

"You're a child. You keep referring to *our world*, yet you live in the middle of this country. I get it, Henry, this is your life, your entire world, but they raised you to believe lies as truth. To allow your fellow young women to be raped for money, hunters abducting women to bring to your farm. A part of you has to realise it's wrong."

Eli placed his hand on my arm and squeezed; the heat spreading throughout my body refused my mouth to keep shut. "Nicol will be raped tonight, at your so-called celebration. Does she know her virginity is for sale?"

"How else will she prove her worth?"

Thirty-one

Henry was raised to never ask questions, to abide by the laws his forefathers had written and proclaimed law. As I stared over the forest towards the ravine, I wondered if we aren't all the same at his age. Then again, technology gives us other input and not only the rules of our parents. With the dawn of social media, a lot changed for people; it made the lonely feel connected, gave us a place to showcase our highs, and sometimes, if you're authentic, your lows. It became the place to show others that their lives lacked what we showcase as reality when more often than not, it's a smokescreen. Teenagers are led to believe they should measure their worth in virtual likes, and not in what they contribute to society. It created a breeding ground for hate and trolls to spew hurtful words with no ramifications. Cowards hiding behind anonymity.

These are only a few of the reasons I don't have a profile on any platform. My life is mine, my highs, my lows. I am who I am and don't need validation from people liking a photo or a post while they sit on the toilet.

The flip side is that the internet brought us the ability to research any matter we wish to gain knowledge on, for better or for worse. The people of Pepper Gorge didn't have this luxury. Yet someone in their midst used the dark web to sell young women's virginities.

Sevens Hunter used the same technology to bring attention to the farm. Perhaps posting his own murders for the world to see. Why would he slaughter innocent young men? Why not rather annihilate the Originals?

Five young men had been murdered, that we knew of. Five Originals. Five men. Henry, the son of an Original, their future leader as the preacher.

The back door opened, and I cringed, desperate to focus on Pepper Gorge rather than going another round with Gabriel.

"They cancelled the celebration, the four cars left six minutes ago." Eli stepped closer.

"Did they cancel because of Henry's disappearance?"

"No." Eli took the chair to my left. He lowered his voice, "Someone tipped them off."

I turned to him, trying to read his eyes. "Not about Henry's abduction?"

He shook his head, his eyes locked on mine.

"They know we are on to them. Who?"

Eli's eyebrows lifted as he shrugged.

Gabriel or Tom? I returned my focus to the trees. Gabriel? Plausible, but what would he gain if something happened to me, or the child he believed would validate his existence? Tom had mentioned no prior knowledge of Pepper Gorge. What could he gain from informing people he had never met that we had their future preacher locked in a steel cage?

"How?" I asked.

"A phone call."

So much for their way of life being free of electronics. "Who took the call?"

"A certain Mister Metzger."

I shook my head. "That doesn't make sense, they should all have the same surname."

Eli stood and walked to the edge of the porch. "Unless they go by their role in the community."

In my ear, a throat cleared. "Metzger is German for butcher," Quinn said.

I tried to remember whether Eli spoke German. He knew I didn't, only a word here and there, and more swear words than conversational. Eli turned to face me. "Butcher in German."

"There aren't enough cattle and livestock to justify having a butcher." Henry's words filled my mind. *The meat tastes off.* "Eli, are they...?"

"From the little we have learned about them, maybe. In the

book it states nothing is to be wasted."

Confused, I marched into the house, heading straight to the dining room. I ignored Tom's question. The book lay open on the table. On the screens, life on the farm continued as per their normal. Nothing about that place was normal. Not the hunting, not the blood sports, not orchestrating the rapes of young girls who should learn about make-up and dreaming about going to university and their lives beyond their parental homes.

Hours passed, the book a longer read than expected. No illustrations apart from the family tree, which was a succession line for the five positions within the community. I wondered if their decision to use different surnames was nothing more than a desire to be individuals or to keep the truth from their paying customers.

Parson the preacher. Metzger the butcher. Bailey, Feldman, and Dresser remained.

Eli placed a cup of coffee to my left, and as I lifted my eyes from the words which blurred, I realised night had come. The wall clock remained a visual reminder I was running out of time to meet my self-imposed deadline. *Five hours left.*

"That first day when I was in the restroom, Nicol said she would be Mrs Bailey. Henry is her friend's brother. How can he become the preacher if he's the son of the person responsible for the farm's security?" I had done a quick internet search for the meaning and origin of the surnames the Originals had chosen years ago. Tom had kept a watchful eye, as if I planned an escape. Not before he kneeled in front of me, the muzzle of my Glock pressed against his forehead.

"Are you thinking what I'm thinking?" Eli asked, and positioned the mug closer to my hand. I thanked him and took a sip. No caffeine to help my exhausted brain.

"Don't stand too close to Henry's cage."

Eli laughed, shaking his head. "Perhaps it's time we take our friend his dinner."

"No meat for him."

"I think it's safe to say neither of us can stomach the sight of meat tonight. Lizzie made minestrone soup."

A sigh of relief escaped me. Not until the possibility of meat laying on my plate came up had I considered the reality. "Eli, we ate there the first time."

He placed his hand on my shoulder. "Neither of us ate any protein other than eggs. Unless they have some freaks living there, you don't get those kinds of eggs from people."

Henry lay on his side, facing the opposite wall when we entered the garage, his prison, Gabriel's arsenal. Eli slid the plate through the bars; I picked up on his quick retreat. It's not like us meat-eaters take a bite out of every cow, sheep, chicken or fish we see. Then again, there are cultures who consume living creatures. I understood Eli's reluctance to find out for himself whether Henry and his people shared in these practices.

"Your dinner," I said, taking a seat. A pungent smell hung in the air. The kind one expects when a plastic bucket serves as a toilet.

Henry didn't move. Eli glanced at me and stepped closer to the cage.

"Don't." I scoured the shelves and found a broom behind the wooden pallet stacked with the bullets which had been the catalyst to Gabriel attacking me. May have been my filterless mouth.

Without time to sharpen the end, I pushed the stick through the bars and poked a young man. This was no time for a dirty joke about how I had spent some of my nights at university. Henry didn't make a sound, no matter the force I put behind the thrust of the broom. Eli placed his hand on my arm; the broom shook.

"He's dead, Fin." Eli dragged the cage away from the wall and stepped around to get a better look at Henry's face. "Foam at his mouth. He's been dead a while."

"We brought him lunch at 1300 hours. A little over six hours later, five since we left him. How can he be dead? We gave him food, water, he appeared in good health."

"Cyanide doesn't care about any of that." Eli dropped into a squat and stared at Henry's lifeless face.

"Cyanide?"

"Yes, it's over there on the second shelf to the left of the door. It's too high for you to see." Eli, being a good twenty-five centimetres taller than me, saw things I couldn't. More often than not, being on the shorter side counts against me.

"He didn't walk out of the cage and take it himself."

"No, he did not. The lock is still in place."

"Eli?"

He lifted his arm to his face, the wristwatch a constant reminder we were never alone. "I don't know what to tell you."

"Did you do this?" I stepped backwards, away from him, away from death caged between us.

"Come on, Fin, I want answers as much as you do." He nodded with a smile.

The tactical knives were not out of my line of sight. I grabbed a K-bar and marched back to Eli. *This ends now.*

"Maybe Henry had a capsule hidden in a capped tooth. I've known a few people who keep poison in their mouths." Eli rolled his eyes as I closed the distance between us.

"I've had enough of your lies. You did this, killing an innocent young man for fun. Eli, who are you?" The blade sliced through the air.

"Calm down, Finley! I didn't kill him."

"The hell you didn't. Gabriel isn't here, and you're the only other person who knows the code to unlock the door. You want me to believe my sister, or Tom, could be responsible for this? Lizzie is my height, and, as you know, she isn't the type to kill for fun. Unlike you and your best friend."

The blade angled towards his chest. Eli lifted his arm. I advanced. Eli didn't retreat. One cut; it fell to the floor.

The sound of destruction filled the silence.

Thirty-two

Gabriel returned as Eli and I stepped out of the garage, leaving Henry's body to continue doing what dead bodies do. From the dining room window, I watched him unload the SUV. The only person who wasn't there when Henry had died.

Gabriel carried in more bags of clothes than either Lizzie or I needed. I had no intention of being in this place much longer and would need an extra suitcase to get all of it back to Marcel. For our return I would fly, no way I would drive back in Gabriel's SUV, locked in a confined space with him. Where would Tom sit? Between Lizzie and me? No.

If things didn't work out for Gabriel in hell, personal shopping might be his forte. He had listened when I told him black, maybe dark grey or navy if he couldn't find black. Lizzie beamed at the variety of colours of clothing he had bought her. How different can two sisters be?

Henry's murder hung heavy in the air as we ate dinner. For the baby, I forced myself to eat the soup. Someone sitting at the kitchen island had killed a defenceless young man whose only mistake had been to be born into a cult. After dinner, I returned to the dining room while Gabriel and Tom cleaned and loaded the dishwasher. I monitored the screens, realising somewhere, someone did the same thing. Watching us, watching me. Not Quinn, or Aidan, but someone complacent in the destruction of our lives. A faceless entity. The Puppet Master. Finley Williams-Walker, nothing more than a caged animal people watched for their entertainment. Even as a child, I hated going to the zoo.

"Do you need anything before I go to bed?" Lizzie placed her hands on my shoulders. "Is this better than how you normally hunt murderers?"

I covered her hands with mine. "No. This isn't my world, Liz. One day I will tell you what hunting them is like, but it's not this. I can't get inside their minds if I see them the whole time. This book is too big."

The wall clock mocked me; three hours left to midnight. The answers I had found only opened the door to more questions. I couldn't go back to Pepper Gorge and get answers the only way I knew how. Not without risking my child's life. The ache for Aidan intensified with every passing minute. To talk it through with him brought clarity. I didn't even know where he was or the danger he faced.

"Have Eli carry the book to your room. Sitting here, you're getting too much input. It's what I do when I need to make decisions or work on a new formulation with the Research and Development team. We step away from it all, away from our computers, phones and just breathe, think it through. Finley, I...I will bring you hot chocolate."

"Liz, have you been to the garage?"

"No."

I squeezed her hands and pushed to my feet. The two-dimensional people in front of me were turning in for the night. Nicol had served dinner with a smile on her usually solemn, typical teenager face. To escape rape would put a smile on anyone's face. I wondered if she saw it the way I do.

In self-defence, I hoped Lizzie would be able to take a life, but she doesn't have it in her to kill, not in cold blood. Gabriel had been away since lunch.

Later, as I sipped the hot chocolate Lizzie had brought, I wondered what motive Tom could have for killing a person he had never met.

Quinn answered when I said Aidan's name. "Dr Walker can't come to the phone right now."

My heart sank, my knees gave in, and I sank onto the white tiles covering the bathroom floor. "Not now, Quinn. There's a body in the garage. I'm not convinced I know all there is to know about Pepper Gorge, but more than anything, I miss my husband." My hands covered my belly, I had never been so frustrated. If only I could get into my car, take a drive to the lake house, and clear my head. Here I sat, a prisoner, wondering when I would suffer Henry's fate. Powerless to protect the child growing inside me. Unable to hear my Aidan's voice.

"I'm sorry, I'm trying to lift your mood, that's all."

"Thank you for trying, but now isn't the time. I need Aidan, I need to talk this through with him."

"Finley, he isn't in a position to talk to you, but I am. Maybe I can add more than Aidan. I see what you see, hear what you hear. Good job on Eli's wristwatch."

"Hasn't helped at all, as we haven't had time to talk again since we left the garage."

"Where is your mind at?"

"Everywhere. That's why I need to hear Aidan's voice and know he's safe, so that I can focus on trying to make sense of all the puzzle pieces scattered throughout the book."

"I didn't have enough time to read all of it. I took a few photos of interesting looking pages and read them later. Left me more confused."

"Most of it's a record of the marriages and births of the Originals. Let's start with that. It makes little sense, considering how royal families have been doing it for ages with all their cousin marriages and uncles marrying their nieces, etcetera."

Quinn listened as I told her about the fornication laws penned in the book which is the guide to life for those confined to Pepper Gorge. Before handing over the reins to the next generation, the current Originals school their prodigies in their ways, as I had said to Henry. Originals may not have sex with their Original wives, yet they bear the children of the Originals before them. Uncles impregnate nieces. A practise which started when the first Originals set foot on Pepper Gorge. *No signs of inbreeding.*

Every Original wife bears only one child, always a son, destined to be the next Original. Five young men had been murdered. The next generation of Originals. Where did this leave Henry? "I need to check something."

After fifteen minutes I found the rule pertaining to what I suspected. Closing the bathroom door, I continued. "Henry had a fraternal twin brother. The boy Gabriel found looked enough like Henry to be his brother, but they weren't identical."

"How does hunting season work?"

"It's nothing more than the future Originals staking their superiority and mating rights over the other young men. Their half-brothers? Half-cousins? Point is, they send the hunters who survive hunting season into the world to abduct women and bring them back to Pepper Gorge. A practise the first Henry Andrews' grandson started. He was the third preacher. This is what I had wanted to ask Henry tonight. If he's a Bailey, how can he become the preacher? The preacher goes by the surname Parson."

"Perhaps you haven't gotten to that part in the book yet. How many laws can one small community have?"

"You would be surprised, and I think the current holders of power aren't penning all of their rules. Over the years, the penmanship obviously changed, no one lives forever, even though Henry believed he would." Did he realise eternity wasn't in his cards as the cyanide had forced his organs to shut down? Something else Henry had said sounded in my mind. "Quinn, who owns this house?"

"You need to get to bed, these late nights aren't doing you or the baby any good. Things might look different in the morning."

"Why won't you give me a name?" My eyes burned, and I blinked to regain focus. The yawn caught me off guard. "Last we spoke, you mentioned Gabriel's employer owns it. Give me a name."

"Above my clearance level. I'm sorry, Finley, when you learn the truth, you will understand why I couldn't tell you. Nothing personal, pet."

I raised my fist in front of my face and extended one finger. The sound of her laugh cleared the fog in my mind and heart.

If not for Quinn, I don't know how I would've coped with being held prisoner again. Lizzie and I were free to roam the property, but never to leave unaccompanied. This time I wasn't hurt or left chained, bleeding in the dust and dirt. Some nights I awoke to my screams, reminded of the filth which had once covered my body, my soul. Without fail, Aidan would take my hand and lead me to the shower where he washed me and blow-dried my hair before taking my hand and leading me back to bed where he held me until sleep returned.

"Finley, go to bed. We can discuss Pepper Gorge tomorrow morning."

"I don't think we will know the extent of what's happening there now, or over the last couple of years, unless we talk to the people."

"I can't wait until we have resolved our other matter and head out there. I'm going with you."

I didn't consider the shambles of my own life more pressing than the lives of the people being controlled, boys killed to assert dominance, girls raped to prove their worth, young women brought there to be murdered. "I need to end this for them, Quinn."

"And you will. For now, rest; things might look different in the morning."

"Nothing is to be wasted." I quoted the book. Bile rose in my throat. "They are rapists, killers, torturers. And cannibals."

Thirty-three

Somewhere over Europe. Location: Classified.

The sun would rise soon, casting its light on a country whose people couldn't fathom the magnitude of what had transpired while they slept. The monster in their nightmares had forever changed. Same face, different values, vision, and outcome for the people. Freedom, economic stability, personal security – things most take for granted.

The man stirred; Etomine-induced sleep kept him. The dosages administered at predetermined intervals; the injections given by the only person on the team with a medical degree, the others no less capable. They had all done it before.

Aidan had known his face, but sitting across from him, he expected more. Maybe it would change once the Puppet Master opened his eyes.

"We're ready for takeoff." Ryan settled in the seat next to him and fastened his seat belt. "Are you?"

Aidan kept his focus on the sleeper. "Am I what?"

"Ready to hear what he has to say?"

"It's possible he won't tell us a thing."

"Yes, well, there are ways around that, aren't there? Finley has her own way of getting people to talk."

"I don't want her to hear what he has to say. She won't believe he's behind it. Ruastan is free. My wife will be bound by the weight of truth forever."

Ryan nodded and closed his eyes. It had been a long night. To the front of the plane, Heather sat with Liam, Rowan in the pilot's seat. They only needed Nathan and Finley and they could head off to one of their secret locations for a family vacation. A place where they can, for a few days, isolate themselves from the horrors of the world, even though they would never be able to forget, no matter where they went.

Aidan turned towards the window, unable to stomach the sight of the man responsible for the destruction of his wife's life. For now, he found solace in every member of the team being safe. The operation had gone down with no injuries or casualties.

"You need to make peace with whatever she decides to do to him. I won't stand in her way, neither will your mother. This despicable creature deserves far worse than what Finley can do to him."

"Have you spoken to Sergio?"

"No, we won't unless it's necessary. He's no longer Sergio, remember?"

Aidan turned his head and faced his father. Unable to stop himself, he rolled his eyes.

"Yes, I know. You were the one who came up with this strategy which has not failed us once over the years. You miss her more than you're letting on."

"The eye roll gave it away?"

"Correct. Once we reach cruising altitude, I will get us some coffee and croissants and then I think we should both sleep. This isn't over, not yet."

Aidan nodded. Despite the knot in his stomach, coffee and food sounded good. Breakfast in bed with Finley sounded better, making love to her until they were both starving again for food. His appetite for her would never be satiated. Those were the moments he would cherish forever, the times they could simply be. Not a doctor and a profiler. Not a sniper and a vigilante. Aidan and Finley. Husband and wife. Partners in all of it, even the burden of truth she stood on the verge of picking up and living with for the rest of her life. If he could spare her, he would, but she needed to know what had happened the night her parents had died. She deserved the truth.

The Puppet Master stirred. For the first time in weeks, joy filled Aidan's soul. This part he liked. The split second it took for them to realise they were about to pay for all they had done. When Finley learned the extent of his depravity, she would make him pay for all of it. This man had destroyed the lives of countless people. Never again would any person suffer because of his sadism, or his lust for power.

Startled, the Puppet Master awoke, scanned his surroundings, his eyes coming to rest on Aidan's. Aidan decided against greeting the prisoner in his native tongue.

Thirty-four

A knock on the door; again, I opened my eyes to a room that wasn't mine. Not even the clothes Gabriel had bought I considered mine. I needed it to cover my growing bump and hide the baby Glock. I could donate them as soon as I was free. Burning them would be a waste and only add to the filth enlarging the hole in the ozone. Again, the knock. "Yes?"

"Fin, I brought you lunch," Lizzie said from the other side of the door.

I pushed off the bed and walked to the door. Adequate rest and waking up to my sister's voice lifted my mood. Until I remembered Henry's body lay in the garage as I reached for the door handle. "What happened to breakfast?"

My sister's smile greeted me, but not her normal teeth-baring smile. A grin might be more accurate. "You slept through it." She pressed her lips to my cheek and stepped inside.

"I need to speak to Eli."

Lizzie placed the tray on the bed, keeping her back to me. "He should be back soon."

"Where did he go?"

"They took the body to Pepper Gorge."

"What?"

Lizzie's hands covered her face. I moved closer and wrapped my arms around her, placing my forehead against the back of her head. "You saw the body, didn't you?"

She shook her head. "They carried him out in a body bag."

Those I didn't see in the garage, but then again neither had I seen the cyanide. I wondered what else I had missed. *Damn genetics.* "I'm sorry, Liz."

"When can we go home?" She snorted a laugh. "Oh yes, we don't have homes to return to."

I hugged her tighter and asked her to join me in the bathroom. After sleeping what I calculated to be close to nine hours, there were things for me to take care of. Lizzie followed and closed the door. I held up my hand. "Quinn, you said things will look better this morning. I'm not seeing it."

"Because you haven't been outside yet, sleepyhead."

"You told me to get rest, so that's what I did." Without trying to.

"This is weird," Lizzie said, a mix of confusion and curiosity on her face. "Tell her I say hello."

"Tell Liz I say hello back."

I lifted my hands, palms facing the ceiling. "We're not playing telephone here, ladies. Focus. Pepper Gorge. Our lives in ruins. My husband is – Quinn knows where but won't tell me. And we woke up to another day in this hellhole. I'm done. Quinn, you tell Aidan, or Ryan, or Heather, I don't care who, this ends today. I can't do this anymore. As long as I'm a prisoner here, I can't get the authorities involved and launch a full-scale investigation into Pepper Gorge. We must close that place down before they hold another celebration. Which is a sugar-coated word for a rape orgy."

Thirty-five

A gentle breeze rustled the leaves, the sound a reminder of memories made here. Even the bad memories were good. A few metres to his left, the spot where he had saved her life, and ended that of the Angel Taker. A few metres to his right, where he had stood when one of the Scarecrows had turned his gun on him, the day Finley had saved his life. The oversized leather couch in the living room, where they had made love the first time. By accident. Still his fondest memory of the times they had spent here.

The house had been purchased by her parents years before and left to her in their will. What was once her father's wine cellar, she had turned into an interrogation room. Some might call it a torture chamber; Aidan understood her reasons. One of the many things he loves about her – she has the stomach to do what's needed to protect the innocent people of this world. His wife's valorous deeds know no bounds.

Aidan stared out over the lake's calm, dark water. He loved this place almost as much as Finley. The reason Tom didn't give the order for it to be destroyed, Nathan Walker had found. Lizzie would've, if she knew. He clenched his fists and pushed them into the front pockets of his jeans. The answer Nathan found was never hidden here.

He would've liked Duncan Williams even more had he been able to meet him, and Victoria. Remarkable people, philanthropists, loving parents, both brilliant in their own rights. They had given their all for their fellow man, their greatest sacrifice for their daughters.

The sun warmed the top of his head and he repositioned the sunglasses over his eyes. It was a beautiful day. The air filled with the scent of the coming rain blowing in from Marcel.

If only Finley stood next to him. He ached to hold her, but not more than his need to keep the truth from her. As Aidan promised, they had neutralised the Puppet Master. His fate now lay in Finley's beautiful, deadly hands.

Halfway down the jetty, Aidan stopped and turned to face the house. "I'm sorry, Fin, for destroying this place filled with your best childhood memories. Our memories. It should never have come to this. The lies we tell are more often than not to protect. I will protect you and our child until my dying breath. I love you."

Finley didn't hear his words. She was in the bathroom speaking to Lizzie and Quinn. Discussing another horror inflicted by men. The puppet masters of Pepper Gorge.

Aidan smiled, remembering the moment he had laid eyes on her that night in Alias; a lifetime ago. In that moment, he knew life with her would never be boring. An air of mischief, adventure and passion had hung around her that night, and with every passing day it intensified. A lifetime with her would never be enough.

With heavy feet he returned to the house, and one last time he checked the C4 and wires.

A deafening sound filled the silence.

Birds scattered.

Debris and meat tore through the air.

As dust, dirt and smoke cleared, the first raindrops fell.

Thirty-six

Lizzie and Quinn spoke at the same time. "A what?"

The last thing I had read before falling asleep were the details of what their celebrations entailed. A grotesque annual induction of the young women into their version of womanhood.

I lowered myself onto the side of the bath and dropped my gaze to the floor. "They force the girls to perform sexual acts on each other, to the point of orgasm, and then the Originals take turns raping the girls. Their laws state only in the presence of a man may a woman orgasm, if stimulated by another woman." I couldn't call teenaged girls women; they are children.

Lizzie gagged. "What if they orgasm during sex?"

"They're killed. In the Originals' eyes, the five perverted men who rule every generation, women who orgasm during intercourse are filled with a spirit of lust. The only way to cast the spirit out of their community is to kill said woman."

"That makes no sense. Sometimes it's more physiological than emotional. I've read of women who orgasm while being raped and the horrendous, devastating impact it has on them. They feel as if their bodies have betrayed them."

"Women are tools for procreating, whose sole purpose is to serve men." Quinn added, "*That* I read in their book."

"The only slight positive, even if I can call it that, is that the women who are killed because of this escape being served up as meat. They're burned alive and buried high up in the mountain. If they don't perform the burning ritual, the spirit of lust will find another female host." I dragged my hands down my face.

"What's wrong?"

"Other than what I just told you?" I asked Quinn.

"Yes."

"I don't think they kill these women as they make the others believe."

"I don't understand."

"I skipped a few pages last night, before I read this part, but there's a detailed list of things a man needs to adhere to in order to either be allowed as a guest, or to have a woman sold to him. One specific point is far worse than the others. Most are based on financial means, social standing, which I think is to ensure they won't want the truth about their dealings with, and actions at, Pepper Gorge coming to light. My biggest concern is another list – names of the women they claim had the spirit of lust in them. I have no way to confirm my suspicion, but I think they're faking the number of women who orgasm. The burning ritual is a private event, attended by no one other than the Originals. What if they're doing something else to these women?"

"For now, let's focus on the men. What's the one thing they need to do?" Quinn asked as Lizzie took a seat next to me and placed her arm around my waist.

"A man has to impregnate the girl he buys. The child is to stay at Pepper Gorge. Once this poor young woman, child, gives birth, he may take her to do with as he pleases."

"That doesn't make sense. You know more than I do on the matter. Can your average fertile woman conceive every month?"

"No, Quinn. All things considered, these girls have a thirty percent chance of falling pregnant in any cycle. The men can't stay indefinitely. They might arrange the rapes during the time the girls are most likely to ovulate. Still thirty percent. It's possible they sell the girls multiple times to be raped by different men every month, lying about them being virgins."

Who would've guessed my infertility would help answer questions about a cult? Even less so talking to someone in my ear, while sitting in an abattoir-inspired bathroom with Lizzie next to me.

My sister who had known for years who I am, what I'm capable of.

"I wouldn't put it past them to do just that. But, if they sold some of these women, and they made it out, why haven't any of them escaped and gone to the police?" Quinn asked.

"Because they're never free. They're slaves to the teachings of the Originals; they don't see themselves the way we do. They don't realise they're victims of a sick cult, of twisted individuals who have been free to do this for 209 years."

I drew a deep breath. Defeat and frustration made way for a sick feeling in the pit of my stomach. "The only record of women being sold started three generations ago. Give or take a few years, but I estimate seventy-five years ago, based on the handwriting. I don't know how many of their practices are still in play, just no record of it being kept. The outsider men who were at Pepper Gorge, one of them is the captain of the Coopersville Police Department. The other is a well-known athlete and the other two are from prominent families, with international businesses."

Lizzie leaned her head against mine. "This may explain why we haven't seen the deformities you would expect after so many generations of inbreeding."

"All the women are married to an Original. Marriages to the soldiers or the hunters are prohibited. Although, the daughters, slash first wives, of Originals may have sex with the soldiers. But only twice a year."

"No wonder that bloody book is so big. They have an insane number of rules." Quinn exhaled hard.

"Most of them are rules about when you may walk outside, dress codes, work allocations, what they may eat and on which day of the week. A vast number of pages went into the ramblings of who I believe was the third preacher."

"Have you figured out why Henry, a Bailey, could become a Parson?" Quinn asked.

"They're given their surnames when they take on the responsibilities of their role. So, their surnames are more an indication of their role in the community rather than the way we use it."

"What happens to their predecessors? Are they killed off, or allowed to live in the free world?"

"They send the previous Originals into the forest to live the remainder of their years close to nature."

"And the women? I didn't see any old people walking around town." Lizzie tilted her head back.

"They are to, one last time, give their all in service to the community."

"The butcher." Quinn hissed.

"Yes." Thankfully, Lizzie hadn't brought me chicken or pork for lunch.

Tom called us to the living room with a strange expression on his face. He waited for Lizzie and me to take a seat before switching off the television. "You can pack your things. Tomorrow morning, we'll head back to Marcel. It's time to go home."

I grabbed Lizzie's hand, confusion rendering me mute.

"Uncle Tom, I don't understand, why now?" Lizzie asked.

"The threat took care of itself."

"You're not making any sense." Lizzie placed her other hand over mine. "Get to the point, what happened?"

Tom smiled, unveiled victory in his eyes. "You took off your ring, said you're done with him. Whether you meant it or not, we will never know."

"Tom, stop your petty games and tell her." Eli placed his hand on my shoulder.

"My dearest Finley, it pains me to tell you this, it does," he said with a sneer, "Aidan Walker is dead."

Four words stopped time.

I pushed to my feet, desperate to keep my balance as the room spun. With my arms wrapped around my stomach, I made my way out of the room, away from *them*.

My lungs ached for air, but I forced out the words. "I need to be with my in-laws."

"They're not your family, Finley; we are. We've always been your family," Tom said to my back as I headed to where the keys to Gabriel's SUV lay on the kitchen island.

"Ley, wait. You're in no state to drive." He ran up behind me, placed his hand on my shoulder. All I could feel was the gun nestled against my breasts. I ached to unleash my rage through its barrel.

"Take your hands off me!" He complied, and I continued in a haze towards the kitchen.

"Ley, calm down. We're free. We can go home, start our lives over. Prepare for the birth of our child."

This time the projectile did not hit the wall. Blood trickled from his right eyebrow. Who would've guessed my aim would be better with keys than a mug?

Gabriel pressed a dishcloth to the miniscule wound. "Nice arm."

"You go wherever you want and do whatever the hell you want. I'm going to my in-laws. Their son died. They need me to be there for them. I have to be at Aidan's funeral, see for myself that he's dead and then, only then, will I think about my future, and my child's."

"There isn't much to bury," Tom said from the living room. "He blew himself up, took your lake house with him."

I stared up at Gabriel. *The truth always comes out.* My nails dug into my palms as anger tore through me. If I had to stay in that house for one more night, I would kill them with my bare hands. "I'm leaving, Lizzie will come with me, Eli can take us. Then you have your friend to keep an eye on us."

"Ley, let me come with you. You need me to be there for you. After the funeral, we can start our life. You're free to love me again."

The laughter came out of nowhere. "My husband is dead. The man I loved, and who I learned never existed as I knew him, has killed himself, and you're standing here talking about us. Love you *again*? I never loved you." I turned my back on the assassin, a dumb move I realised the second I did it. "If you love me at all, if this child means anything to you, let me go and get the closure I need. The closure I deserve."

"Okay."

I spun around, ready to keep fighting, but the look of resolution in his eyes caught me off guard. "Okay?"

"Yes, go. Do what you have to. Grieve for the life you hoped to share with him and heal. When our child is born, he will need his mother's full attention. He needs you to be whole."

A sadness filled his eyes and an understanding I had never seen before. The empath in me had to know. "What happened to your mother, after your father's arrest?"

"She didn't stop to take stock of her life, she had me and my brother to think about, she thought returning to Tel Aviv would fix her."

"I'm sorry."

Gabriel laughed, the sound hoarse.

"I'm sorry, Gabriel, for the little boy who had to find out his father wasn't a hero. You lost him when you learned the truth, and in many ways, your mother."

He nodded, averting my gaze.

"Where's your brother?"

Gabriel shrugged, the movement pained.

"I'm sorry you lost your brother, too."

He lifted his eyes to mine and stepped forward. "I can't lose you again. Will you come back to me?"

I reached for his face, my smile sincere, the reasons for it not. "I promise you that we will see each other again. Thank you for understanding this is something I must do. I never got to bury my parents; I need this for more reasons than I can count."

With his thumbs, Gabriel wiped away the tears streaming down my cheeks and pressed his lips to my forehead. "I'm sorry you're hurting. I hope you allow me to make you happy again, even if it's only to be the best father our son can wish for. Ley, I'm many terrible things, but I love this child." Again, his lips connected with my skin. "I love you."

I nodded and stepped back. "Thank you for not fighting me on this." He had, but I was winning, so I kept my mouth shut.

Aidan had died in order for me to leave that mountainous hell.

My biggest nightmare became my reality.

Thirty-seven

The entire drive to the Douglasdale airport, the duration of the flight, and from the airfield to my in-laws' house in Wild Bay, I didn't breathe. The pressure on my chest made it impossible. Lizzie reminded me countless times to breathe, if not for me, for the baby. Eli had arranged for a private jet to transport us from Douglasdale to the airfield a few kilometres outside Wild Bay. A car waited for us at the airfield. When I saw the driver, I realised Quinn hadn't said a single word since we last spoke. I wondered where she was and when she had heard of Aidan's death.

The front door opened as I walked up the stairs. Ryan and Heather's eyes were not swollen or red like mine. They both hugged me to the point of making me feel like a toddler's favourite stuffed animal, then did the same to Lizzie and Eli.

"Fin, go shower or take a nap. I prepared your room," Heather said.

I needed to be alone. As much as I enjoy my people, and their company, the only person I can stomach spending every minute with is Aidan. Was Aidan.

The room we all referred to as mine and Aidan's since before we were married, yet it had been the same room in which he had slept as a boy. The Walkers' home away from home. A mansion, not unlike the one I grew up in. Although, none of our houses came with an underground shooting range or the state of the art security system which most presidential homes lack. The places state secrets are kept and C-Max prisons don't have what's considered standard in this home. The cherry on top of this black-ops cake – a private beach with underwater motion detectors.

I closed the door and stepped closer to the king-sized bed.

A bed bought for Aidan and me before our first weekend spent with his family. He had refused to let me sleep in the bed in which Kate had. I never replaced her, not in the family, not in his life. The fact that they appreciated Kate had strengthened my respect for the Walkers and Aidan. Regardless of their broken marriage, she had been his friend, and the mother of his first child.

I stroked my belly, desperate to touch a part of Aidan. Our child – his biggest legacy, living proof of our love, our commitment to each other, and the promise we had made to keep fighting to right the wrongs.

"Hello, Wife."

I spun around, lost my footing, and stumbled backwards onto the bed. Aidan rushed to my side and pressed his mouth to mine before I could savour the moment. *He will always protect me from my nightmares.*

I eased him back and cradled his beautiful face between my palms. His boyish grin undid the knot in my stomach. The depth of his eyes restored my breathing. His scent filled my soul, pushing the weight of the fear from my shoulders that I had been carrying since the last time I saw him.

"To tell you I missed you won't do justice to what I experienced the days we spent apart," he whispered. "Lay on your back." His eyes sparkled with mischief and joy.

"Dr Walker, I believe this is a high-risk pregnancy and we can't have sex."

He rolled his eyes. I laughed. A raw, real, zestful sound filled the room. I realised I hadn't truly laughed since I last saw him. The dark cloud which hung over me had altered even my laugh. "We need to talk about Pepper Gorge. The Puppet Master. All of it."

Aidan pressed his mouth to mine and drew a deep breath. "Yes, but first I want to kiss my daughter and tell Ainsley how much I love her." He pressed my shoulders down on the bed, lifted my shirt and placed his mouth against my skin. "I'm so proud of Mommy for keeping you safe. I love you, Ainsley.

You're the culmination of answered prayers, of hope, and the love I have for your mother, and she for me. Baby girl, may you know that all of this, all of what we still need to do, is for you, my love. To give you a life filled with freedom, without fear, the best Mommy and I can do."

I made no attempt to wipe the moisture from my stomach, or my cheeks. I had only seen Aidan cry once, the day he had told me how he had lost his unborn son. "She's the luckiest child in the world to have you as a father. Thank you for being you, Aidan Walker, love of my life. My life will always be you, Ainsley, us. Typical, a few seconds with you and I already feel lighter. Grounded. Whole."

Aidan kissed my belly and moved upwards till his lips met mine. "I know, Mrs Walker, I feel it too. Let's go do a sonar because I need to see for myself that you're both okay."

He helped me up, not that I needed it. In months to come, I would ask for it. "And you just happen to have a sonar machine standing around here somewhere."

"My parents didn't, but they got everything ready the day I disappeared. Followed my instructions to a tee."

"You knew we would end up here, together?" Aidan brushed away my tears with the back of his fingers.

"I promised you." He eased me back down, lifted my shirt, and again kissed my stomach until I was breathless.

"Your beard is tickling me."

"Good."

I ran my fingers through his hair and as he lifted his eyes to mine, I saw what the weeks apart had done to him. Unshaven, dark circles prominent under his eyes. "Thank you."

"Are you thanking me for the beard or for tickling you? Or kissing our girl because you can't?"

My head fell back on a heavy sigh. Aidan got to his feet and asked me to turn on my side. He held me, drawing lazy circles over my tummy with his fingertips, and feathering kisses along my neck.

"You look as tired as I feel." His warmth spread to every

part of me. I had never felt safer.

"You don't look your vibrant self either."

"Way to compliment your wife, dude."

Aidan pressed his face to my nape. His entire body shook. "Back to the dude?"

"Yes, I've missed my dude. Ached for him, for this, to breathe and feel safe. It isn't over. When will you take care of Tom and Gabriel?"

"Already being transported to their forever home if you wish to leave them breathing."

I rolled away and turned to face him. Aidan placed his hand on my lower back and pulled me against him. My face pressed to the hollow of his neck. His scent brought an overwhelming calm. "How?"

"Minutes after they waved you off, they were both stung by insects and within seconds, they fell asleep."

"Mosquito drone thingy?"

"Not the name given to it by its creator, but yes. I prefer your name for it, it's shorter and an adequate description."

"You're mocking me, Mr Walker."

"I missed doing so, Mrs Walker." He pressed his lips to my forehead, tightening his hold.

"Not that I don't appreciate what you've done, but this is a little anti-climactic. No big shoot out, no chance of maiming them."

Aidan took a deep breath. "I couldn't risk another member of my team, under my command, getting injured or dying. Believe me, nothing would've pleased me more than to shoot those bastards down where they stood, but they can answer your questions. My sincere apologies for this plan not meeting your expectations, but just like I put your safety first, so I do that of my team."

I wiggled upwards and brushed my lips against his. "All this talk of your team, and safety, and you being in command, it's sexy," I whispered against his mouth.

Aidan pulled his head back. "Stop looking at me like that,

no sexy time for you, young lady."

"Hold on, I look exhausted, but at least you consider me to be a young lady? That isn't it. You don't want to tell me how much you enjoyed working with your father's organisation again. I won't be able to call you Dr Walker anymore. What should I call you now? Sir? Fearless leader? Big daddy?"

He pursed his lips. "Did you remove the *thingy* in your ear?"

"No, got used to it. Where's my imaginary friend?" I removed the earpiece and placed it on the bedside table. "Thingy?"

"Again, the correct name isn't as cute as what you call it."

"You're avoiding my question. You've never thought it cute when I name stuff what I want. For example—"

"Finley, did you destroy the earpiece?" One of his eyebrows raised.

"No."

"Then Quinn can still listen in." He reached past me and slammed his fist on the bedside table. "Could."

"Your future employment aside for the moment. Aidan, I think Tom killed the young man Gabriel abducted. Tom's the only one who had access if he knew the password to the lock. He had the means, but what could be his motive?"

"Tom went into the garage, we have footage of him entering, and seven minutes and thirty-nine seconds later, he exited."

"Why would he kill Henry? Did he place the call to Metzger to warn him?"

"You can ask him when you see him."

The longer we spoke, the more I realised we weren't out of the woods, not yet. "Where are they? And who is the Puppet Master?"

"All three of them are being kept in a secure location. When the time is right, we will go to said location and get the answers you deserve."

"Secure location meaning a black site?"

"Yes."

"How many of these secure locations does your father's

organisation own?" I traced the curve of his jaw with my fingertip and pressed my lips to his eyelids, cheeks, nose, ending at his mouth. A luscious full kiss which left me craving more of him. To be one with him.

"What was the question?"

I rolled my eyes at him and his eidetic memory. "Aidan, we need to end Pepper Gorge. I need to speak to Captain Taylor, he'll know who we can trust."

"He should be here within the hour. Quinn briefed him as per your request."

"Once the people there are safe, we can focus on Tom, Gabriel, and the Puppet Master."

Aidan pushed his fingers through my hair, his eyes fixed on mine. "You always put others ahead of yourself, your own needs. Have I told you it's one of the qualities I love most about you?"

"Let's go shower, before Captain Taylor gets here. Perhaps there's a way I can show you how much I love you, how much I missed you, without putting our baby in danger."

"Before you give me what I hope you're planning on giving me, I have something of yours."

"If it is what I think it is, I'm going to make you tremble like you always make me."

"I believe the only thing that will make you tremble right now is strawberry-flavoured anything. As far as I know, it doesn't taste like strawberries."

"I like the taste of your skin much better."

Aidan pushed off the bed and came around to my side, his hand extended. I stared up at him, remembering waking up every morning in that house, missing him to the point that my heart broke more and more each day.

"I'm not craving strawberries because of the pregnancy. The first morning we had breakfast together, you ordered strawberries and whipped cream with your pancakes. I looked like a rabid raccoon, with my mascara-smeared eyes and wet hair, as we had just gotten out of the pool. You came around the table, pulled me to my feet, and kissed me the same way you had kissed me the night before, as you had kissed me in the pool. You weren't kissing me to get me into bed, *you* took sex off the table, you weren't kissing me because I looked presentable. Aidan, you kissed me, the person I am without make-up, or dry and styled hair. You kissed me until my stomach could knot no further."

I reached for my husband's face, touching my fingertips to his lips. "Aidan, I craved you."

Thirty-eight

To sit around a table, share a meal, and make small talk with people you love is priceless. During dinner there was no talk of Pepper Gorge, or the hunt for the Puppet Master. We discussed everything and nothing. Heather had refused Lizzie and I help with anything. All she had said was, "My grandchildren need their mommies well rested. You two have been through so much," and kissed both of us on the forehead. They had accepted Lizzie as part of the family, and the feeling was mutual.

After dinner I found Aidan, Eli, and Ryan standing on the porch and joined them, even though they looked deep in conversation. It was too nice a night to be inside, no trees to obscure my view of the ocean illuminated by the full moon. My soul felt at rest, despite all of it not being behind us quite yet.

"Gentlemen, who will be the one to tell me how Eli came to be part of our team?" I asked, stretching my legs out on the couch.

"Eli, you do the honours. If not for you, we wouldn't have known." Ryan patted Eli's shoulder and joined me on the couch.

Eli and Aidan each took a chair across from the couch; I waited.

"Where do you want me to start?" Eli covered his face with his hands.

"I guess the night we met."

Eli cleared his throat and told me the story of a man who got paid to insert himself in not only my life, but that of my sister as well. He had received no orders other than to make Lizzie fall in love with him and do whatever was needed to stay in her life, and mine.

"Hold on, you're saying you were like a sleeper agent, inserted in our lives until the day your mission would start. What's the mission?"

"I asked, but they didn't want to tell me. Then Gabriel got sent away on another mission and I was ordered to remain in your lives."

I turned to face him; the tiles were cool beneath my bare feet. Below my cool exterior, rage simmered. "Your entire relationship with Lizzie has been a lie. When are you going to tell her? Eli, I trusted you with her."

As I came to my feet, Aidan gave me a look which forced me back down. "Finley, let him finish."

Eli dragged his hands over his face. Desperation filled his eyes. "I love Lizzie, and our child." He hiccupped a laugh. "I fell so hard for Liz, nothing else even mattered, only that I will do whatever it takes to keep her, and you, safe."

"Why were you instructed to infiltrate our lives?"

"I have no idea. Gabriel failed his mission when you ended your relationship, that's when he contacted me. He knows I will never hurt a woman, and my only instruction was to infiltrate and remain in your lives. It was easy to fall for Lizzie, and to become your friend. When Gabriel left, I received no further instructions, and by then I had already begun falling for Lizzie and had the utmost respect for you when you brought down that ring of serial killers which led to the Angel Taker being identified."

"Why was Gabriel sent away? You said he chose to leave, and he had me believe he was a hero, set on infiltrating and ending a human trafficking ring."

"The hero part they wanted you to think. He ended the traffickers' operation, but I'm not sure why. A few things are becoming clearer. As for why he was sent away, it was twofold. One – he failed in his mission. The second – his employer gained something by him infiltrating the traffickers."

"His failed mission being me ending our short-lived fling?

We got back together, and then he got the phone call. It doesn't make sense."

Eli turned to Aidan, and Aidan nodded.

"Finley, Gabriel being sent away was punishment for him being with you the night the Angel Taker tried to kill Riley. That's all I know. Gabriel has to tell you the truth about what his orders were. If he doesn't, I'll make him. Not only did he lie to you, but to me as well. He got me involved in all of this, I never signed up for any of it."

Eli came around the table and dropped to his knees in front of me, taking hold of my hands. "When Gabriel asked me to help frame Aidan for murder, I did it, only to find out what they were up to, him and Tom. On my way to Tom's house, to go over the details of their plan, I had contacted Aidan. Please believe me. I love Lizzie, I love you, and Aidan is my friend. I never got involved in this to hurt anyone, it's not who I am. Soldier, yes, hacker, yes, but not someone who destroys the lives of innocent people."

I cupped my friend's face between my hands. This man who is the closest I have to a brother. "Gabriel deserted you in the middle of an operation, he phones you out of nowhere, offers you money to infiltrate two women's lives. You had to know it wasn't for any good reason."

Eli dropped his head forward. "I had no choice. My friend had gone missing, presumed to be in Marcel or Wild Bay. The opportunity handed to me to travel to Marcel and get paid while I searched for her was too good to pass up. What would you have done in my position? If for one second I suspected you or Lizzie were in danger, I would've told you. When the Scarecrows abducted you, I did everything to get you back. Tom stalled on the information I wanted to give Captain Taylor. When I realised this, I went to Captain Taylor."

"I can vouch for him, Finley. If not for Eli going behind Tom's back, you wouldn't be sitting here tonight," Captain Taylor said from behind me.

***

Captain Taylor listened without interrupting as I relayed all we had learned about Pepper Gorge. Eli showed him the live stream from the cameras still in place. No indication of any rape orgies being held soon. The silver lining of a tar-black cloud. Aidan returned from our bedroom with the book and placed it on the table in front of Captain Taylor. "You're sure the Coopersville Department's Captain is involved?" he asked as he dragged the book closer.

"Yes, in the rapes. For all we know he might be complacent in the murders." I covered Aidan's hand with my own. My wedding ring back in its rightful place.

"Eli, can you show me the footage of the young man who was murdered?"

I couldn't bring myself to watch when Eli showed Captain Taylor the brutal slaying of a child, I had seen enough death to last me until the end of that week. Deep down, I hoped someone had loved this boy, that his entire life living in the cult hadn't been only cruelty and rules.

Captain Taylor turned to me, his familiar frown a reminder that there are other people fighting the evil in this world. Over the years, I grew fond of him. "I take it you want to be there when we arrest and question the Originals? I can set it up for you to speak to the people, sorry, the victims."

"Once you arrest the Originals, and they are in the holding cells at Douglasdale police station, then Finley may question them. Sorry, Dr Williams-Walker, but I will not allow her to be present at the raid."

"Aidan Walker, you're a party pooper. As my husband, you have no say. I'm, after all, a profiler consulting for the Marcel Police Department."

"As the medical doctor under whose care you are at this very moment, I do."

I laughed. "You saw for yourself that the baby and I are both in perfect health." Aidan and I had both wiped our eyes when he had done the sonogram. Our little girl had been awake, moving her tiny arms and legs, my cervix still holding.

All we could do was pray I would carry to term, which we had before dinner.

"Yes, but raids are dangerous. There are too many variables to consider. We didn't go through everything we just went through, are still going through, for you to get injured, or worse, because one cult member is a little trigger-happy." Aidan squeezed my hand.

With a heavy sigh, I conceded. No point in fighting him when what he said made sense. "On one condition. Every SWAT member wears a body camera. I want a front-row seat."

"Liam and I want in," Rowan said as he straddled a chair. Since the day we had met, there was something familiar about him, his voice, his calm nature. I couldn't put my finger on it and wrote it down to the traits he and Aidan shared. "I'm sure you can persuade Commander Elliot to allow us to join his team. He and I have a classified past, and he owes me for letting him get that redhead. It was a done deal for Liam, poor guy."

Men. "Is there anyone alive who doesn't owe you Walkers a favour?" I asked.

"A few," Ryan said, his face taut.

"Dad, what's wrong?" I asked.

"All these years and no one cared, countless women raped, young men killed, people slaughtered. I don't even want to think about what they did to the female infants. No way every Original wife birthed a son."

I pushed to my feet, walked to the head of the table, and wrapped my arms around him from behind. "We're doing something now. Together we will end this, right the wrongs, help the victims, and avenge the dead."

I turned to Captain Taylor. "We need trauma counsellors; Heather can brief the counsellors on how to work with people who have lived in cults. They might not realise what they were subjected to. Adapting to outside life will be hard on them. It's imperative they get adequate care and support. I wish Tabby Manor was closer, but the stress of flying and being in the outside world may prove too much for them."

"I never tire of working with you, Finley." Captain Taylor lifted his hand. "Yes, I realise you might be a stay-at-home mom for a while after the baby is born, but of all the profilers I've worked with, I respect you and your heart the most."

My mentioned organ filled, and I could only smile at the compliment. "I don't want the Originals with the general population and keep them separate from each other. From what I read, they see themselves as one and not five individuals. Separate them and I will have a better chance to break them." As the men who captured me and my squad had done, except for when they had murdered one of us in front of all the others. "Unity is strength, a collective mind is stronger than that of the individual."

Aidan held out his hand and pulled me against him, resting his cheek against my chest. "Your strength, resilience, and devotion to others, three of the things I love most about you," he whispered as I bent down to press my lips to his hair. "No rabid-raccoon eyes can ever steal my focus from your soul."

"Aidan died for me to leave that house safely. Do the Originals need to survive the raid? Knowing the Originals are out there might make the victims clamp up out of fear. If they die, we might have a better chance of learning the truth."

"We operate in the grey, Finley. What you're proposing is to be like them. Their deaths aren't justified if we can get the victims out without incident." Ryan leaned forward in his chair, resting his elbows on the glass table.

"I'm more concerned they might keep preaching their doctrine from within prison walls. Charismatic men like them, they can garner a following, one we might not be able to control. Don't tell me you don't have a place where we can keep five men until nature takes its course? They don't have to die; they can appear dead. Lock them in a cage, kill them, I don't care. Their perversions must end with them." I turned to Aidan. "You still owe me a bedtime story, Dr Walker, or is it Commander Walker?"

"Neither, and yes, I do."

Heather stepped out onto the patio and asked Liam to help her carry the coffee. "Decaf for Finley."

I no longer needed caffeine. Surrounded by the people I trust, I felt more energised than I had in weeks. Aidan placed his hand on my stomach and turned to me as I took my seat next to him. "Do you feel that?"

"What?" I covered his hand with my own. Leaning forward, I lifted my mouth to his ear. "Are you still trembling from our shower?"

He pressed his lips to my cheek. "I tremble every time I think about it."

"Every five seconds?"

"Three. There, do you feel that? If I can, you must."

"I'm used to getting this twisty sensation in my stomach whenever I'm around you." I pulled my head back and stared into his eyes.

"It's the baby, Fin."

My heart clenched. "Aidan, we need to end this. Now. We deserve to enjoy this pregnancy, after everything we've been through. Don't we deserve just a bit of time to enjoy this miracle without facing the darkness which will always be there? We both know we will not turn our backs on the plight of millions, but don't we deserve to breathe? We already lost one child. Ainsley deserves our attention and I want to enjoy this pregnancy even with the stress that she might be born early." I kept my voice low.

Stress there will always be, but I wanted to be selfish for once and allow myself to enjoy the miracle we had prayed for. Enjoy this phase of our marriage, even though we were homeless and by the look of things, unemployed. Before dinner, while Aidan and I had dressed, he said he knew patients would never want a doctor who had been accused of two murders, even when he would be cleared of all charges. Listening to my husband, the brilliant medical doctor, letting go of his dream, rage had pushed itself higher. The darkness inside me shifted into its protective stance. Tom and Gabriel had destroyed Aidan's calling. Another thing for which they would pay. Would anyone trust the judgement of a profiler whose husband had been accused of murder?

"Finley? Did you hear me?"

The flap of the darkness' wings drowned out the voices around the table. The scent of the ocean breeze was replaced by the familiar copper smell. The Reaper's odour.

"Finley?" Captain Taylor tried again. I turned to him, my eyebrows raised. "Tomorrow night."

"What about it?"

"The raid will happen tomorrow night. Which gives us twenty-four hours to get everything in place. I will pull as many strings as I can. After we conclude here, you, Heather, and I can discuss what we need to have in place for the victims. You will be the first to talk to the Originals, and Ryan will make arrangements for their transportation to an undisclosed location."

"The men who had paid to rape the young women. We need to hunt them down. They might rape other girls in their home cities and countries. I need DNA samples of every single person at Pepper Gorge, and we need a lab to process it." I pushed to my feet and slammed my fists onto the table. The reinforced glass held. "I want these men hunted down, outside the law, and I want them annihilated. Raping children is not a grey area. Either you help me, or I will do it on my own, but they *will* die before they hurt anyone else."

"I'm in," a familiar voice said.

I spun around, marched to her, and wrapped my arms around her. "I knew we were going to be best friends."

"Calm down, babe, we aren't braiding each other's hair just yet." Quinn hugged me tighter.

"Only because mine isn't long enough. What about a pyjama party? But Aidan has to be there because I haven't slept next to him in weeks and you need to meet Lizzie. She won't watch thrillers with us, but she makes good popcorn and margaritas."

"Being your friend is going to be tiring. Man, I miss living inside your head."

I held her at arm's length. "Thank you for getting me through this, and for being the one to hunt these bastards down. I will help as much as I can. I doubt a certain Mr Walker will allow me out in the field, but I can still hunt."

"You got that right, and no sleepover tonight. Quinn has spent more time with you than I have and tonight I want you all to myself. Speaking of which, shouldn't we be wrapping things up here so we can all get an early night? Tomorrow is going to be a long day." Aidan started placing mugs on the tray.

Quinn hugged me. "I'm glad you're safe, and that you got out. I'm sorry I couldn't tell you about Aidan's plan. This friendship thing is new to me, but I believe we're not supposed to keep secrets from each other. Consider that the last."

"Deal, and the sleepover we will do once Aidan and I find a home. You and I are going to be spending a lot of time together identifying the rapists and taking them out."

A sinister, yet familiar, shadow lurked in Quinn's eyes. Perhaps we had more in common than I had first thought. "I look forward to hunting with you."

Captain Taylor cleared his throat. "Officially, I was never privy to this conversation. Unofficially, I will make every resource at my disposal available to you. I've been at this long enough to know sometimes death is the only way to keep someone safe."

Aidan and I stared at each other. His eyes held an answer to a question I had pondered since the Sophia Blake investigation.

After Captain Taylor, Heather and I discussed what we would need for the victims, I made my way to the guest bedroom. Laughter welcomed me as I knocked on the door. Lizzie sat on the bed, clutching the photos of the sonogram Aidan had done after he finished checking on our daughter and a certain part of my anatomy I had never given much thought to before

I had heard it might prove problematic.

"Can I see the photos again?" I asked as I sat down next to her. She handed the strip to me and I took in the sight of a baby I didn't carry but loved as much as my own. "Why were you laughing?"

"Eli reckons the baby is a boy, and as clever as I am because of his enormous head."

"I said we can only hope he has her intellect," Eli corrected. "He's only a few weeks old and will grow into it."

"Her intellect, cooking skills, your bravery and selflessness." I held out my hand to my un-biological brother and wrapped my arms around him. "Does Lizzie know?"

"Yes, he told me. I won't lie and say I'm not a little ticked off about how he came into my life." Lizzie reached for Eli's hand, lifting it to her mouth. "I love you, and that's all that matters. Eli, I will never throw how you came into our lives in your face. If our love, and this child, is the good that comes out of others' plans against us, I'm glad things worked out the way they did."

I always thought Lizzie was too forgiving, but she lived a more carefree life for it. She can let go and move on. I envied her. "Where are they being held?" she asked.

Eli squeezed her hand. "I don't care, as long as they never see the free world again. My focus is on what lays ahead for us."

"I need to know." They both turned to me, and I shrugged.

"Will it change anything?" Lizzie placed her hands on mine.

"Yes, it will. I need to know why Tom wasn't who he led us to believe, why he brought Gabriel into my life, Eli into yours, and why he framed my husband for murder. He tried to destroy our lives, why?"

"Knowing the reasons won't change what happened, or where we are now. Just let it go, focus on rebuilding your life."

"I can't." I pulled away from her, moved off the bed, and stopped in front of the window. The ocean a black mass, the moon no longer illuminating the rippling surface. Darkness watched me. "Why did they try to destroy our lives? They need to answer for what they've done, for what they planned to do if not for Eli and Aidan stopping it. They will tell me how the one who pulled their strings factors in."

"Who is he, the one you've been calling the Puppet Master?"

"Aidan said he will tell me tonight. As soon as we're done at Pepper Gorge, Aidan will take me to where they're being held." The material of the curtain crumpled into my fists. Rage coursed so ferociously my muscles trembled.

Eli placed a hand on my shoulder. "Ryan won't let you kill them. He doesn't strike me as the type to stand back and let you take more deaths onto your conscience."

"It's not for him to decide. He, Aidan, and their team brought them to me. Their fates are in my hands now." I released the curtain and smoothed out the creases. "I better get to bed before Aidan comes looking for me and drags me off."

"You can't do this, Finley." Lizzie wiped her face. Desperation filled her eyes.

"I will do whatever it takes to protect the ones I love. I always have, I always will. You don't have to be there when I interrogate them. I would prefer if you weren't."

Lizzie grabbed my arm and wrapped her arms around me. "They also tried to infiltrate my life. I'm in this with you. Whatever you do to them, I support you, one hundred percent."

"Even if I kill them with my bare hands?"

Thirty-nine

Aidan pulled me closer, my body snug against his. The safest I had felt in weeks, always felt, was when I lay next to him. I closed my eyes, drew a deep breath, savouring the seconds before I would open my mouth and ask the Puppet Master's name. He shushed me before I opened my mouth by feathering kisses along my neck, ending at my shoulder. Goosebumps rippled across my body.

Aidan touched the back of his fingers to my cheek. "Can we not just have tonight? I understand you need to know. Oh, this is pointless, you won't wait until morning. Can't fault you for it."

I turned to face him in the dark, his stubble pricking my lips. He had shaved while I had spoken to Eli and Liz. "I need to know."

"Who, I can tell you. Why, you need to hear from them. We don't have enough answers for me to even begin to tell you."

I never thought he would lie to me, least of all while I lay in his arms. "Is the truth so terrible you want to keep it from me?"

"What I learned, yes. If I could keep it from you for the rest of your life, I would."

"What's the worst I can do?"

"It's not what you can do, Finley. It's what it will do to you." His breathing remained calm, but his hold increased.

"As long as we have each other, we can face anything, get through anything. Not this?"

"We will. In time, you will. But at what cost to your soul?"

I tried to pull away from him, but he held me tighter. "Aidan, please, they almost destroyed our lives. We lost the home where we planned to raise our daughter, and the home

236

my parents left me you destroyed in the process."

"I was waiting for you to bring it up."

"Couldn't you have blown up anything else? Was it because of what Gabriel had said that night?"

Aidan grunted a laugh. "I'm not fond of the idea of you two doing what we do, but I'm not jealous. Your past is just that." Aidan isn't the jealous type; protective to a fault for certain, but not jealous.

"For the record, my darling husband, he and I never made love. You and I always make love, no matter what we do or where we do it."

He pressed his lips to my forehead. His body responded to my words.

"Let me love you, Aidan." I reached between us, slipped my hand into his boxers, and stroked his full length. *I missed you.*

His breath caught as I squeezed. "Let me guess, you'll continue loving me if I tell you his name?"

Yes. "No, you sacrificed so much to keep Ainsley and me safe, and more than anything, I missed you, missed this." I squeezed again, eliciting another stifled groan from him.

"I want to make love to my wife."

"After my six-week check-up, we can ask your mother to watch the baby while we go at it like we did before I fell pregnant."

"Not then, I want to make love to you now. I want us back, Finley. No talk of death and destruction on our first night together. No mention of the lies you were fed by a man you trusted, a man who had watched you grow up."

"Then don't talk. Keep the answers till morning. Thank you for carrying the burden for me, but come tomorrow, I need to take up my share of it." I threw off the duvet and made love to my husband as best I could, with every part of me that didn't put the baby at risk. More than anything, I made love to him with my soul, the only part of me I had never shared with anyone but Aidan.

***

Morning came sooner than I wanted. The seven hours of sleep were the best I had had since last sleeping in Aidan's arms. He woke me up by placing a cup of coffee on the bedside table. His naked torso greeted me; the towel riding dangerously low on his hips. *I'm home.*

"I offer you coffee and answers." He pressed his lips to mine. I smiled against his mouth, remembering the way he had clutched the sheet as I had brought him to the brink, only to let him fall again. "You're even more skilled with your mouth than what I remembered." His smile matched mine.

"I'm keeping score, you better make up for all this once we can have sex again."

"I promise, Mrs Walker. Time to talk, Fin, we've got a long day ahead of us."

I groaned, pushing myself up against the headboard. The truth didn't seem important waking up to my semi-naked husband. The ever-present questions hung heavy in the air as I lifted the mug to my lips. I waited for Aidan to settle next to me and take a sip of his own coffee.

"Where do you want to begin?" he asked.

"His name." I placed the mug on the table and turned to face Aidan. He did the same, taking my hands in his.

"How much do you know about Ruastan?"

"Enough to hold a conversation." I told Aidan what I knew.

A small landlocked country in eastern Europe. Their biggest export over the preceding years had been people, during and after the civilian uprising which toppled the previous president and his regime. The current president had been the General of the armed forces. He had won votes by promising economic stability and growth. President Milat held power long enough to prove he, like most politicians, never have the interests of the people at heart, only his own monetary gain. What was left to gain in Ruastan was anyone's guess. Years of civil unrest and wars with neighbouring countries had left the country destitute.

"Why do you ask?"

"After we conclude the matter of Pepper Gorge, you will meet Ivan Milat."

"President Milat?"

"Yes."

My mouth fell open, my mind raced. "How does he factor in?"

Aidan moved closer and pressed my face against his chest. "Fin, he's responsible for the deaths of your parents." I tried to move, but Aidan held me tighter. "The accident wasn't an accident. We believe your parents committed suicide."

"Why would they do that?"

"Hours after they learned of your rescue and that you were in a critical, yet stable condition, Tom told them you were dead."

I pushed away from him and grabbed his hands. "Why would they commit suicide? And after they learned that I was alive? Lizzie told me what utter hell they went through during the time I was held captive. And what it did to them to see the footage of me being tortured. Why would Tom lie?"

Aidan shut his eyes and took a deep breath. "I think your parents did it to protect you and Lizzie. Tom took on the role of liaison between your parents and our military. The military played no part in your rescue, as the government refused to launch a rescue mission in Ruastan and risk an international incident. My father's organisation, however, operates without diplomatic red tape."

I scampered off the bed and paced the length of the room. "Tom lied about me being dead." I mulled over the information and turned to Aidan where he remained on the bed. "How did your parents get involved? Aidan, did you know? When we met, did you know?"

He darted across the room and wrapped his arms around me. "No. Finley, I swear to you when we met, I had no idea. After Eli warned me that Tom and Gabriel were framing me for murder, I approached my parents and they told me there might be more to it. They only told me about the circumstances of your rescue after you left Marcel."

"The government refused to acknowledge our squad had been ambushed and taken as prisoners, how did your parents find out?" I laughed, despite the hurricane of emotions erupting inside me. "Your father's organisation, he has to know what's going on in the world."

Aidan stepped back and held my face with both hands. "They need to tell you the details, but Fin, your mother asked for their help."

In a daze, I showered and dressed. This day was supposed to be about ending the atrocities of Pepper Gorge. An evil decades, if not centuries, old. I found my in-laws in the study, and Aidan closed the wooden doors.

Heather wrapped her arms around me and pressed her lips to my still damp hair. "I'm sorry you had to learn the truth like this."

I pulled away from her. "The truth? I have more questions than I have answers. Tell me how my mother came to ask for your help, and help with what?"

Heather led me to the couch, not releasing my hands. "We learned about a squad taken hostage. Ryan put out some feelers and found out it was a squad from our army. Your name came up, and I, of course, knew your parents through the fundraisers held for Tabula Rasa. At one of these events, I approached your mother and asked why it hadn't been made public. At first your mother denied it. I wouldn't have any of it and told her we could help with our connections. You understand our need for secrecy in this line of work."

I nodded, desperate to hear the rest.

"A week later I was having lunch at The Marcella, and this time your mother approached me. Victoria said more was at stake than only your life. She told me as much as she could, and I promised we would get you back alive." Heather pressed her lips to my forehead. "I kept my promise. Why Tom had lied, only he can answer."

A knock on the door yanked my mind back from that time. Rowan pushed the double sliding doors open and closed them before joining us in the sitting area.

I turned to Heather. "From the first time Aidan mentioned my name, you knew who I was. Why didn't you say anything?" She moved back as I yanked my hands free from her grip.

"We were not aware of Ivan Milat's involvement, or anything more than that your squad had been ambushed and were being held in Ruastan. At the time we thought it was a normal occurrence of war, if there even is such a thing. There were many para-military groups in Ruastan who wanted to show their reach, their strength. All our intelligence pointed to this."

"Why did Tom lie? How did he get involved?"

Ryan stepped closer and sat on the coffee table. He placed his hands on my knees. "Aidan *never* heard about it from us. The rest of the family wanted to spare you seeing us and knowing that we know what you went through. You can ask Tom why he lied to your parents, and about his role in your abduction. Finley, I will not stand in your way. Get the answers you deserve from all three of them, whichever way you need to."

"The rest of you?" I lifted my eyes to Rowan's. He gave a slow blink and took the space Ryan vacated in front of me.

Rowan placed his hand on my neck and pulled my head forward until our foreheads touched. "I will never see you as the naked, brutalised woman I carried out of that compound. Sergeant Williams was a fellow soldier, and my orders were to bring you home, by any means necessary."

He eased back as unshed tears threatened to spill from his eyes and mine. "Finley, my sister-in-law, you're the woman I met on your wedding day. I never confuse the two of you. Please don't ever think when you catch me looking at you that I'm remembering what you looked like, or that you were naked. When I stare at you, it's because I wonder how the hell Aidan got so lucky to find a woman like you. You survived horrendous torture, and here you are today, the most amazing and strongest woman I've ever met." Rowan glanced over his shoulder at Aidan. "And one of the most beautiful."

"Don't forget *happily* married," Aidan muttered under his breath.

Rowan rolled his eyes. His smile matched mine. "When my father called to say he needed my help, that it involved you and Aidan, I was on the first flight back. Not only for my brother and my sister-in-law, but also for Sergeant Williams who I had held in my arms when she had known nothing but the cruelty of men for months. You trusted me then, so trust me now. I will never see you as anything other than the magnificent, intelligent, and wonderful person you are."

I pressed my lips to his forehead and wrapped my arms around his neck. Rowan's long, dark hair was tied on top of his head. The tears didn't stop, no matter how hard I willed them to. Countless times I had wondered what I would say to the man who had dressed me and carried me out of the dust, away from horror. I had never even asked his name, not that I could have, as I was semi-conscious at the time. "Rowan, I..." The words caught in the back of my throat. Thank you just didn't seem enough.

"Not necessary, Sergeant Williams. Neither from my sister." He held me to the point of suffocating me. "There's nothing I won't do for you, Finley, and not only because you love my brother despite his quirks. If he doesn't take care of you the way you deserve, I'm waiting to prove to you that the youngest is always the best, the most skilled, and the most passionate."

I laughed through the tears. Despite us not spending much time together because of his undercover work, Rowan knew me well enough to know making me laugh is the only way to stop my tears.

"Let's go hunt some murdering rapists, this finger of mine sure is itchy today." Rowan wiggled his trigger finger as we released our hold on each other.

"Liam?" I asked and got to my feet.

"My objective was to locate you and get you out. Liam ensured they paid for what they had done to you, and every member of your squad."

From what I had been told, none of the men responsible for the murders of my squad had been left alive. The world is a better place without them in it.

Before we left for our flight to Douglasdale, I spoke with Lizzie and Eli. They would remain in Wild Bay and meet up with us when the time came to confront the men responsible for not only destroying our lives but also the deaths of my and Lizzie's parents.

The Walkers promised to let me be the one to tell Lizzie the truth. I couldn't say anything to my sister, not until I had an answer to every question.

Forty

Night fell, and so did the rain. A moonless night devoid of thunder and lightning. Rowan held the umbrella for me as I fastened the Kevlar to Aidan's body, praying he would return to me unharmed. It irked me that they seemed to have forgotten that I'm a warrior, but Ainsley changed everything, for all of us. If there had ever been a time to make the world a better place, it was now, for her. And continue our fight for every other child in the world. Pepper Gorge was as bad a place as any to start.

I pushed onto my toes, wrapping my arms around Aidan's neck. "You better come back to me. Rowan, you keep your brother safe. Aidan, keep your brothers safe. That's an order."

Aidan smiled against my mouth. Excitement pulsing in his eyes. I wondered if this same look had hidden under the mask he had worn when hunting as the Marcel Sniper.

During the flight from Wild Bay, I had watched my husband transform into a person I had only ever heard of. To see him take command of the team, give orders, the authority in his voice, I had been more than a little turned on.

Aidan kissed me hard and jogged towards the waiting Black Hawk. He waved as the helicopter lifted into the darkness and disappeared. Without a doubt, Aidan's days of bringing new life into the world were over. The call to protect the innocent too loud in his ear, his soul. With me by his side, Aidan can be whoever he wants to be, and so can I.

"It's time for us to head out," Ryan said, and together we walked to the armoured vehicle where Heather waited.

From the airfield, we drove to the nature reserve bordering Pepper Gorge and waited for the familiar sound of a helicopter approaching.

"He's going to be fine." Heather placed her hand on my knee. I didn't realise my leg jumped.

"I know." I hoped. "I'm worried about the people's reactions, their willingness to assist us, and to accept our help."

"It's a brilliant idea to keep them here until the reality sinks in."

"Once the Originals are neutralised, we can prove to the people we mean them no harm." I glanced at the time displayed on the vehicle's console. In less than an hour, physical darkness would retreat.

"Finley, sweetie, what happens in the next hour isn't in your hands. Armed men guard that farm, ones who will die to protect the only home they've ever known. I will not have my sons killed because of the doctrine by which these poor people live."

Ryan stepped back into the vehicle and closed the door behind him. "Listen to your mother, young lady. Why don't you get some sleep? I'll wake you up when everyone is in place."

"No, thank you. With the amount of adrenaline pumping through me I won't be able to will my eyes shut." My heart drummed to the rhythms Lizzie and I had danced to in our youth. Minus the flashing lights, smoke machines, and drug pushers.

"Aidan mapped it out during the flight and briefed the team twice." Ryan poured himself and Heather a cup of coffee from the thermos, before producing a second and filling a mug which he held out to me. "Decaf, I'm sorry."

"When are you going to tell us the sex of the baby?" Heather asked.

"When my husband can share in the news. I'm not going to tell you without him present, in the middle of nowhere, and an operation. Good job on getting my mind off what Aidan's heading towards." I blew on the warm liquid in the mug.

"I hope our other sons marry women who aren't inclined to your psychological games. The idea of having more than two of you in the family is going to make me go bald."

Heather ran her fingers through Ryan's full head of hair. "You have three of us in the family."

Ryan eased back in his seat. "Ah, Quinn. Yes, well, she's more playful than cunning."

"Don't underestimate her. I look forward to working with her when we hunt down the men who raped the girls at Pepper Gorge." I sighed. "Both of us will have to make peace with it, going in, that we might not track all the men down."

"One less rapist on the street is still one less. Who knows how many lives you'll save by taking one out?" Heather patted my knee.

I nodded, not yet able to make peace with knowing for every head we cut off, more will grow in its place. A war we will wage for as long as the earth remains. "Thank you." Heather and Ryan kissed my temples at the same time.

"We adored your parents and believed in their causes. I'm sorry they didn't get to see you again, that you were robbed of the chance to say goodbye to them. Most of all we regret that they'll never see the woman you have become, the profiler, and mother to our first grandchild." Heather leaned her head against mine, her arm warm around my shoulders.

"Thank you for sending clothes with Rowan." I breathed in her scent. It had become home to me over the years. The same way my mother's scent had enveloped me whenever she hugged me.

"Oh, sweetie." Heather's voice caught. "I didn't think of it. Your mother begged me to spare you further humiliation."

A simple sentence, filled with my mother's heart, her love for me, my mother's last maternal act towards me. I closed my eyes, savouring the feeling of the tears streaming down my face. *Whatever the truth, I will avenge you, Mom.*

Ten minutes after I got my emotions under control, by pushing them straight into the eagerly awaiting hands of my inner darkness, Aidan's voice filled the vehicle. "In position, going live now."

Ryan pulled down the overhead screens and switched them

on. Aidan's view became mine. Darkness tinged with the vertigo-inducing green hue. Not even from the body camera mounted to his chest could I stomach the sight. "Fin, breathe through it, focus on a single point."

"Yes, sir."

Aidan's laughter filled my heart, releasing the knot in my stomach. Within minutes, people might die. *Aidan might die.* Death may claim more of the ones I love. I realised Aidan never shared his strategy with me, only with his team. *Where is he?* I focused on the screen in front of me, desperate to piece it together.

"In position." An unfamiliar voice said.

"Keep it steady." The barrel of Aidan's rifle came into view as he dropped to his knees and onto his stomach.

I covered my microphone and turned to Ryan. "Where is he?"

"In his element."

I rolled my eyes and focused on the screen. The image changed. A solitary greenish figure walked across a clearing, not knowing my husband and I had him in our sights. I covered my mouth with my hand. Not because this person had wondered into a sniper's line of sight. The sniper? Airborne.

The figure fell. Another came into view and fell. Over and over until none of Pepper Gorge's guards were left standing. The night remained quiet, devoid of the familiar sound made by chopping blades.

"Aidan, where are you?"

"About to breach. Once we touchdown, radio silence."

Heather placed her hand on my fist. "Aidan's wooing you."

A little late for that – his child grew inside me, his ring on my finger, his surname hyphenated with mine.

"You've heard of Aidan the sniper, but you've never seen him in action."

I had, sort of, when we were both broken versions of who we were now. Still, Heather was right. I had never seen Aidan in action. How could seeing him like this make me want him more, when I already had all of him?

The screen flashed and again my eyes gazed from Aidan's chest. He turned to look at his team. Smiles filled their faces as they nodded. I smiled too, not because night vision was no longer needed, but because captives were about to be freed. Freedom gifted to those who didn't realise they were slaves because humans are capable of immense evil. I doubted they would see their freedom as a gift. At first.

Trees streamed by on the screen in front of me. A real-life video game. It isn't a game when people are raped for the sadistic pleasure of monsters, or the monetary gain of equally despicable creatures. Death had plagued this farm for too long. *It ends today.*

Aidan stopped, obscured tree bark my only view. I glanced at the time display. The hour didn't matter, but the time did. Seconds ticked by; time stood still. Aidan moved, gliding between trees and over rocks. His every move precise, his breathing controlled.

The backs of five men came into view. Their daily routine so strict you could set your watch by it. Aidan's SIG lifted in front of his chest.

I glanced at the screens holding Heather and Ryan's attention. The same view filled their screens, relayed from the rest of the team's body cameras.

As one, they stood. As one, they fell.

The blood of the Originals was the only shed that day.

Forty-one

A blond teenage girl stepped through the door. Her eyes fell on the empty chairs as she made her way to where I sat, waiting for her. Rowan stood sentry at the door, Aidan next to me. Brothers, so different in appearance, yet their mannerisms so similar. Aidan placed his hand on my thigh, a reassuring gesture. I planned to do much more to him once we were alone than offer him comfort, or a pat on the back for a job well done.

The girl's eyes met mine. I smiled, she didn't. As she neared the table, Aidan stood and pulled a chair out for her. She smiled at him. "Hello, Nicol."

She threw herself down in the chair, a typical teenage expression on her face, even though she had never experienced the normalcy of being a carefree adolescent. "The people are hungry, could you not have waited until after breakfast?"

"You can be glad we waited until daylight." The reason? I believed a siege to be less terrifying during the day than the middle of the night. A game of trust. A fragile thread. "We are handing out food parcels to everyone. You can either eat yours now or after we talk."

"What's there to talk about? You said you would help, here you are. Now what? The Originals are immortal, they will continue this somewhere else." She glanced at Aidan as he pushed a mug across the table towards her. Again, she smiled.

I removed the phone from the front pocket of my jeans and held it up for her to see. Nicol choked on her tea. "Are they...?"

The gaping holes made by the bullets exiting their foreheads were answer enough.

Nicol leaned back in her chair and crossed her arms over

her chest. "How do I know those five bodies are the Originals? You could be lying."

"What would we gain by lying to you?" Aidan asked.

Her calm response to death surprised me. "You saw the bodies in the woods." For a moment, our stares locked. "Why hasn't anyone spoken about Henry's disappearance? Remember your future fiancé? Not once did you mention his name after he went missing."

Nicol shifted in her seat. "Him going missing isn't a tragedy." She didn't ask how we knew that no one had spoken of him since his disappearance.

Aidan reached across the table, placing a hand on her forearm. I didn't appreciate the look she gave my husband, despite knowing what he was doing. "You're safe now. Nicol, I promise you, I won't let anyone hurt you again." Aidan moved his chair closer to hers. Her eyes followed his every move. "We're not with the police. Whatever you tell us will stay between the three of us."

Again, she smiled, a young girl's attempt at a seductive smile. A young woman who couldn't comprehend that an older man could talk to her and not want more than answers. She turned to me. "Where's your husband?"

"Next to you."

"I thought..." She dropped her eyes to the table and eased away from Aidan.

"You thought what I needed you to think. The man next to you is, and always will be, my only husband. I don't share him, he doesn't share me. It's how we want our marriage to be. Just like you never wanted to share Henry."

The statement caught her off guard, and the defiance in her gaze hinted at an answer I still had to formulate a question to.

"Nicol, I need your help. In time we'll move all of you away from this place and help you integrate into the outside world. I believe you're ready for it, but a number of people won't be as accepting of the truth. Help me. Help me understand the significance of the carvings made in the bodies of the young men murdered in the woods. Why was the word 'no' carved into their foreheads?"

"There weren't any carvings in their heads." Too young to understand what she had stepped into. A puddle of truth, one I didn't want her to drown in. Not when I understand the need for survival at this primitive level.

I pushed my chair back and stepped around the table. As I placed my hands on the back of her chair, I whispered, "You saw all five bodies, the carvings in their bodies and in the trees. Who is he?"

Nicol's back straightened. "The true saviour of this place. You didn't help us. You being here, it was his plan all along."

Aidan moved to the chair I vacated; his hands flat on the table's surface. "Henry's dead, Nicol. You're alone now."

"Henry didn't strike me as the type to get his precious future preacher hands dirty. Who helped you?" I asked.

Her silence answered me. Two killers. One taller, because the shorter was a woman. A teenage girl.

"Help us understand what happened here. We won't tell anyone you helped murder five young men, not if you tell us the truth. Aren't you tired of all the lies?"

"If Henry's dead, there's no reason for me to tell you who *he* is. He's safe, so am I, as well as the rest of our people." She tried to stand, but I pressed her down.

"What was the end game? Why would you and the one who calls himself Sevens Hunter murder five of the six future Originals?"

"You answered yourself."

I lifted my eyes to Aidan's. The restrained calm in his eyes a gentle reminder I couldn't use any of my prior interrogation techniques. Let alone on a child. Neither could I not learn the truth. I closed my eyes, allowing what I knew to take form. "Henry didn't want to share power. He wanted to be the only Original."

"Congratulations," Nicol said. "May I go have breakfast now? All this talk has made me even hungrier."

"As soon as you tell me what you got out of murdering for Henry?"

"Freedom." The word sounded pained coming from her mouth.

"Who is he, Nicol? Sevens Hunter. Your brother or lover? Although around here, it's the same thing, isn't it?"

"What they did to us here is wrong. In your world, people aren't forced to have sex with men who want to hurt them. The Originals called it a celebration, but your world calls it rape. You're free to make your own decisions, live your own lives, go where you want, and eat whatever you want. Did anyone force you two to marry each other, or told you that you can't love each other?"

Tom tried.

Her use of the word rape caught me off guard. "How do you know so much about the outside world?"

"He who you call Sevens Hunter taught me. It's my fault all of this happened, but we're free, and we stopped Henry. Even as a young boy, Henry was *different*. How did he die?"

"Poison." I offered her no more.

"Coward, he was all big talk, but he would've been the worst of the Originals. He would've killed us all. Hate grew in his heart even before he took his first breath. Imagine, the greatest of the preachers had to share his mother's womb. Henry hated his mother, his brother, even me."

"If he hated you, why would he let you go to pursue a life in the outside world?"

"I offered him the one thing he craved."

"Power," I said. "Without getting his hands dirty."

"I hope whoever killed him burned his body."

"Why?" Aidan asked as I stepped around to his side of the table and took the chair that he pulled closer.

"The evil living inside him must be stopped."

"Nicol, he was eighteen years old. What evil things could he have done if not yet in a position of power?"

She laughed. "They sent him away because of the things he

did. Henry returned worse, scarier. Whatever happened to him in the outside world increased his lust for power."

"Why was he sent away?"

"The things he did to the animals the Originals laughed away, but its despicable. When he did the same thing to his mother, they couldn't make it off as him trying to hone his skills as the potential future butcher. You need to understand, back then, there had been no indication that the preacher spirit lived inside him."

Aidan leaned forward, holding a napkin towards Nicol. Without thanking him, she pressed it to her eyes. "We all heard her screams. Everyone tried to get to her in time. When we got there, he had already started eating the part of her which should've been only for him."

I swallowed hard, pushing the bile back down, and focused on keeping my voice level. "He raped his mother and ate her womb."

Nicol nodded. I stood and wrapped my arms around her, held her as the fear no child should live through echoed out of her. I couldn't fault her for turning to murder for a chance to get away. Until you've been that desperate, you can't understand what true fear is. As her screams calmed, I hugged her and pressed my lips to her head. I would ask Heather to be Nicol's therapist. I didn't trust anyone else to help Nicol make peace with what she had endured, or what she had done. "Nicol, where was Henry sent after he killed his mother?" I found it strange that they had punished him. The Originals were all part of this incestuous, murderous cult. To them, Henry should've been the epitome of a future leader.

"The man who speaks funny. He was here when it happened. For as long as I can remember, he comes here every year, for two weeks. Every year he takes two of the girls the hunters brought here with him when he leaves."

"Where did he take them?"

She shook her head. "Henry bragged about going with the man to a house Henry said isn't far from here. He only told the others to show them he was different, that he had privileges they didn't."

I didn't tell her I believe the reason the Originals sent him away was because Henry wouldn't have waited until it was his time to rape and kill. He enjoyed it too much. A child capable of raping and murdering his mother is capable of inflicting unspeakable horrors on others. What did he do while in the outside world? What would he have done once he held control of Pepper Gorge?

"Tell me about this man?" Aidan asked, his voice filled with understanding.

"He didn't speak like us, or the other men who come here. He took my sister once. She said he spoke of a place she hadn't heard the name of before, a different country. His friend spoke like us. My sister called his friend the Watcher. Because he liked to watch and not touch her or do anything with her."

Under the table I grabbed Aidan's hand, remembering Henry's words about us being at *his* house. Ruastanians have a very distinct accent.

The Puppet Master.

Forty-two

The guards awoke to a different world, one where their services were no longer needed. Their entire existence had been rendered redundant. Aidan decided to keep them restrained until he felt they posed no threat to our team or the surrounding people. In the minds of these twelve men, they had failed to protect their community. The enemy had overpowered them and were at that very moment offering them water to help them through the grogginess as the tranquilliser wore off.

Aidan joined me where I stood on the veranda of the building which had served as a church. This had never been a place of worship. The people's fear hung heavy in the air, uncertainty their new norm. What they didn't realise was that they no longer had to be afraid. Yet, not knowing what the future holds always brings a certain degree of trepidation. We must embrace it, accept it, and lift our heads.

One guard did this as Ryan approached with his hands behind his back. His stride more of a march than his usual relaxed demeanour. Strange how someone who lives his life confronted with the dark reality of this world on a daily basis can exude this level of calm, control, and demand respect with the mere tone of his voice. Next to me stood a man with the same characteristics. A born leader.

"I wonder when Nicol will realise what she's done. A part of me hopes she never does." I rested my head against his chest as Aidan wrapped his arm around me.

"You've been on your feet too long. Time for us to head back to Douglasdale. Our flight leaves early tomorrow morning. How about dinner and a movie in bed? Just the three of us." Aidan placed his hand on my stomach.

"I don't want to leave before I'm certain every person here

accepts the truth and embraces the freedom we brought them. Or as Nicol said, perhaps it wasn't us, but Sevens Hunter."

"You played your part, Finley. It's time for the Douglasdale police and the therapists to take over. My mom will stay in Douglasdale for the next week for daily sessions with Nicol."

"Where is Sevens Hunter? Should we even try to locate him?"

"He isn't that different from what you and I used to be." Aidan pressed his lips to my hair.

"Neither of us killed innocent children."

"From his point of view, they were destined to be monsters, just like their predecessors. In his eyes, he did his people a favour. Why am I telling you this? You hold the doctorates in criminal psychology."

I bit my bottom lip. My focus had been on the Originals, and the people born into this cult, so much so that I had forgotten to consider Sevens Hunter's point of view. I hated not knowing his name, or his face, but not because I wanted to bring him to justice for the murders. It was up to the police now to hunt down a ghost.

Aidan stepped around me, placed his fingers under my chin, tilting my head up, my lip still victim to my teeth. "Stop second-guessing yourself." He ran his thumb over my mouth; I pressed my lips to his finger.

"I should've given him more thought as an individual."

"Finley, you would've if you could've. It has been days since you stumbled onto this place and here we are. The people are free. You did all this while being held captive yourself, with your and our daughter's lives to worry about. You did good, real good."

"But not good enough. Children were murdered and raped on my watch." I increased my hold on him.

"There will always be people we can't save, another assault we can't stop. Does that mean we'll stop trying? Never. No one died today except the five men who subjected these people to unspeakable horrors. Today is a win."

I stared at the mountain rising beyond the tree line. "We need to send the team up into the forest. I won't rest until we're certain we know everything about this place. Some pages are missing from the book."

"Aidan, you're going to want to see this." Rowan stepped onto the porch and handed a leather-bound book to Aidan. The leather unlike any I had ever seen. "I found it in a crawl space hidden under the preacher's house."

"What is it?" I asked as Aidan started flipping through the pages.

He didn't have to answer. Quinn and my hunt had just become a lot easier.

Rowan stepped back and turned his attention to where Ryan sat, speaking to the guards. "A few of the names I'm familiar with, some are no longer alive. One stands out. Third last page. Tenth from the top."

Aidan and I spent the evening alone. We showered, ordered room service, and ate in bed. The rest of the night we spent talking, either clutching onto each other or while I paced across the bedroom. Neither of us were in the mood for a movie, our reality much stranger.

We compromised on what I could or couldn't throw around the room in a hotel his family didn't own shares in. I ended up throwing pillows and doing about as much damage as a marshmallow shot from a bazooka.

The dark rage festering inside me had remained leashed for far too long. I ended up crying and hating myself for it. No matter how many times I thought it through, or we spoke about it, it didn't make sense. How can the name of someone I knew, a person I once trusted, be written with the names of men who had paid to rape the young women of Pepper Gorge?

A few hours after breakfast, I faced him. The man Nicol's sister called 'the Watcher'.

Forty-three

I pulled Aidan's face to mine, letting my lips linger against his. A desperate attempt to stall. Behind three doors truth waited, or rather, the versions they would tell me.

"I'm ready when you are, Mrs Walker." Aidan smiled against my mouth.

Without knowing, I had waited years for this very moment. "How am I to get the truth from him if you won't allow me to take a weapon in?" I forced out my bottom lip. I loved having both my guns strapped to my body, where they belong.

"Finley." Ryan raised an eyebrow.

I rolled my eyes for being spoken to like a child, but I was theirs now and, on some level, this had to be difficult for them. The Walkers love Lizzie and me like they love their own children. During the flight to the black site, Heather had confirmed what I had long suspected – the youngest son wasn't biologically theirs. Heather said it was up to Rowan to tell me his story.

With both my Glock and SIG placed on the table, I turned towards the first room's door.

"Finley, the rest," Ryan said with a smile.

This time I refrained from going adolescent but liked him a bit less for knowing me so well. Aidan would've strip-searched me if he had to. What a splendid mental picture...until I remembered who waited on the other side of the door.

This game show had been rigged in my favour, and despite the security measures, it's never a good idea to torture your prisoners during the first interrogation. Ryan had promised to step back and allow me to do what I believe I do best – turn off my conscience and get answers no matter the personal cost.

The Ontario MK 3 Navy Knife Aidan had given me for

our first Valentine's Day, the Karambit I bought, and the Ari B'Lilah Eli had gifted me on my birthday joined the Glock and SIG where they lay helpless on the table.

I turned to Lizzie; her jaw tight. "You don't have to be here for this."

She stepped forward. "They were my parents, too."

Lizzie and Eli had waited for us upon our arrival at the black site, which appeared to be a private island complete with a house and an airstrip, to anyone who flies over. The airspace wasn't restricted but monitored and secured by surface-to-air missiles hidden amongst the vegetation. The Walkers truly are my kind of people.

Eli met my stare. "Promise me if it gets too much for her, you will take my sister out of this room."

The monitor behind me would show Lizzie everything that happens inside each of the three rooms. She would hear every word. Even though I'm eleven months and a few days younger than Lizzie, I will always see it as my duty, my privilege, to protect her. Even from the truth.

For a split second I considered leaving the three of them to rot, to keep their lies, or perhaps the truth, to themselves in order to protect Lizzie. And myself.

Lizzie wrapped her arms around my neck. "I'm stronger than you think. I survived growing up with you. If you need me, I'll be right here. No matter what happens, I will always be by your side, Finley Duncan Williams-Walker."

I hugged her tighter, buried my face in her golden hair and decided it was time to change my name. Duncan had to go. *Dad will roll over in his grave. A grave he shouldn't be in.*

Lizzie released her hold, and I scanned my family's faces. Lizzie, Eli, Ryan, Heather, Rowan, and Liam. My husband took my hand and pulled me against his chest. I inhaled his scent and the thundering of my heart calmed, the knot in my stomach loosened. This man, the one I call my own, the father of my child, made this moment possible. If that isn't proof of his love for me, I don't know what is. For most of my life, I believed myself unworthy of this kind of love, yet here I stood, safe in Aidan's arms. His daughter growing inside me. Aidan and Ainsley deserved this chapter of my life to end.

The only way for me to be free of the lies which had bound me for far too long. My parents deserved the riddle of their deaths answered.

"My people are looking for me. It's a matter of time before you beg for my mercy." Rich coming from a man strapped to a metal chair bolted to the concrete floor. Never mind the fact we were on an island. He didn't know he was being held two storeys below sea level. A part of me hoped he only screamed once I left the room. I prefer my ears ring-free.

I glanced at Aidan and nodded. He switched on the monitor and waited for the realisation to worm its way into the psyche of the man who stared unblinking at the screen.

With no table between us, I crossed my legs and let my arms hang at my sides. My relaxed appearance didn't match the adrenaline splashing in my stomach. I stared at his face, the man Aidan and I had dubbed the Puppet Master. "Do you need another minute, Ivan?"

His eyes fell on mine. Rage simmered below the surface. "President Milat." His distinct accent heavy.

"No, Ivan, that there is President Milat." I pointed to the monitor. "You're nothing more than the man responsible for the deaths of my parents." I pushed to my feet and walked to a corner in the windowless room. As I turned to face him, I smiled. "Ruastan will be the country the people voted for, had trusted you to create. They will never realise the man they'll grow to adore isn't you."

"How?" His eyes darted between Aidan's and mine.

I wondered when he would realise that I was his judge and jury, and whether he lived to take another leak lay in my hands and mine alone. With the right words, I might even get him to take that last leak where he sat. *Self-challenge accepted.*

"I'm going to tell you a story, Ivan. Be a good boy and

listen, don't go falling asleep on me now, okay?" I pouted.

"Why do you let a woman do the talking?" he asked Aidan.

Aidan's head tilted to the right. Without seeing his face, I felt his smile. It changed the energy in the room. "You know who she is, what she's capable of. Play nice or I will leave the room. Let her do what she does best."

Milat shook his head.

"The President of Ruastan went to bed and got out of that bed the following morning. You, Ivan Milat, fell asleep, and slept a little deeper thanks to an aerosolised sedative. Hours later you opened your eyes to the most beautiful face in the world, the same one sitting across from you now. Must have been the most splendid awakening of your life. My mornings always start better when I open my eyes to Aidan's gorgeous face. Then again, men aren't your thing."

I walked along the wall, coming to a stop behind him. I leaned forward; my breath warm on his neck. "Young girls – that's your thing." Ivan didn't rape the children and women he trafficked before becoming president of Ruastan. "For some strange reason, you prefer to pay to rape. I don't believe for a second you stopped making money from selling human beings. No, you're a greedy little bastard." I flicked his ear with my middle finger.

"You have no proof. Let me go and I will tell my people to kill you quick."

I flicked his other ear. Such stupidity can't go unpunished. "Ivan, you saw for yourself, the President of Ruastan addressed his nation. It was a live feed, you know, unless you're so thick you didn't get that part. Let me sum it up for you."

This time I flicked both his ears and told him how he came to be here, leaving no detail out. The hotel he had stayed in was owned by the same people who gave him accommodation now. He had gone to sleep, and from a hidden compartment underneath the bed, Sergio had climbed out. The switch was made. From the room below the penthouse in which Ivan had stayed, Aidan's team lowered his sedated body. How they had moved him out of the hotel and onto the awaiting aeroplane were details Ivan could wonder about for the rest of his life. However long I decided it to be. No amount of torture could cause enough pain to equal the torment he had caused others. We might never find all the victims he had trafficked or avenge the ones who didn't survive their captivity.

"What do you want?" Milat tried to look at me, but my hands wound around his neck made it impossible.

"The truth. I enjoy having options, and I believe in offering it to others. So, here are your two options. One – you answer my questions, and you'll live here until nature gives you a ticket to hell. Two – you don't tell me the truth and nature will still give you that bloodstained ticket. I might make the time it takes for nature to get here a little more uncomfortable. I'm good at that, Ivan. I enjoy it more than you do. See, the difference between you and me is I believe filth like you deserve the worst there is to bestow on them. I don't relish in it much…okay, I do. There's no peak moment for me, no climax, I can keep going long after you give up. You're aware Aidan is a medical doctor; he will administer the adrenaline and I'll keep going. We make a good team, despite your friend's efforts to keep us apart."

"You can't do this to me. I did nothing to deserve this!" He thrashed against the barbwire restraints. The barbwire had been my idea.

Aidan and I looked at each other. The expression on my face mirrored his. We had never done this together. Having him with me brought even more calm than I had felt doing this on my own.

Worked-up Finley, the one who craves vengeance, is scary, even though I love her to bits, but calm Finley, the one I am whenever Aidan is around – I'm terrified of her.

"Ivan." I sighed. "As much as I enjoy seeing your face, I'm getting bored. Bored-me is not your friend. Bored-me will leave you here, sitting in your own filth. I might bring some flies to keep you company. Or rather bees." His bee allergy was public knowledge.

I walked to Aidan and rested my hands on his strong shoulders. I could still swoon over my husband's perfect body while staring at the face of a self-made monster. "This little game I have always hated doing with suspects, but you're not a suspect. You're as guilty as your bladder is full. I'll go talk to your friend, Tom, hear his side of the story. Whoever spills first might live another day without having pieces of his flesh stripped out by my fork."

When my hand reached for the door, he spoke. "Ask Tom what he did with the videos of you while you were being held by my men. The videos Duncan and Victoria never saw. It's a pity they never saw how much it took to break you. They would've been proud of you. It gave me some respect for you. You lasted much longer than any of my whores ever did."

"Breathe," Aidan whispered. He stood so close I felt the rage radiating off him.

Forty-four

Gabriel's face filled with joy as I stepped through the door. "Ley, you're glowing."

"Like a firefly, whenever I'm around him." I tilted my head back.

Gabriel stared past me. "You're dead."

"Sorry to disappoint you, but *you* might be soon," Aidan said.

"I saw you blow yourself up."

"You did."

"I saw you detonate the bomb, the blast before the cameras went out."

"You have much to learn about the art of deception. A camera trick, a delayed feed. An already dead body blown to smithereens."

Aidan had told me the body in question was that of a known drug pusher who sold crack to children as young as ten. I didn't care to ask how said pusher ended up en route to push daisies. They would never find enough of him to even cremate.

I didn't plan on staying long. Instead of sitting down, I stood behind the chair next to the one Aidan took, placing my hands on the backrest.

"You look good, Ley. How is our baby?" Gabriel resembled a puppy. I bet if he had a tail, it would've wagged.

"Oh, Gabriel, have you still not figured it out?" I waited for him to put two and two together. He didn't. Instead, he kept smiling. "Not your child growing inside me. Your sperm went swimming down a drain, or wherever they send waste." I could ask Aidan later whether its termed medical waste. The sperm of an assassin would probably be labelled *biohazardous*. "This baby is Aidan's."

"I don't understand…" Gabriel tried to shift in his chair.

"Dr Walker, do you mind explaining the assisted-reproductive birds and bees? I don't have the patience to explain to this con artist that we beat him at his own game. Wait, maybe I can put it in terms he will understand. Gabriel, you're an assassin, therefore, you understand death like few other people do. Your sperm is dead. They're in Sheol now."

Aidan laughed at my reference to hell.

"Ley, I love you. Everything I did was for you. For us."

I let out a long, exaggerated breath. "You infiltrated my life to help Ivan Milat with his diabolical plan to become president of Ruastan. I was nothing more than a job to you. I came to gloat, and to tell you there's nothing you can say to change my mind about the punishment you will receive for the crimes you committed."

"Ley, I broke protocol for you. They punished me because of what I did for you." He thrashed against the restraints. The thin metal cut into his arms.

"What do you want? A thank you? A box of chocolates? Or a pat on the back? You knew what was going on, yet you deceived me. Framed my husband for murder. Be thankful I'm still deciding whether I'm going to execute you or let you suffer a fate far worse than death."

"Do you remember the night I shot the Angel Taker?"

I nodded. Bored. The yawn I didn't fake.

"They gave me strict orders not to kill him. Tom knew his identity and told him you were hunting him. Don't you get it? Tom wanted Tony Andretti to kill you. I shot him to give you a fighting chance. They punished me for protecting you."

"Protecting me?" My knuckles turned white. "Protecting me would've been you telling me what was going on, not maiming a child murderer Aidan had to kill to save my life!"

Gabriel turned to Aidan. "At last, the truth. You're the Marcel Sniper."

"Sniper, meet Assassin. Assassin, meet Sniper. There, you're acquainted." I lowered myself onto the chair, placing my hands on my bump. Gabriel stared at my hands. "You got sent away, you claim as punishment, to annihilate Ivan Milat's biggest competitor in Europe. To an assassin, a kill order isn't punishment, it's a job."

"Not being with you, losing you to him." He glanced at Aidan and spat on the concrete floor. "It killed me."

"Don't be dramatic, Gabriel, you're still breathing. For now."

"I will die if you walk out of this room and I never get to see you again. You already ripped my heart out by telling me you're not carrying my child. Dammit, Ley, I love you."

I pushed to my feet and walked to the door. "Tony Andretti killed two more little girls after that night. Because you didn't do the right thing and kill him. Or at least give me his name." I balled my fists, remembering the little blonde girls with their wet, white hair. Riley, who had only recently stopped having nightmares. "For every single day since we met, you will spend a day in a white room. Eat white food. Wear white clothes. You will have no contact with anyone. I don't need to explain the psychological effects of white torture to you. After you have served your punishment, I will award you with the opportunity to take your own life. In the same manner the Angel Taker killed the two girls you chose not to save."

Before I could open the door, Gabriel spoke. "Finley, I need to tell you the truth, but only if you switch off the cameras."

"There's nothing you can say that will keep her in this room another second." Aidan walked up beside me, placing his hand on my lower back.

Gabriel stared at the floor. "I can tell you what happened the night your parents died. I was there."

Forty-five

Tom didn't look at me when I entered the room. He sat unmoving thanks to the restraints keeping his arms and legs pressed against the steel chair. I had asked Ryan to start the party trick before I opened the door to face the man who had been my father's best friend, as well as Lizzie and my godfather. The flannel covering his body would offer little protection against Heather's brilliance. Soon, scorching water would flow through the pipes which made up the chair. My mother-in-law scared me for reasons no mother-in-law ever should. *I adore her.*

"Tom," Rowan said, and waited for me to sit before he took the other chair, straddling it. I had asked Aidan to wait in the observation room. It might work to my advantage if Tom believed Aidan is dead. If he was as thick as Gabriel.

I couldn't sit. My body trembled. I got to my feet and stood behind Rowan, to hide my clenching fists and uncontrolled breathing. I closed my eyes, remembering my parents' faces when we had laughed together. Tom Anderson had betrayed my father. A crime for which no punishment would ever be enough. This was my life, my and Aidan's life, Lizzie's life, my parents' deaths.

I could no longer fight the darkness' call. It deafened me.

She flapped her dark wings. A primal drum beat.

Rage screamed for release. For war.

"You're the Watcher." I opened my eyes. "Your friend," I laughed at the irony as my father had believed Tom to be his, "Ivan Milat, is in the room next door. He tells an interesting story of how the two of you met. Poor Tom, erectile dysfunction kept you from joining in, didn't it?"

He shook his head, his gaze fixed either on Rowan's shoes or the floor.

"It's nothing to be ashamed of, Tom, erectile dysfunction that is. Watching children being raped, and being complacent in their murders, well, that's despicable." A stronger word evaded me. The flapping of wings, the deafening drum, controlled my mind.

"I will not sugar-coat this for you, my once darling uncle. What I'm about to do to you won't be pleasant. You brought that man into my parents' lives. You tried to destroy my life, my sister's, and for what? Three million Ruastan Dollars? With the rate of exchange as it was at the time my parents were murdered, it wasn't even enough for you to retire on."

"Your parents weren't murdered, they died in a car accident. Stop your childish games and just get it over with, you murderous bitch." His eyes met mine. "Kill me."

I sat down on the chair, desperate to keep the darkness controlled a little longer. Next to me, Rowan breathed hard. I laughed to remind him, and myself, that I remained in control. We were in control, the darkness and I. Sticks and stones and all that. Nothing Tom said could hurt me more than learning the reason my parents had died. I stretched out my legs and crossed my arms over my bump. "Ivan Milat, at the time not yet President of Ruastan, had a problem – the voters didn't like him. Too many rumours going around about his illegal dealings." I lowered my voice. "Rumour is he operates one of the biggest trafficking rings in Europe. Don't tell anyone, but it's true."

In my best British accent, I said, "Prepare the gallows. At dawn he will hang for his crimes." I laughed; the sound ominous. A veiled lie. Hanging is too quick.

I had other plans for this little trio of cheats, deceivers, rapists, and murderers. To my knowledge, Gabriel had never raped a woman, but a man who can assault the woman who he believes carries his child, the woman he claims to love, is capable of anything.

"Speak." Rowan's voice was low and hard. I expected Tom to bark or burst into tears. He did neither.

"What does it matter? Your parents are dead. By some miracle you survived, and here I am. I hold no hope of seeing Ashley, or Hope, again. You won, Finley. Despite losing your homes and your precious serial killer husband."

I shot to my feet, and my fist connected with his face. I gritted my teeth, breathed through the pain searing through my hand. "You adopted a survivor of trafficking, yet you spent two weeks a year watching other men rape young girls. Don't you dare say her name ever again. If possible, I would cut all of her memories out of your brain. Don't even think my best friend's name."

As Tom spat blood on the floor, a realisation struck me so hard, my vision blurred. "You like watching. Ashley's recovery, having her in your house, she was a constant victim in your eyes. You could look at her every day and imagine what they had done to her. How did I never see you for what you are?"

Rowan placed his hand on my lower back. I stepped backwards until my legs pressed against the chair. He gripped my arm and pulled me down to sit.

"Ivan Milat had a problem, one you knew Duncan Williams could solve. How did you find out about the research he conducted? Did you put listening devices or cameras inside his homes?" Rowan leaned forward, resting his elbows on the back of the chair.

Tom wiped his mouth on his shoulder, leaving a red smear to taunt me. He hadn't spilled enough blood. Not yet. The flapping of wings drowned out every rational thought.

"I overheard him talking to the epidemiologist he worked with. Duncan was too trusting of people; he always left the front door open. I stood outside his office door and heard every word."

"Dr Klein, did you target him first?"

"I didn't know he had been diagnosed with stage four pancreatic cancer. There was nothing I could say or do to get him to help Ivan. He overdosed on painkillers and took his part of the research with him to the grave. Not even a single note left in his office, home or on his computer."

"Help Ivan?" Anger bounced from the soundproofed walls. "You call genocide *help*?"

"It would've helped Ivan become president." Tom shrugged.

I couldn't fight the darkness' call any longer. I leapt to my feet. The K-bar I kept hidden rested on top of Tom's left ear.

Blood covered his clothes. His ear? On the floor.

Behind me, the door opened, and Heather placed her hand on my shoulder. I stepped back, still gripping the knife. She took it from me and handed it to a smiling Aidan. When our eyes met, he winked.

Heather asked Tom to stop screaming and stabbed a needle into his thigh. "For the pain," she said, and wrapped his wound with gauze and bandages. From the look of it, not sterile ones. An infection would be the least of Tom's worries, despite his protests of having someone else's dried blood pressed against his gaping wound.

I turned to Aidan, approval in his smile. "I wondered when you were going to pull it out."

As I waited for Heather to finish bandaging Tom's head, I thought about the work my father had done. Work none of us knew about at the time. He and Dr Klein cultivated various diseases to find cures, altering bacteria and viruses to be ready to save lives, should the need ever arise. Ivan Milat would've killed millions had he gotten his hands on the aerosolised cholera my father and Dr Klein had created. With a vast amount of the population falling ill at the same time, no country's health system would be able to save them all. Nathan found my father's research hidden behind a painting he and my mother had left to Lizzie in their will. The painting was still in storage.

One more question remained for Tom. After Heather and Aidan left, closing the door behind them, I asked, "The videos Milat's men made of me being raped, my parents never saw it. You kept it for yourself, didn't you?"

Tom smiled. "You didn't scream, you didn't cry, you said

'no' and tried to fight, but being tied down, you should've known it was pointless. I give you ten out of ten for fighting. A part of me believed, and still does, that being tied down like that is a turn on for you. Admit it, Fin, you liked it?"

To the air around him, Tom said, "Tell me, Aidan, does your wife like being tied down, being taken like that? Or does she fake who she is with you? If you want, I will tell you where I hid the flash drive. You can see for yourself what a spirited little whore your wife is. Thank goodness I remembered to take it before my house got blown up."

The door didn't swing open. Aidan too controlled to be baited.

Tom turned his focus to me. "Of all the rapes I've witnessed, yours brought me the most pleasure. I asked them to do it and record it for me. As you said, I didn't get a lot of money, I had to get something priceless for helping Ivan." Tom shivered, and glee filled his eyes.

Before I could get to my feet and wrap my hands around Tom's neck, the door opened. Tom stared past me.

No time for me to turn around. Gunshots drowned out the darkness' calls.

Bullet after bullet ripped into Tom's face.

Forty-six

Lizzie sat on the beach drawing circles in the sand as she gazed over the ocean. The wind played with her hair, and seeing her so at peace, I forgot the way hatred had transformed her face. I took a seat next to her and wrapped my arm around her shoulder. "It's time for lunch."

"I hope Ryan made lasagne. Remind me to ask him for the recipe."

My sister shouldn't be talking about exchanging recipes a week after she had taken a life. I'm not sure how I expected her to react, but this wasn't it.

"Do you think we will ever know the truth about the night Mom and Dad died?"

I pressed my lips to Lizzie's temple.

She turned to face me, her eyes devoid of tears. "I should've waited for Tom to tell the truth. Made him tell us, and then killed him."

"Knowing won't bring them back, it won't change what happened or where we are now."

"I need to know, Fin. All these questions are driving me crazy, and it all comes down to one simple question – why?"

"I told you everything I know, from what we can put together. I believe Mom and Dad realised that it would never be over. Tom had told them I was dead after Heather informed them I was safe. That's when they must have realised Tom was involved, that it would not end until Milat got his hands on the cholera."

I pushed her hair behind her ear. "They died protecting not only the two of us, but millions of Ruastanians. Aidan read through Dad's work and he explained the just of it to me. Dad and Dr Klein created a biological weapon, a potential monster of war in the wrong hands."

Lizzie stared out over the ocean, drawing her knees to her chest. My heart ached. I didn't want to keep any detail from her, but I couldn't tell her what Gabriel had said before I left the room. Contrary to what's written in the official accident report, my mother had died in the driver's seat. Gabriel had checked her pulse, finding none. Whether my father knew about my mother's plan, we will never know. After all this time, the why had been answered. In the same breath, Tom had told my parents of my supposed death and forced my mother's hand. Tom had said Lizzie would never last as long as I did. 'Is it worth losing another daughter?'

"Perhaps I can continue with Dad's work, let some good come out of this at least."

"No. You will *not* continue with Dad's work. Never, Elizabeth Williams. Do you hear me? Someone will hear about it and we will be right back in this mess because I will protect you to my dying breath. An aerosolised cholera that can be dispersed over vast areas, one as fast-acting as this one, no. Biological weapons are the coward's way to wage war." I took her hands and rested my forehead against hers. "Thank you."

"For what?"

"Avenging me."

Lizzie pulled back, unshed tears in her eyes. A hint of a smile tugged at the corners of her mouth. "It's what sisters do."

She never asked why I didn't tell her about the daily rapes I had endured. I guess, in her own way, she understood.

"Is it helping you to talk to Heather?" I asked, and got to my feet, holding my hand out to her.

Lizzie placed her hand in mine and eased up from the soft sand. She kept her attention on the ocean. "I'm not losing any sleep. It was a justifiable kill. If I didn't do it, Aidan would have. I stood closer to the door."

***

The Walkers and Eli waited for us on the porch where Heather had set the table for lunch. She still refused our help. Instead, Ryan played second to her culinary command, although she had allowed him to make his infamous lasagne.

Liam handed me the bread rolls. "I can't believe I didn't tell you, Ivan peed his pants when you sliced off Tom's ear," he said so that only I could hear.

Happiness filled my soul, not because I won my self-challenge by getting Ivan to urinate on himself. *That word.* The smile from a place of joy. Lizzie and I were part of a family again, both of us pregnant. Our babies growing strong. My heart was full, even with an unknown future ahead of us. No house to call home just yet.

I couldn't go back to being a profiler. Aidan had already taken up a position with his father's organisation. A decision I supported. Seeing Aidan in charge, and to hear him give orders, is sexy. Could've been due to my hormones running amok…the no-sex thing sucked. *Again.*

Aidan reached for my hand. "It's time, Wife."

I grabbed his beautiful face between my hands and pressed my mouth to his. Butterflies returned to the space the knot had occupied for far too long. "I love you, Aidan Walker, more in this moment than ever before."

"It was me sniping out of a helicopter in the dark that made you fall for me, wasn't it?" He smiled, and so did I.

"You wish. It's going to take more than that to make me fall in love with you."

"Woman, you just said you love me. I have witnesses."

I kissed him again, a kiss filled with the promise of spending the rest of my life with him.

Ryan cleared his throat. "Some of us are trying not to lose our appetites. Your kissing can wait, let's say grace. I'm famished."

"Don't you want to hear the gender of your grandchild?" I asked, my eyes still on Aidan's. The butterflies scurried inside me.

"Do you want to do a video call, then Quinn, Nathan, and Rowan can hear at the same time?" Heather asked as she stood to retrieve her phone from the kitchen. "Nathan won't be here until late afternoon."

Both Quinn and Rowan had returned to their undercover assignments. Ryan had given me and Lizzie strict orders that in the event we recognise Quinn in Marcel, to call her Andrea Logan. As for Rowan, Ryan wouldn't tell me where his youngest son was, or about his and Quinn's assignments. Their world completely new to me. Intriguing. A puzzle I wanted to be a piece of.

As Heather returned, Lizzie said, "I look forward to seeing Nathan, and thanking him in person for his part in ending this and getting us answers. If he wants to stay on at Williams Pharmaceuticals, I would love to continue working with him."

"He has no intention of ending his employment with you, but I believe he might have some ideas of his own to add considering the work your father did." Ryan leaned back in his chair.

"No. Lizzie will not work with biological or chemical weapons or anything microscopically small that can kill millions of people. I forbid it." I thought better than to slam my fists on the table, despite my verbal tantrum.

Everyone turned to me. Aidan spoke first, after he wrapped me in his arms and huffed a laugh. "You're cute when you throw tantrums. If our daughter is anything like you, I'm going to have my hands full and we might have to revisit having more children." He laughed.

"It's a girl?" Heather covered her mouth with both hands.

Aidan pulled me to my feet and placed his hands on my bump. "Family, meet Ainsley Victoria Walker. Baby girl, this is your family. Even though you can't hear a word I'm saying, just know we all love you and your cousin. We will fight to the death to give you and as many children in the world, as we can, the best life. One free from monsters and darkness."

"I want to be right next to you, Mr Walker. Commander

Walker? Boss? Sir? Whatever I need to call you."

Aidan pressed his lips to my forehead. "You can call me Aidan, because you will work alongside me and not underneath me."

I pulled my head back, stared up at him, biting my bottom lip. "Where's the fun in that?"

"You owe me a holiday," Heather said to Ryan.

"I don't mind losing a bet to you if it means Finley will take over from you as head of interrogation and profiling."

"I will what?" I spun around to face them; Aidan wrapped his arms around me.

Ryan stood. "Aidan and Eli have already signed on. We have prepared two of the units in the apartment complex used by our operatives when they're in Marcel, for you to live in until you find new homes. In reality it's a fortress, and you can stay as long as you want. Nathan is driving down our gift for Lizzie. Heather and I realised the four of you lost everything in the explosions, it's our way of trying to help. Yourself, Aidan, and Eli will have use of the company vehicles. Quinn's Mustang is off limits, even when she's out of town."

My father-in-law held his hand out towards me, and I grinned, placing my hand in his. He offered me a chance to continue the hunt, continue fighting for the innocent, to protect those who can't protect themselves.

Finley Williams-Walker – super spy. *It has a nice ring to it.*

"I have questions. How do you make money? Enough to own a prison island, aeroplanes, and everything else I don't know about yet?"

Ryan smiled, one eyebrow raised. "You need to sign an employment contract before I tell you anything."

I pushed my fists into my sides. "I have a signed marriage certificate, your granddaughter growing inside me, and your surname. What difference does an employment contract make?"

Aidan turned me to face him. He cupped my face and pressed his lips to mine. "We will have to put a few strict, and some very naughty clauses, into your contract."

Waves crashed in the distance; the wind found us on the porch. A single tear slipped down my cheek. We were free from the lies which had bound us for years. The man I love stood in front of me, offering me a lifetime of what we do best.

I lifted onto my toes, wrapping my arms around his neck, my bump pressed against him. Our daughter safe between us. "Yes, sir." I smiled against his mouth. "Last question – what's the organisation's name?"

Aidan pressed his lips below my ear, and whispered, "Fortius."

Acknowledgements

To my family and friends – for their continued support and belief in my imagination and ambition.

My first pass readers – Maricka, Nicolina, Tania, and Yolanda. Thank you for continuing to share in Finley's story. It isn't over...

Megan Pereira, my editor. Thank you for your support, patience, and keeping true to Finley's voice.

Marcel Koortzen, my proofreader. Thank you for allowing me to name a city after you, and for being the last pair of eyes. You are my writing's last line of defense, and on some days that of my sanity.

To my husband for believing in me and helping with scenes for this novel. I love you.

Most of all, to God. All I can ever offer in gratitude is my life.

All mistakes are my own.

About the author

Mariëtte Whitcomb studied Criminology and Psychology at the University of Pretoria. An avid reader of psychological thrillers and romantic suspense novels, writing allows her to pursue her childhood dream to hunt criminals, albeit fictional and born in the darkest corners of her imagination.

When Mariëtte isn't writing, she reads or spends time with her family and friends.

Visit www.mariettewhitcomb.com or find her on Facebook or Instagram.

www.ingramcontent.com/pod-product-compliance
Lightning Source LLC
Chambersburg PA
CBHW052032240626
47153CB00006B/2044